Gaye Hiçyılmaz is the author of a number of highly praised books for children and young adults, among them *And the Stars were Gold*, *Smiling for Strangers* and *Girl in Red* – the book that inspired *Pictures from the Fire*. After twenty years living in Turkey and Switzerland she returned to England where she grew up, and now lives with her husband on the Pembrokeshire coast, where she writes overlooking the sea. She has three sons and a daughter, all now grown up.

Also by Gaye Hiçyılmaz

Girl in Red
Smiling for Strangers
And the Stars were Gold

Pictures from the Fire

Gaye Hiçyılmaz

Dolphin Paperbacks

First published in Great Britain in 2003
as a Dolphin paperback
by Orion Children's Books
a division of the Orion Publishing Group Ltd
Orion House
5 Upper St Martin's Lane
London WC2H 9EA

Reprinted 2004

A catalogue record for this book is available
from the British Library.

ISBN 1 85881 896 6

Typeset at The Spartan Press Ltd,
Lymington, Hants

Printed in Great Britain by
Clays Ltd, St Ives plc

For Nick, with love
and thanks for all his support

Contents

Picture 1
The View from a Yellow Room

She was locked in again.

Once more, Emilia's parents had left her alone in their rooms in the hostel, and had gone out without saying goodbye. They hadn't even waved. As soon as her mother had cleared away the breakfast things, they'd put on their outdoor clothes and got ready to leave. Her little brother, Zoltan, had started leaping around their feet like a pup that's been shut in too long. Emilia had stayed where she was. She'd watched her father unlock the yellow door of the flat and step into the corridor outside, closely followed by her mother and Zoltan. She'd watched her father kick the door to make it shut. Yesterday, when he'd tried to close it more quietly, it had stuck. Today, he'd learnt the trick, and kicked.

And today, Emilia didn't try to go after them. She stayed in the room, perched on the edge of the sofa and holding her breath. Today, she didn't grab at the handle, desperate to escape. Today, she stayed where she was and listened to the sound of the key sliding round in the lock. She didn't kneel by the door and try to peer past its yellow edges. She knew, now, that she couldn't see through because the thick paint had wrinkled and run like mud.

Today, she knew there was no point in trying to get out, so she leant back on the sofa and tucked her feet up under her red skirt. She put her fingers in her mouth and bit off another piece of skin as she listened to the sounds of her family leaving her alone.

Yesterday she'd cried. Today, she understood. She'd learnt that the yellow door was double-locked and that she didn't have a key. Yesterday, as she'd knelt by the crack, she hadn't seen through to any light, but she'd seen the bright brass bar of a new lock glide across the space as easily and sweetly as a soft, sucked thumb slips back into the waiting mouth. And that was that. The lock had slid across, and she was locked in. Once more her family was walking away from her, along an unknown winter street.

And might never come back.

She bit more deeply into the flesh at the side of her nail to stop herself thinking like that. Even though her parents had threatened to abandon her several times, she didn't really believe that they would. They couldn't do that. Even though they were so ashamed of her that they could barely bring themselves to speak to her, they still wouldn't leave her behind. Or not yet. And anyway, they hadn't taken their things.

She shut her eyes, and imagined them walking away down the corridor towards the lift. Her father would be feeling up under his shirt, for the keys. She'd already seen him fasten them to the red striped bootlace which always hung round his neck, under his clothes. Now, he would be settling the keys against his skin, which was the only way, he'd always said, to be completely safe. Gypsies had to take extra precautions and keep secret things skin close, because anybody, even the most respectable-looking person sauntering down the street, might in reality be a pickpocket or a thief.

So Emilia knew that when her father had arranged the keys to his satisfaction, he would carefully engage the zip on his leather jacket and pull it right up to his unshaven chin. That would protect the keys even more securely. And it would also protect him. Her father, Daniel Radu, had always detested bad weather, and he knew that he'd soon be outside amongst the wet gusts of wind which were blowing winter rain along this street to which they'd come. Previously, he'd complained about the cold winters in their home town of Bucharest, but since they'd left that city and come west, he'd complained even more about the bitter weather in these foreign places. There was, he said, a different, harsher sort of cold, here in the west.

Now, she pictured him pulling his scarf from his pocket and winding it carefully round his throat. He'd be tucking in the ends, while he stabbed the lift button again and again, with the stubby forefinger of his other hand. Behind him, her mother, Elizabeta, would be watching his jabbing hand. Although they'd lived in England for several months, Elizabeta had never got used to the lifts. Now, if they were going to live in this town, she'd have to get used to them all over again. When this lift began its descent, Emilia knew that her mother would let out a feeble, frightened shriek. Then she'd snatch at her son, trying to drag him close. He'd scowl at her as he tried to pull away. He would complain that his mother made too much fuss. Recently, Zoltan had started complaining about fuss, like his father complained about rain.

At the entrance to this building, where the authorities had brought them three nights ago, her father would pause on the bottom step and look around cautiously. He'd lean against the wet black railings as he looked. 'A gypsy can *never* be too careful.' That's what her father'd always said and though Emilia had always silently doubted this wisdom before, now, after what had happened in England, she wondered if he'd been right all along.

Now she refolded the edge of her red skirt over her feet and imagined the scene on the steps. As he leant against the railings, her father would glance up at the low grey sky and run his fingertips through the dark curls at the back of his neck. Then, he'd catch hold of the crown of his hat, and raise it, before setting it back on his head and tapping it into its place. He'd tap the top with two fingers, until he'd tilted the brim into its correct position, over his eyes. Yes: that's what her father'd be doing as he stood on the step outside. It was what he always did when he went out. Emilia could picture it so vividly that she almost saw the flash of light from the diamond ring that nestled into the folds of flesh and wiry hairs on the fingers of his left hand. If she'd had a pencil in her own hand, she could have drawn his portrait perfectly and she could've drawn her mother's too. Elizabeta would be on the steps above, still hanging on to Zoltan, who'd be wriggling and trying to get free.

Daniel would continue tapping down the crown of his small black hat. Only when he was sure that the street was absolutely safe would he finally snap his fingers at his family, and step down onto the pavement below. Then, once he'd made his move, he'd walk off as smartly and elegantly as a dancer, in his pointed cowboy boots. Her mother would follow, but always several steps behind. Elizabeta never ran, but she never gave up either. She was heavy and awkward, and though she never appeared to be hurrying, she always caught up in the end.

Zoltan would be hopping from foot to foot, trying to break away. In the flat, he'd been excited at the prospect of going out. He'd longed to be near the bright lights of the shops and supermarkets, and near people once more. He'd always hated being shut in.

Yesterday, Emilia had pressed her face against the window in the front room and watched the three of them walking away down the straight, wet street. Her father had moved swiftly along the pavement and past a white wall. He'd passed the fronts of the tall, joined-together houses that stretched to a corner, at the far end, where this street ran into another much busier one. A tree grew out of the pavement at the corner where the two streets met, and yesterday, her father had stopped under the tree, and waited for Elizabeta and Zoltan to catch up. Yesterday, Emilia had felt the chill of winter seeping through the glass as she'd watched her father stop beneath the tree. He'd raised his cupped hands to his face as he lit another cigarette, and she'd known that he wouldn't only be protecting the flame from the wind, he'd also be looking through his fingers, carefully taking stock.

Yesterday, that had been Zoltan's chance. Emilia'd seen him snatch his hand from his mother's, then dash, splashing and stamping through the puddles in his green plastic boots. He'd caught his father up but hadn't taken his hand.

5

At nine years old he was now too grown-up for that. Instead, he'd just stood close and watched his father struggle with another spluttering match. Then the two of them had set off, walking side by side, in the direction that Daniel had chosen, and Elizabeta had followed on behind. Her wide back had been bent against the wind and her long flowered skirt had dragged and darkened in the rain. As Emilia'd watched her mother had pulled her cardigan more tightly around her shoulders as she'd tried to keep out the cold.

And yesterday, Emilia had stayed at the window long after her family had turned the corner by the tree and gone out of sight. Today, she hadn't watched them at all. She'd just hugged her feet as she'd thought about them, and rocked gently to and fro as she slid her fingers into her mouth and bit off another strip of skin. Then she'd got up and walked round the rooms once more, although there wasn't far to go. There was only the bedroom where her parents and Zoltan slept, the tiny kitchen with the bathroom next door, and this room, with its table and television and its window, overlooking the street. She had been sleeping in this room, on the sofa by the door. She thought it was the nicest room, despite its colour, because it was the only room which had a view. Emilia now realised that the whole flat must have been newly painted. Everything was clean and bright, but she hadn't noticed that on the night they'd arrived. Then she'd been overwhelmed by the smell of the new paint, and hadn't appreciated anything else.

They'd been travelling for so long, and she'd been so tired, that the smell of paint was the only thing she'd noticed. Now, after being in the rooms for a few days, she felt smothered by their colour, but couldn't smell the paint at all.

They had travelled constantly after leaving England, because her father hoped to meet up with people he'd known in Bucharest, but it hadn't worked out. Finally, at the end of the third or fourth day, as the sky outside darkened into night, they'd been taken off a train when it stopped at a quiet station. At first, Emilia had thought that the uniformed men and women were removing them because their train tickets weren't right. She'd suspected that her father hadn't bought enough tickets, and this was why they'd been turned off. However, once the train had gone, and they'd been left standing by themselves, it had become clear that something else was wrong. The people in uniforms were joined by others with big, red-tongued dogs, and though nobody had shouted at the family, and the dogs had only whimpered, it had frightened Emilia a lot. She had been so deeply asleep in the nodding warmth of the railway carriage, and so suddenly startled awake, that she would have given anything to lay her head down, and go back to sleep. But there hadn't even been a place to sit.

They'd stood on the empty platform for what had seemed like hours. The chill evening had blackened into a clear, frosty night. Stars had glittered overhead, and a sliver of moon had been set into the sky as if carved there by the sweep of a swift, sharp knife. Her feet had ached with cold as she'd seen other trains rushing past to places that she would now never see. Sometimes, a curious face had turned and looked back, and once, a woman sitting in a corner seemed to have met her eye. But that was all there'd been.

Emilia'd hugged her arms around her and bitten her lips, but she hadn't been able to stop her teeth chattering or her legs from trembling with cold. Since leaving England on Christmas Eve they'd been on the move continually, and she'd lost any sense of where they were. She'd stopped caring too. The only thing she'd wanted to do, as they'd stood on that platform, was close her eyes and sleep.

She must have slept as soon as the police car arrived and they'd been persuaded in. She wasn't sorry. The car had been warm and comfortable. She'd told herself that she would only lean her head back for a moment, but she must have fallen asleep instantly, because even now, she couldn't remember a single thing about the final drive to this place. It could have taken minutes or hours. All she remembered was a sudden rush of freezing air on her face and throat, as someone had opened the door.

'Go *on*, can't you?' Zoltan had kicked her ankles as he'd scrambled past, determined to get out first. She'd closed her eyes. When she'd opened them again she'd been the only person left in the car. Her parents were climbing the steps into a building. Elizabeta was staggering with their bags, while Zoltan and her father went inside. Emilia had shrunk back into her seat and closed her eyes. For one second she'd willed them to forget her, and leave her behind. She could have stayed in that warm car forever. She'd dreaded stepping out into the freezing night, just as much as she dreaded moving on. But it hadn't done any good. A firm hand had reached in and grasped her elbow and although she hadn't understood the words the woman used, she'd known she must get out of the car and follow her family up the stone steps and through the waiting door.

She'd entered a tiled hallway where a crowd of people stood around and talked. The lightbulbs were unshaded and the voices of the people echoed from the shining walls and the sharply patterned floor. When Emilia had stepped inside she was convinced that a hush had fallen over the crowd, even though the sounds of their voices had soon rolled back and then seemed even louder than before. She'd blinked in the bright light, then hung her head. Her first impression was of a throng of different people from all the different countries of the world, but when she'd dared to look again, it had seemed as if almost all the people in that hallway were young, dark-eyed men. She'd been relieved when the woman from the car had led them away from the crowd and into a separate office with a cracked glass door. A young man with long fair hair had been sitting behind an overflowing desk. He'd looked up and smiled as he'd pointed to a couple of chairs. Zoltan had scrambled onto his mother's lap. The young man had continued to write. Daniel, who hadn't shaved since they'd left England, had sat on the other chair and scratched the bristles on his chin. On the wall behind the desk, the hands of a large clock jerked and ticked.

There'd been nowhere for Emilia to sit, so she'd stayed where she was, in the middle of the room. She'd longed to look behind her, because she'd sensed that the men in the hall were now watching through the door. She'd been convinced that they were staring at her and when she couldn't stand it any longer, she'd glanced behind her. Then, she'd met a wall of their curious eyes, with the crack in the glass door running across their faces, like a wound.

The young man behind the desk had finished what he

was writing and put a stack of papers into a file. Then he'd taken out a new, printed form from a pile in front of him, and asked her father questions about who they were.

'Name?' he'd asked, glancing up. He'd continued asking questions in English and in other languages too, whenever her father hadn't replied. Daniel had spoken as little as he could, and sometimes he'd just shrugged and tapped down his hat. Emilia had understood almost nothing, but she'd begun to suspect that the whole building was filled with other people like themselves: people who'd left the streets where they'd been born, and now had nowhere safe to go.

'This is an *asylum hostel*. Yes?' The young man had repeated these words several times as he'd looked at her parents. 'It is *our* hostel and for now you will make it *your home*. We hope that it is for you a very happy place to be.' He'd reached up and taken two keys from a row of hooks on the wall. When he held them out, Emilia'd noticed that the palm of his hand was as soft and pink as a child's. At the sight of the keys, Zoltan had slid from his mother's lap and reached out, but Daniel had pushed him aside and pocketed both keys himself.

The young man had led them back into the waiting crowd, which had seemed even noisier than before. This time, Emilia had noticed two young women. They'd been talking in a corner, and their voices had been too soft for anyone to hear. A boy was bouncing a ball against one wall. Zoltan had paused to watch. The young man spoke sharply. The little boy instantly edged behind the adults and put his hands behind his back. In the sudden silence, the ball had rolled on across the tiled floor and no one had moved to pick it up.

The lift had taken them to the second floor and as soon as she'd stepped out, Emilia had smelt the paint. She'd watched her father fit one of the keys into the lock. When he'd opened the door, the strong smell had made her step back.

'You're in luck!' the young man had grinned. 'These rooms were only finished yesterday, so you're the first to move in. It is very smart, very good. No?' He'd marched about pointing to taps and switches in the bathroom and kitchen and was probably explaining how everything worked. Elizabeta had watched his hands touching the things that they would later use and her lips had curled in disgust. Daniel had frowned too, but he'd nodded his head as though he understood what was being said. Zoltan had stopped in front of the television, then knelt down. He'd immediately started pushing its buttons, and when it sprang into life he'd laughed. Emilia had stood apart from the others in the furthest corner of the yellow room. She'd felt wheels still turning beneath her and the smell of the paint had made her cough.

Now, as she returned to the window, she saw the wind blowing the rain up the street. It hit the glass in gusts and fat drops slithered down. The room was warm but she was shivering as if the window had been left open and the wind was howling in. She took her fingers from her mouth and touched the skin on her neck. This wasn't the first time that she'd shivered because she'd felt an icy wind that wasn't there, but each time it happened, it startled her anew. It took her back to the moment when she'd felt the blade on her throat, when that woman had cut off her plaits. Now she let her fingers play amongst the scraps of hair that were left. She'd tried to smooth them down, but she knew it was no good. She was so ugly: her head of slashed-off hair was grotesque. That's why her father didn't want to see her face.

Outside, the grey street was quiet, but the building was restless with the sounds of many people held in behind its doors. She could hear the beat of different types of music and the thin wail of some baby who could not sleep. Once she thought she heard the sound of drums, but when she listened more carefully, she realised that the pounding was in her head.

Yesterday, while her family was out, one of these other people had come and knocked on their door.

'Herr Radu?' A man had suddenly spoken from outside. 'Herr Radu? You are in there?'

She hadn't made a sound.

'Herr Radu? It is I, Michael, from the next door?'

She'd been overcome by fear.

'Herr Radu.' The voice had been quite clear. 'You like to drink a coffee with me? Now?' A hand had tried the door.

She'd fled across the room, crept under the table and crouched down, making herself as small as she could. The door handle had moved again. She'd shut her eyes and held her breath and tried to make herself so small she wasn't there. The man had spoken once more, then must have given up and gone.

She'd remained under the table long after he'd left. She'd realised that if the door hadn't been locked, that strange man, whoever he was, might have walked straight in. She'd let out a careful breath, and reminded herself that at least for the moment she was safe. Silently, she'd moved her toes and been grateful that her father had double-locked the door. When she'd dared to move again, she'd noticed that the cleaners had missed a small patch of carpet around one of the table legs. It was grey with dust and other people's crumbs. She noticed a blue thread on it, and a long black hair caught in between. Sweat had trickled down her back as she'd wondered if anyone was still around, but she'd told herself that such a thought was stupid and she'd forced herself to draw another, calmer breath.

For the first time she'd wondered about the people who'd been living in these rooms before. How long had they stayed here? And had this been 'a happy place' for them? Then she'd noticed the brilliant spots and runs of yellow paint on the table legs. Someone, redecorating too hurriedly perhaps, had shaken out their brush, or spilt the paint and carelessly let it drip down. She'd reached up, and run her fingers over the blobs of colour, and that was how she'd seen the book.

Someone had taped it to the underside of the table, directly above her head. She'd instantly realised that it must have been a secret, because why else had it been so carefully hidden there? The people who'd repainted these rooms couldn't have known it was there. And why should they? How could anyone have discovered it unless they'd been hiding under the table, like her?

Thick brown sticky tape had been stretched across it, from corner to corner, like arms held out, but she could see that it had been a nice book, once. The pages were gold-edged and although the cover was shabby and stained, it had once been deep blue. She'd scratched at the tape, but her nails were bitten down and she hadn't found the end. Finally, she'd forced her fingers underneath and pulled on the book so hard that it had torn free. Then, when she'd turned it over she'd been upset to see that a jagged piece of its blue cover had been ripped off as well.

She'd taken the book to the window and been turning the first pages when she'd heard the sound of the key in the lock. She'd only just hidden the book under the sofa when Zoltan burst through the door.

'You'll never guess what *I've* seen!' He'd pushed his mother aside in his eagerness to get in first. 'You'll never guess, because *you* weren't there! But it was huge! It was the biggest one in the world. That's what Dad said.' Zoltan dropped his anorak on the floor before kicking off his boots. Then he'd leant against a wall and extended a limp foot so that Emilia could straighten his sock. His toes had felt cold and damp and his cheeks had been beaded with rain. She'd pulled one dirty sock back over his heel, and pushed his curls out of his eyes, before either of them had remembered that they weren't supposed to be speaking to each other now. Her parents were so ashamed of what Emilia'd done in England that they didn't trust her with Zoltan any more. She'd glanced at her mother, then they'd sprung apart.

'It *was* big, wasn't it?' Zoltan had turned to his mother and grabbed her arm, but she'd shaken him off.

'Wasn't that bar of chocolate the biggest one in the whole world?' He'd appealed to his father but Daniel Radu hadn't replied either. He'd been busy taking off his leather jacket and shaking it to get rid of the rain. He hadn't known where to put it because the space behind the front door was very small and at that moment Zoltan had been everywhere, getting in everyone's way. Cautiously, and with her head bent down so that she needn't meet her father's eye,

Emilia'd taken his jacket from him and laid it over a chair. He'd turned his face away and hadn't looked at her at all.

Later, when Elizabeta was in the kitchen and Daniel was switching between channels on the television, Zoltan had sidled back to her, and touched her sleeve. 'It *was* big,' he'd muttered resentfully.

'What was?' She'd forgotten what he'd been talking about. When he'd pressed close, she'd smelt the rain on him, and he'd reminded her of a small wild animal, caught out in a storm.

'The *chocolate* was!' In his excitement he'd spat. 'Honestly, Emi, the bar of chocolate we saw in the shop was much bigger than *this*!' He'd held his arms as wide apart as he could. She'd smiled at him. 'Emi' was the name everyone had called her in the English school and she was grateful he hadn't forgotten. He'd smiled too, and begun a whispered description of a gigantic bar of chocolate they'd seen in a shop window in the town.

'And, Dad promised – ' Zoltan's hand had flown to his mouth as though he would have stuffed the words back in. But, when they'd looked at their father, he was staring at the screen and smiling too. He'd found a musical show. A girl singer with spiky pink hair and a sparkling pink dress was moving about in front of a band. He was drumming out the beat with his fingers and hadn't noticed them talking at all. As Emilia had watched him, Daniel stretched out his legs and called Elizabeta to come and pull off his boots.

'Dad *promised* he'd get one for *me*, as soon as he could,' Zoltan had started whispering as soon as his mother returned to the kitchen. 'But . . .' he'd frowned.

'But what?' Emilia'd asked.

'But how can I get such a big chocolate into this *room*?'

She'd shrugged.

'And how can I eat it, if I can't get it in?' His expression had been dark with worry.

She hadn't known what to say.

'I know!' Suddenly, his face had lit up and he'd grinned. 'I know what I'll do! I'll get a hammer, or an axe!'

'Why?' She'd been even more puzzled than before.

'So I can smash it up, of course!'

'But . . .'

'Oh, you're *so* stupid, you ugly potato head!' He'd snatched at a wisp of her hair and pulled as hard as he could. Previously, she would have plunged her hands into his curls and pulled until he'd shrieked, but yesterday she hadn't done that. She'd bitten her lip, as her eyes watered with pain, but she hadn't fought back. The things that had happened in England had changed her: it was as if they'd slashed off her courage as well as her hair.

Zoltan had giggled as he'd stared at the tuft of her hair he'd pulled out. Then, he'd dropped it on the ground and rubbed it into the carpet with his foot. 'I'll tell you what,' he'd muttered, not looking at her, '*when* I get my big chocolate, and *when* I've smashed it up, I'll let you have the crumbs, and I bet there'll be lots.'

'OK,' she'd mouthed at him and smiled, as if his idea had been good.

Today, she checked the rooms once more, to be sure she was alone. Then she looked along the street just in case her family was coming back. Finally, she knelt down and felt under the sofa until her fingers closed over the edge of the book. She blew dust from its gold edges before taking it to the window and opening it up. The first pages were covered with writing but gradually there was less and less. Halfway through, the writing actually stopped. The beginning was neatly written in dark blue ink, but as she turned over the pages she saw that other sections were scrawled in red and black biro. Some were in pencil or something that had smudged. It was quite a large book, larger anyway than the exercise books which the students had used in the English school, but apart from the black lines which divided the pages up, there were no thin blue lines to help the writer keep straight. Towards the end, some of the writing was very wild. It looked as though the writer had been working desperately and at too great a speed, or even in the dark. She couldn't understand the words, but there was something about the sameness of the way the marks were made that convinced her that it had all been written by one person. As she turned through it, the book reminded her of something she'd seen before, and suddenly she knew what it was.

Yasmina, the girl who'd been her best friend in the English school, had had a book like this. Of course, it hadn't been exactly the same. Yasmina's had been newer and smaller than this, and had fitted into the front pocket of her rucksack, but it had had those same black lines, printed across, and those rows of little numbers. Yasmina had explained that these were 'dates'. She'd called her book 'My Diary', and those words had been printed on its cover in silver. Yasmina had written in her diary constantly. She'd filled the pages up in breaks and tutor times, and even in lessons, when she was bored. She'd covered pages and pages with fast flowing words and gradually Emilia had come to understand that this book held a record of all the things that were happening in Yasmina's life. It had been Yasmina's secret voice and she'd written things in the diary that she hadn't wanted to say out loud. When Emilia turned through the pages again, she'd realised that the difference between this diary and Yasmina's was that hers had been almost finished, whereas in this one, more than half the pages were left clear.

Now, Emilia pictured Yasmina sitting in class. She'd always had her elbow curved protectively round the book and her head bent over, so that no one else could see. Emilia turned through the pages again, and was even more sure: this book *was* a diary too. Someone had been writing it, here, in this room. Then they'd hidden it and gone away, leaving only these words which she couldn't read to carry the secret story of their life.

Until she'd gone to England, Emilia hadn't realised that other people did things like that. She knew that there were books, of course, although none of her family and very few of their neighbours or relatives could read or write. Her father could speak to people in languages that were different from the one they used at home, but he'd never felt the need to read, or write anything down. He believed that writing was a trap and he insisted that it was safer, especially for people like them, to keep one's thoughts, unwritten, in one's head. Putting an idea on paper was as risky as putting money in a bank. One day, when you went to count it, you might find that a thief had got there first. 'A deep grave is the only place safer than silence,' was what Daniel Radu had always said.

Emilia moved slowly to the table and sat down. There were pages and pages of this book empty, and waiting to be filled. She felt in the pockets of her skirt. Her pencils and pens were still there. Some of the coloured chalks had crumbled up and their dust was on her hands. She turned to a fresh page; a noise made her jump up, but it wasn't the sound of her parents coming back. It had come from the room above. Her heart was beating fast as she sat down. She hadn't drawn anything since she'd left England, days ago.

Now, if her parents didn't come back, and if she dared, she could draw. She looked at the clean page. Her fingers had left a smear of yellow chalk, but she knew what to do. This would be her diary and it would begin here, in this yellow room. This wasn't where her story had begun, but this room, with its yellow walls, had given her this book, and it was the place from which she could look back to those earlier days in Bucharest. The door out might be locked, but at least the room had a window, with a view.

She found the yellow chalk and converted the smear into the window frame.

Outside, rain still ran down. She knew she must draw quickly. The rain was unfortunate. It wasn't only her father who hated it. Her mother did too. Both of them continued to believe that rain always brought mud. That had been true of the streets in Bucharest, but it hadn't been true of England, and it didn't appear to be true of the streets outside. Here the pavements and road sparkled like polished stone, but she knew that her parents would never notice that. They insisted that rain was dangerous because it brought mud and hardship and disease, so on a wet day like this they might return any time.

In Bucharest, Elizabeta had been one of the gypsy women employed as street sweepers. Her job had been to sweep the huge square in front of the President's palace. It had been hard work which never ended, so she'd swept and swept from morning till night, through all the seasons of the year, but the square had never been clean. Emilia had usually gone with her, and ever since she could remember, she'd watched her mother sweep. Sometimes she'd just watched, but as she'd got older she'd learnt how to beg. Usually, she'd tried to wander a little way off, then she'd squatted down, and drawn pictures in the mud.

She couldn't remember when she'd started to draw. It seemed to her that she'd always done it. It had always felt as natural as running away at the bark of a dog. All she knew was that she had to draw. So her mother had swept, and she'd drawn, and people had walked past, treading indifferently on what they'd both done. If a passer-by had ever looked down, they would only have seen another gypsy and her kid, messing around in the dirt. It was what they'd expected because that's what gypsies did. Emilia had known that they hadn't been worth noticing, and in that huge, bleak square, no one had. They'd trampled across her pictures and trodden on her skirt. When they'd kicked her ankles, they'd sworn at her for trying to trip them up.

She hadn't cared. She'd continued to draw in winter mud and summer dust, but she'd remembered what her father always said: 'A deep grave is the only place safer than silence.' She'd made her marks cautiously, one on top of another, so that she was the only person who understood what they meant. She'd been as careful as any gypsy could. Even when the sun shone and the pictures dried out, she'd known that she'd be safe. Nobody, not even the secret police, could have suspected that these lines in the mud were detailed pictures of the streets and buildings that she'd seen around her in Bucharest.

She used her fingertips to smooth in part of the yellow wall, then put the chalk aside and picked up a felt-tipped pen. She ran a fine black line along the edges of the kerbstones that she could see in the street beyond. She made the line curve towards the far corner, and the tree beneath which her father and Zoltan had stood. Then she glanced out of the window again: there was a blue door set into the corner building. Now she coloured it in. The tree on the corner still had Christmas lights amongst its branches. She hesitated about how best to draw them in.

When she looked out of the window again, she saw Zoltan running down the street. Her parents, with their heads bent against the wind and rain, were following behind. Instantly, she pushed the book under the sofa and wiped the chalk dust from her hands. The first entry in her diary wasn't finished, but she didn't mind. At least she had begun.

Picture 2

Still Life, with Chocolate Cake

Two days passed before Emilia could get back to the book because the rain that had driven her parents back to the hostel had later turned to sleet, which pattered and fluttered like hands on the glass. Then, when darkness sank down on the street, she'd noticed that the Christmas lights on the tree were shining on flakes of snow. She'd watched white mounds settle along the black branches and heap up in the nooks and forks between. Beneath the coloured lights, the snow-covered boughs were like bits of a rainbow that had been broken up.

By morning, the edges of the kerbstones had disappeared beneath deep drifts of white. The view from the room was beautiful, and she could have stayed by the window and watched the falling snow all day. The rest of the family were not pleased. Elizabeta paced restlessly between the rooms and would not go out. Zoltan was bored. He ran around and jumped from the sofa to the floor until somebody banged on the ceiling, and then banged again. When Zoltan had kept on jumping, they'd all heard an angry shout. Emilia had sat by herself and tried to keep out of their way. At mealtimes, her mother had passed her plate across and she'd continued to eat her food alone.

Only Daniel Radu had continued to come and go. He was spending his days at the railway station, watching for another gypsy family from their old district in Bucharest. He had heard that this family were also on their way west, but no one like them had arrived. He was irritable. They owed him money from way back and he'd been sending them messages that now he must be repaid. Each morning he'd stamped out of the hostel and in the evening he returned in a worse temper, and empty-handed, with his boots soaked through to the inside. He blamed the foreign snow.

Then one morning Emilia woke to hear the sound of cars moving swiftly along a wet street, and the steady drip, drip of a thaw. Once again, a silver light shone on the grey ridges of the roofs opposite and sheets of melting snow slid down and fell onto the pavements below. Her father now insisted on taking her mother and Zoltan to the station with him. They needed Elizabeta to beg. They'd already finished the small amount of money which the hostel manager had given them, and if their neighbours from Bucharest didn't arrive soon, he didn't know how they could get more cash.

So once again, Emilia was waiting for her parents to leave. She sat on the edge of the sofa, biting off fragments of nail, and listening for the sound of the key turning round in the lock. This time, she didn't dread being left alone. This time, she wanted them to go. When she heard the door shut, she jumped up, then made herself wait. She must be absolutely sure that they'd gone. If they returned unexpectedly, and caught her drawing, they'd be even angrier than they'd been in England. This time they might do what they'd often threatened and turn her out of their home. Now, she concentrated on the sound of their receding steps while she felt the shapes of the pencils and crayons through the cloth of her skirt. So long as she still had these, she knew she could wait. She had taken them from the school in England, and nobody, least of all her friends, had ever suspected that she stole. At the time she'd been ashamed of herself, but today she was glad. Today, she needed them more than she'd ever thought she would.

Now, she remembered how she'd walked round and round that fenced-in place they'd called the playground, in the school. She'd linked her arm to the arms of those other girls she'd loved so much, and who had been her friends. They'd liked her and she'd liked them, and none of them had ever guessed that, secretly, she was a thief. They'd smiled as they'd said their version of her name. 'Emi . . . Emi . . .' they'd giggled, and she'd giggled too, returning their smiles and laughing with them at things that seemed like jokes, even when she hadn't understood. She remembered the soft pressure of their bodies against hers and the smell of their hair and skin. For a moment she recalled the smoky warmth of their breath, the sounds of them shrieking and the colours of their strange dyed hair. She heard the sound of the school bell and then the thunder of their feet on the stairs in huge black shoes like hooves. They'd been so kind and now she missed them so much. Yet none of them had ever guessed she was a thief. She stared at the yellow walls: would they still have liked her, if they'd known that her pockets concealed pencils and little tubes of paint which she'd stolen from their school?

It made her feel bad. She hadn't taken the things in handfuls, but one by one, and only now and then. She'd known that it was wrong, but the longer she'd stayed in England, the harder it had become to face a future where she might never draw with things like that again. That's why she'd taken them: not to use while she was there, but just in case. She'd kept them hidden in the pockets of her red skirt and so long as she'd had them, she'd felt more secure. Whenever her father had talked of moving on, she'd gone into the English school next day, and stolen something else.

Now, she shut her eyes and pictured her family approaching the far corner of the street. Soon they must be out of sight.

'One-two-three-four-five-six-seven-eight-nine-ten!' She counted their imagined steps as slowly as she could. That way it took more time. Anyway, now that she'd learnt the numbers in English, she didn't want to forget. She counted again: then reached under the sofa, but pulled back her arm. Supposing they'd forgotten something: then they'd come back. She ran to the window, but there was no one in the street outside. In fact, there was nothing there at all.

The view that she'd drawn two days before had disappeared. For a second she wondered if she was awake, but when she pressed her face to the glass she realised that the scene had been unmade by mist. The kerbstones, the tree on the corner and the blue door in the building had all vanished. They'd melted away as silently as the snow. For another moment, even the hostel was still, as if all its other inhabitants had vanished as well. In front of her, the white mist shifted and rolled, and she felt as dizzy as if she was floating too. She was as scared as she'd been on the ferry, when she'd looked down on the heaving sea. Now, she gripped the window ledge and tried to look through the mist, but it was too thick and nothing like a safe horizon came into sight.

Then she heard something. She heard a child's cry and she thought of Zoltan. She imagined him lost in the mist and calling from the street below. She struggled to open the window, but the catch had been painted over, so she couldn't make it move. She pressed her hands to the glass. But it wasn't her brother's voice. She'd heard some other child who'd called her from some other, much more distant place.

Quickly she retrieved the book, and examined the drawing of 'the view from a yellow room'. She was content that the picture remained unfinished: that was how it should be. The yellow walls did shut her in, but they also enclosed a safe place from which she could look back to other places and other times that she had known before. It was enough and she was glad.

She signed her name under the first picture, just as they'd shown her in England. Then, she turned over and began a new sketch.

She drew another entrance, along another winter street. She set another door into a darkened wall, but this door wasn't blue. In her memory, it had no colour at all, except the unreflective surface of its dirt. Beside it, she drew the child who had been calling out. She used a flash of red on the girl's skirt. Then, using the finest pen she had, she looped in her two fair plaits that had swung down to her waist.

Emilia had always worn her hair long and in two thin plaits. All gypsy girls did. Yet, even then, she'd been different from the others, because she'd been fair and pale, while they were strong and dark. Her hair had always been colourless and now it reminded her of the ugly, cut-off stems of bunches of flowers that have been thrown out by the flower sellers. In Bucharest, women had teased Elizabeta a lot. They used to ask Elizabeta what terrible fright she'd had before the baby was born, because that was the reason the poor child's hair was so colourless: she'd been scared to death in the womb. Nevertheless, Emilia's head had itched just as much as everyone else's did. None of the houses in their part of Bucharest had had water and it had been impossible to keep clean. They'd all been troubled by lice. She'd also had a patch of flaking skin behind her ear and another behind her knee. They'd both itched so much they'd driven her mad. The sore spot behind her knee oozed and needed to be scratched. And that's what she'd been doing the day she'd seen two red-haired girls walking towards her in Bucharest. She'd been balancing on one leg while she gave the other leg a really good scratch. She'd also been leaning against a restaurant window, hoping to smell the food. That morning, the itch had been particularly bad. It was always worst when the weather was cold and she'd been out since early morning, begging in the square.

A waiter had already chased her away from the restaurant a couple of times. Once he'd spat at her, then he'd flung a stone. She'd retreated, then returned to her place by the window because a bit of warmth sometimes seeped through the glass as well as the smell of food. Later, the waiter had given up. He'd done his duty and tried to keep beggars from the door, so he'd turned his back on her and begun polishing a pile of knives and forks instead. She'd noticed that he was busy inside and had leant against the window again and sighed with relief as she'd scratched. When she'd looked up, she'd seen the red-haired girls quite close.

She'd first noticed them earlier that morning, when they'd been climbing from a taxi at the far end of the square. They were obviously tourists, although winter wasn't the usual time for such people to visit Bucharest. There'd been four of them: two adults who were tall and clean and smart, and these two girls whose amazing red hair had billowed from their white fur hats like flames from clouds. Elizabeta had been sweeping. She hadn't stopped as the foreigners approached, but she'd held out her hand without breaking the rhythm of her strokes. The strangers hadn't noticed her upturned palm, or hadn't cared, or maybe they just hadn't understood. They'd stepped aside to avoid her broom, but they hadn't put a coin into her mother's hand. Emilia had been nearby, hopping from foot to foot as she'd tried to keep warm. Now, she remembered how she'd stopped hopping as they'd approached, and stared at the colour of their hair. It had been as bright as fire. Then, one of the girls had also stopped. She'd lifted her foot from her fur-lined boot and fiddled with the toe of her green spotted sock. As she did so, her red hair had swung forward, as if a wind had fanned the flames. She'd pushed her hair back from her face and, still balancing on one foot, she'd looked directly at Emilia, and grinned. Then, she'd stepped back into her boot and run after the others who'd continued walking across the square.

They'd approached the President's palace and then

stopped and stared. Emilia hadn't been surprised. It was what strangers always did. The palace had been built by the old President, Nicolae Ceausescu, who'd been shot. Everybody said that his palace was the biggest palace in the world, and Emilia had believed what they'd said. She couldn't imagine any building being bigger than that. It was simply huge, and much too big to be seen in a single glance. She'd been watching it grow all her life and she still hadn't seen it all. Whenever she'd gazed at it, she'd always been startled to notice something new. A few days after the President and his wife had been shot, Emilia'd heard that ordinary people had broken into the palace and stolen some of its things. She'd wished she'd gone too. She hadn't wanted to thieve, but she would have loved to have gone inside, and seen its amazing rooms.

And amazement was what those foreigners must've felt as they'd stood open-mouthed in front of the palace, and tried to take it all in. They'd shaded their eyes, although no sun shone, and tilted back their heads as they'd tried to get a better view. Then they'd walked to and fro, as though there were some puzzle about the building that they hadn't understood. Steaming breath had trailed from their lips like smoke. The man had taken photographs. The woman had turned the pages of a small book with her gloved hand. They'd shrugged their shoulders and pulled faces at each other, as if they'd given up. They'd called the girls, and glanced at the tremendous building one more time. Then they'd turned their backs on it and strolled away across the square.

Emilia had watched them disappear with regret.

'If you'd only asked *me*,' she'd thought, 'I could have

29

drawn you every line, and floor and ledge and arch, almost, because I know the pattern of the palace as well as I know the pattern of my own street.' But they hadn't asked her. Such people never did. With the exception of one of their daughters, they hadn't even noticed she was there. When they'd gone, Emilia had taken a sharp stick from her pocket and drawn another picture of the palace in the mud.

Later, when she'd been leaning against the restaurant window and had got her nail underneath the scab on the back of her knee, she'd seen the family again. She'd been convinced that that was what they were: a mother and father, with two little girls. This time they'd passed so close that they'd almost jogged her elbow and she'd been so enchanted by their appearance that she'd forgotten to hold out her hand. They'd stood out from everyone else because they'd shone with colours that were brighter and better than those around. She'd watched the family climb the two steps at the restaurant's entrance. There, the mother'd hesitated. The father'd pushed open the dark door with its heavy, weary swing. The girls had followed him. They'd looked cold: their little noses were bright pink under their white fur hats and they'd reminded her of a pair of young cats. Halfway through the entrance the younger one had sneezed and as she'd put her hands up to wipe away the snot, the great door had swung back and almost pushed her out.

Outside, Emilia had pressed her face against the window, trying to see in. She'd watched the waiter show the family to an unlaid table at the back. The father shook his head. He'd pointed to the tables with pink cloths and plastic flowers at the front. The waiter smiled, but shook his head.

None of the Romanian diners had bothered to look up. It had always been like that. Even Emilia, who'd never been in a restaurant, had known what to expect. Her father'd laughed at these tourists. It wasn't just the palace that they never understood. He'd always called them poor fools, who'd wasted good money and travelled all the way to Bucharest, but were never able to understand Romanian life. They never learnt the first lesson, which was that you had to pay for everything, even for the right to sit at a table with a grubby pink cloth. Once she'd heard her father complain that if the Romanian government had been able to charge its people for the air they breathed, then they would. He'd also muttered that if you were a gypsy, they'd have made you pay twice. That's what these tourists, who had so much money, never understood.

She'd continued watching this foreign father, whose red hair had faded like cloth in the sun. He'd seated himself defiantly at one of the front tables by the window. The waiter had smiled but pointed to the back. When the mother and girls sat down as well, the waiter had shrugged and walked off. At first they'd waited quietly. The younger girl had reached inside her boots again and fiddled with her spotted socks. The mother'd looked down at the menu, then up at the other customers. She clearly hoped that someone would explain what they should do. But no one helped them because no one ever did. Nearby, the waiter polished knives and forks. The older girl picked up her mother's book. She turned a few pages, then settled down to read. The smaller girl was bored. She was wriggling and had pleated up the cloth. Suddenly, she'd rubbed a circle of window clear of condensation and looked out.

31

Their eyes had met through the glass. Both had been startled and looked away, but when Emilia'd looked back, she'd seen that the other girl's eyes were as green as still water or the first blades of grass. She'd pressed herself as close as she could and she'd been so fascinated by the stranger's face that she'd forgotten about the itch on her leg. This girl, who was younger than herself, had wiped her nose on her sleeve, then suddenly stuck out her tongue. The elder girl had noticed and kicked her sister under the table. The little one kicked back. They'd pushed and shoved each other about until their mother'd given them a look. Then the elder one had made a face and gone back to reading the book. The younger one had fidgeted with her empty plate, then looked up. This time, she'd pushed her cat's nose against the window, poked her pink tongue through her squashed-up lips and licked a drop of moisture from the inside of the glass. Her leafy eyes had sparkled with fun and this time, Emilia had understood. The girl wasn't being horrid or rude. This was her idea of making friends.

Carefully, Emilia'd taken her special banknote from the waistband of her skirt. Then she'd pointed to the waiter and held it up. The older girl had blushed. She'd tossed her red hair over her eyes and hidden herself away. The little girl had wrinkled up her brow, then grinned as if she'd suddenly understood. She'd touched her father's arm and made him look through the window at Emilia and the note. She'd realised that Emilia wasn't begging but was trying to tell them something. The father rubbed his chin on his hand, then got up. He'd shaken his head as he'd realised that if they wanted to be served in the restaurant, he had to offer money first. Emilia'd watched him hand a banknote to the waiter. A few minutes later, the whole family were eating chocolate cake.

The older girl had eaten fast. The younger girl had picked up her knife and carefully cut her slice in two. Then she'd picked up one half with her clean, pink hand and nibbled like a mouse. Emilia'd swallowed and looked away. She'd never wanted to taste the frothy orange drink which was always served as well. Foreigners usually took a gulp of the drink, then looked at each other in surprise and put their glasses down. But the cake was different. Foreigners always finished that and Emilia'd always longed to taste a piece herself.

When Emilia'd looked back at the family, she'd noticed that the green-eyed girl had left her seat and was now snuggling against her father's shoulder and stroking his cheek. He hadn't pushed her away and looked cross, as her father would have done if she'd behaved like that. Instead, he'd pushed his chair back and lifted her onto his lap. She'd put her arms round his neck and as she'd whispered into his ear, her red curls had covered his face. Emilia'd guessed that this was tickling him because he'd laughed and scratched his neck. Then the girl had pointed to where Emilia stood and this time they'd all stopped eating and stared at Emilia through the glass.

She'd stepped back, and, as she'd done so, she'd seen her own reflection in the window. For the first time in her life, she'd been ashamed. She'd never realised how filthy she was. Her skirt was stiff with mud. It had no colour at all. Her nails were broken and black edged. Her hands were cracked with cold. Her cheeks glistened with layers of greasy, smoky dirt. No wonder people crossing the square stepped over her: she wasn't worth a second glance. Compared to the girls inside, eating chocolate cake, she was no different from the rubbish in the street. She'd been so disgusted with herself that she could have cried, except that she never, ever did.

Just then, the restaurant door had opened. A trail of music and the smell of soup had leaked out into the street. She'd already put her dirty hands behind her back and begun to edge away. She hadn't wanted to look at the foreigners any more. When someone spoke and touched her arm, she'd run.

'Hello?' But a cry had followed her across the square.

'Hello? Come back! Please?' Now that Emilia'd been in England she was sure that this was what the girl had said, but that morning, she'd only heard the sound.

'Ple-ease?'

And stopped.

'Please . . .' The younger girl had been running after her and holding something out. With her hands still hidden, Emilia'd gone back. Wind flicked up the corner of a pink paper napkin and she'd seen that it was folded round the half slice of chocolate cake.

'Please?' The little girl had smiled and sniffed. Behind her, both the parents watched. The mother'd frowned and opened her mouth, but before she spoke, Emilia had taken the gift, and the other girl had run straight back. She'd run past her family to the door of the taxi that still waited in the square. Then she'd opened it and disappeared inside.

When they'd gone, Emilia'd hidden the cake in the pocket of her skirt, then retraced her steps to where

Elizabeta still swept the frozen mud with a broom made of twigs. She'd watched her mother work and as she'd listened to the sound of the twigs scratching across the ice, she'd suddenly wondered if there could be other ways to live. There, in the cold shadow of the palace that she'd been watching all her life, she'd felt dissatisfied and angry and she'd known that this was not enough. She'd wanted warmth and colour and things that were beautiful and bright. She'd wanted green socks and chocolate cake. She'd also wanted someone who'd let her whisper in their ear and who would listen to what she said.

Now, as she worked on the picture, she remembered what she'd done that night. When she'd been sure that her family was asleep, she'd taken the cake from her pocket and eaten it secretly in bed. She couldn't remember its exact taste any more, but she could recall its dryness in her throat, that had been followed by a sticky sweetness as it dissolved, crumb by crumb. Today, after living in England and eating real chocolate with friends, she suspected that the restaurant cake hadn't been made with chocolate at all. But that night, in bed, the taste had been darker and sweeter than anything she'd eaten before. She'd sat in the cold room, licking the last fragments from the napkin and wondering what it would be like to climb into a taxi, and be driven away. Hugging her knees, she'd let her tongue search out the last traces of sweetness, while her body had felt hot with an excitement that she hadn't known before. The fever hadn't only been caused by the thought of going away, it had also been caused by her anxiety about eating the cake. As a gypsy, she was forbidden to eat other people's food, because it was unclean.

Her parents would have been revolted and furious if they'd known, and until that night, she'd have agreed and been disgusted too. She'd never copied other hungry children on the streets and eaten food from rubbish bins. She'd known that it was wrong. But that night, as she'd sat in the dark, with the strange taste lingering on her tongue, she'd repeated the sound of the other girl's words, over and over again. 'Pleasehellopleasehelloplease.' Then, like the bad daughter she was, she'd secretly wished that one day she might leave the only place she'd ever known.

As she'd sat there, Emilia'd realised that she wasn't only bad because she'd broken the laws about clean food. She was bad because she'd been deceitful too. She'd never told her parents about the special note she'd hidden in the waistband of her skirt. Another foreigner had given it to her several weeks before. He'd dropped it in front of her and it had blown and fluttered in a breeze. He'd laughed when she'd run after it, but she hadn't cared. She'd already noticed its special colour and she hadn't wanted it to fall into the mud. When she'd caught it, she'd examined the picture and seen that it was particularly beautiful. That's why she'd kept it, at first, though she'd never kept anything before. She and her mother had always handed their earnings to Daniel who understood about foreign money and saved it up. This time, with the beautiful note in her hand, she'd glanced at her mother and when she was sure that she wasn't being watched, she'd folded it into the waistband of her skirt. Later, she'd secretly studied the picture and copied its lines in the mud. That night, after she'd eaten the cake, she'd smoothed the creases from the bank note and the pink napkin, and accepted the fact that she was

36

bad. Then she'd hidden them under a loose piece of board by the bed.

Now, she ran her fingers over the picture that she'd drawn. She wrote the words 'hello' and 'please' all round its edge. She threaded the words in and out of each other, using all the colours that she had. When she was satisfied, she signed her name underneath and closed the book.

Outside the mist was thick and white. She yawned. She was tired, although she didn't know what time it was. She leant her head against the back of the sofa and closed her eyes. Then she whispered the lucky words to herself, just as she'd done as a little girl, to lull herself to sleep.

'Hellopleasehelloplease . . .'

Picture 3

Faces in School

'Please?'

Emilia opened her eyes and looked for the person who'd spoken, but there was no one else in the shadows of the unlit yellow room. She must've been dreaming of Bucharest and –

'Hello?' There it was again.

She put her fingers in her mouth and bit off another piece of skin.

'Hello? You are in?'

Now she realised that the voice came from outside, not from within. And it wasn't a man's voice. This was a woman or a girl.

'Hello?' Someone was speaking to her from behind the door.

Outside, the evening sky flickered with the glow of the town beyond and the swinging lights of the cars. Silently Emilia stood up. Suddenly, she wanted her parents back. What had kept them away so long, with a winter night coming on?

'Hello?' The voice was warm.

Emilia moved closer to the door. Why hadn't they returned? Where could they go in this strange town, where they didn't know a soul? Unless –

'Hello? My name is Zeynep, Zeynep Kara. You open the door? Please?' Then someone tapped.

Emilia tiptoed to the door. Her parents must be on their way back. Unless – she bit into her flesh. She mustn't think like that. Her parents would *never* go away and leave her all alone. Even though they'd threatened to. They couldn't do it, and especially not in winter, and at night. Could they?

'Hello? My name is *Zeynep*. Who *you* are?'

Soundlessly, Emilia rested her head against the door and rehearsed the words she should have said. 'Hello. My name is Emilia Radu. I am coming from Bucharest. I like England very well. What your name is, please? And how old?' That's what she'd learnt from her friends in the English school. She hadn't forgotten the words, but she couldn't say them aloud. Something like fear had snatched at her throat and wouldn't let her speak out. She shut her eyes and held her breath as she listened for the sound of this other girl, breathing behind the door. But there was nothing there. When she heard the clang of the lift a moment later, she knew she'd missed a chance to speak once more.

She returned to the window and rested her forehead against the glass. Then she noticed a figure in the street outside, walking away into the dusk. It was moving very quickly, with head bent down. It could have been a boy, but it might have been that girl, wearing jeans. Every now and then the hurrying figure glanced back, as if sensing that someone was following behind. Halfway along the street the figure stopped, looked quickly all round, then snatched something from the pavement, and ran. As they passed under a streetlight, Emilia saw the flash of a red jacket and the swing of straight black hair. She pressed closer and followed the runner into the night because there was something about their movements that she'd understood.

In England, she'd also walked too fast whenever she was alone. When she wasn't with friends from school, she'd always been anxious that someone would point at her and shout. She'd always been waiting for someone to laugh at her and say that this, or that, was wrong. Usually, people had only stared. Often, they'd whispered to each other as they'd walked away and then she'd been worried that they were criticising her. Yet it wasn't only the black-haired figure's speed that she'd noticed. It was the habit of looking at the ground, then snatching up something that other people had dropped. That's what poor people did, and she had done it too.

In Bucharest, she'd always picked up everything: sticks for the fire, nails that could be straightened out, bottles and cans and rags that could be sold. There'd never been that much left lying around, because most people had so few things, but whenever Emilia'd noticed something useful, she'd acted just like this person. She'd pounced, before anyone else could. It remained one of the puzzles about England, that there was so much thrown onto the streets which no one bothered to pick up. Back in Bucharest, Emilia had always handed her picked-up things to her father, and Daniel had sorted them and sold them on. That was his work. It had been what they'd needed to do. The blue banknote was the first thing she'd ever withheld. After she'd kept back the napkin as well, she'd felt like a thief who'd begun a secret hoard.

It was these things that made her suspect that the person in the red jacket was the girl, Zeynep, who had been tapping on the door. So why had she kept quiet? If the girl at the door was someone like herself, why hadn't she made herself talk? That girl could have been a friend.

Emilia watched the figure run past the lighted tree. She saw her pause on the edge of the busy street, then plunge amongst the mass of cars and flaring lights, where she was swallowed up and lost.

So why had she been so stupid? Why hadn't she answered? It wasn't hard to say 'hello': she'd been whispering that word to herself ever since she'd heard it from the little girl in the square. Now she bit through a thread of skin and despised herself for being such a coward. It didn't matter that the door between them was locked. They could have spoken through. She might have made a friend. This girl could have become like her friends in the English school, who'd looked up and smiled whenever she'd approached.

She shut her eyes and thought of them and saw their faces very close: Yasmina and Katy, and Sam. Especially Sam. If she were to draw their portraits she could bring them nearer still. Then . . .

She pulled out the book, switched on the light, but stopped. This was not the way. She was rushing on too fast. If this picture diary was to make sense to anyone else she must keep her English friends hidden in her imagination and concentrate on her more distant days in Bucharest. She must draw a picture of the Romanian school.

Pictures of the English school wouldn't make sense unless she'd drawn this scene first.

She couldn't remember how old she'd been that day, but she did remember that it must have happened in early summer because the weather had been very hot. And it must have been the summer after she'd seen the red-haired girls, because she hadn't thought about going to school before. It was only after she'd seen them that she'd wanted to read and write. She'd begun to look around and had decided that reading couldn't be that difficult because she'd seen children younger than herself reading books in the park. She'd started to hang around the local school, watching other children going in and out. During that spring, when the classroom windows were thrown open, she'd loitered outside and listened to the students chanting in singsong voices which rippled and billowed like clouds. Sometimes they'd sung. In the mornings, they'd stood in straight lines in the school yard and when a teacher shouted, they'd marched.

Occasionally, when important men came to Bucharest, the students were taken out to line the roadside and wave. When the big black cars approached, the teachers made a sign and some of the children had waved their paper flags at the cars, while the rest cheered and clapped. She'd watched them from a safe distance because a child or teacher sometimes threw a stone. She'd envied the pupils, with their school bags and clean clothes, and she'd wanted to join in. She'd wanted to stand in line with them and wave a real Romanian flag.

Her parents had been annoyed when she'd started asking if she could be a student too. They'd said she was a fool.

Didn't she know that no child ever went willingly to school? Didn't she realise that the teachers carried sticks? Hadn't she noticed that few children from the gypsy district ever started school, and if they did, they'd never carried on? Her father said that neither the teachers nor the pupils wanted a gypsy in their class, so it was hardly surprising that decent gypsy families never let their children go. Emilia'd believed them, to begin with. They'd explained that school was no help to people like themselves, and not safe either, especially for girls, who would marry and have a husband and a mother-in-law to tell them what to do.

But as that spring progressed, Emilia had begun to have doubts. She'd thought about the red-haired girls and she'd watched a rich man's child sitting in a car, reading by himself. He'd been so engrossed in the book that he'd never noticed her creeping up and staring in. Day after day, on her way to buy bread, she'd loitered by a bit of broken wall opposite the school, and watched. None of the pupils had seemed afraid. They were usually laughing and fooling about as they trooped in through the gate. She'd imagined herself mingling with them and slipping past the caretaker unobserved, before he'd shot home the bolt.

Then one morning she'd made a detour and crossed the road. She'd rested her chin on the curves of the wrought iron gate and peered through. A young woman teacher, whom she hadn't seen before, had been walking across the yard with a pile of papers in her arms. She'd been screwing up her eyes against the sun, but she must've noticed Emilia, because she'd changed direction and come towards the gate. She'd been smart, with short shiny hair and a pale, smiling face. She'd smiled at Emilia and beckoned with the fingers of one hand. Emilia had clung to the warm bars and smiled back. 'Would you like to come in?' The teacher had tried to lift the bolt with the toe of her shoe, so Emilia had stuck her hands through and helped. When the gate had swung open, she'd walked into the yard. She would have liked to explain that she'd always wanted to come to school, but it hadn't seemed necessary. When the teacher had repeated her question, Emilia'd nodded and the teacher had looked very pleased. She'd followed the teacher across the sunlit yard and never thought about the bread. She had remembered her father, and what he'd always said about school but she'd only wished he had been there. Then he would have realised that he was wrong about teachers and schools. This teacher was happy that a gypsy wanted to come in.

She'd begun to run towards the building. It had never occurred to her to wait. She'd been certain that in another moment she'd be learning how to write her name. They might even let her draw. If they did, she'd known exactly what to make: it had to be the flag. She'd been startled when the woman took her hand to slow her up. Now, she remembered how awkward she'd felt. She'd been shy of being touched. Gypsies like them had always kept themselves apart. She'd felt herself sweat, but she'd let the teacher hold her hand and she hadn't pulled away. Together, they'd stepped out of the blazing sun and into the shadows of the school. At that time, she hadn't been inside many buildings other than her home so the school had seemed very big and very quiet. The tiled floor was thick with trodden dust and the footprints on it had looked like autumn leaves. A silent corridor stretched in front of them, and the sounds of children's voices were as distant as the drone of flies shut in.

The teacher had stopped in front of one door and given her hand an extra squeeze. Emilia'd felt her heart pound in her chest. When the door opened a rush of hot air had gushed out and Emilia'd blinked, then seen the rows of children packed in behind the desks. As she'd entered, every face in every row had turned. Silently the rows of children looked her up and down. The school had only been two streets from her house, but she'd realised, with growing panic, that she couldn't recognise a single face. She'd been scared and surprised to find herself so alone, but she hadn't thought about escape, even though the door behind her was open and she could have run very fast.

Now, as she leant over the book and drew another row of staring eyes, she realised that even then she'd been braver than she was today. She hadn't enjoyed being stared at, but she still hadn't run away.

The staring children had started to whisper and wriggle about. The young teacher had squeezed her hand again, then led her to an empty place beside a big girl who was scratching her neck and ears, and who smelt of meat. She'd sat down and the big girl had shifted up. The other teacher in the room, who was old and white-haired, had looked across. She'd banged on the floor with a stick. In the silence that followed, she'd laid her stick across the teacher's desk, folded her arms and begun to stare at Emilia as though she'd never seen a girl like her before. The younger teacher had said something and left. The children talked and laughed, but the old one hadn't told them off. She'd continued to stare at Emilia, without moving a muscle in her face. When she eventually turned away, Emilia had noticed that she had a limp.

The children had fallen silent as she'd picked up her stick. She'd resumed speaking in a high, harsh voice which Emilia had found difficult to understand because they never used words like that at home. The children had elbowed each other and whispered as they'd all tried to follow the lesson from a few shared books. The big girl, who was one of the very few to have a book to herself, had edged it away so that Emilia couldn't look. All the time she was speaking, the teacher had limped up and down the rows. Sometimes, for no reason that Emilia could see, she'd thumped one of the students with her stick. At other times she'd brought the stick down on a desk. There'd been a fan on the ceiling but it wasn't turning round and as the sun had moved and shone into the room, Emilia'd felt the sweat trickling down her back and soaking through her clothes. Beside her, the big girl scratched. The teacher had limped and tapped her way up and down the rows, and talked all the time. Emilia had made herself listen but she hadn't understood a single thing.

She'd concentrated so hard that her head had ached. Then, unexpectedly, she'd begun to feel bored. She'd imagined that learning things might be hard work, but she'd never contemplated being bored. She'd stifled a yawn. When she'd looked up, she'd noticed that a couple of children had nodded off. The room had been airless and she'd found it difficult to sit so still. If she hadn't wanted to go to the lavatory so badly, she might have nodded off as well. However, the fear of wetting herself had kept her wide awake, and she'd sat bolt upright, with her legs all twisted up.

46

When a bell had rung suddenly, the other children had leapt to their feet and fought as they'd all tried to get out of the room at once. Emilia hadn't known what to do. She hadn't known if this was the end of one lesson or the whole day at school. She'd followed the others out. Some children were running round the yard. Others had dashed through the iron gate. She'd seen the big girl standing by herself and eating something from a paper bag. When Emilia'd approached, the girl had stuffed most of a sugar-coated bun into her mouth so that her cheeks bulged out. Emilia took the hint. As she'd turned aside, a boy stuck out his foot. She'd tripped and heard the big girl laugh, then choke explosively, through a mouthful of flying crumbs.

When Emilia'd got to her feet she'd run after the boy and slapped his face, then kept on running until she reached her house. She'd never told her parents where she'd been, but had pretended that she'd had to wait for bread. She'd told them that the supply had run out before her turn had come, and they'd believed her lies, because everybody knew that enough bread couldn't be baked because of the shortages of fuel and power.

She'd been disappointed about school, but she hadn't abandoned the idea of going. She'd continued to think that there must be something nice about it that she hadn't yet seen. Why else would those other children have continued going, day after day, when they could have been helping their parents, or working, or just playing in the street? And why did rich people know how to read and write? It'd remained a mystery that she hadn't solved. She'd asked Gizella, the older girl next door, but she'd pulled a face and said she'd never go, even if you'd paid her, because it wasn't safe, especially for girls. Boys who couldn't read or write never trusted girls who could. Then she'd whispered that she'd seen a boy she really liked and she was sure that he liked her. Emilia had concentrated on making her pattern in the dust. She'd listened to Gizella, but she'd always hated conversations about marriage and love, or anything like that. She'd always avoided them, if she could.

For several weeks after that she'd hung around the school gate, keeping watch. She'd hoped to see the young woman teacher again, but never did. Then, one afternoon when both her parents and Zoltan were out, she'd changed into her cleanest clothes, washed her face and hands, and gone back to school. She'd darted into the crowd of children pushing and shoving to get through the gate and managed to tumble into the yard with everyone else, behind the caretaker's back. Then she'd walked down the same dusty corridor and gone into the classroom through the same grey door.

The same rows of children had looked up, but this time the old woman had done more than stare. She'd picked up her stick and limped across. She'd grabbed the collar of Emilia's blouse and dragged her to the front of the class. This time she'd spoken very slowly in her hard, high voice and this time she'd used words Emilia had understood.

Today, the teacher had told her class, there was a new lesson to be learnt. They must all pay close attention to this example of the new lesson, and learn it by heart, before it was too late. And as soon as school was over, they must all run home and tell their mothers and fathers that now, it seemed, these uppity gypsies wanted to come into their school.

As Emilia worked on the picture, she remembered how quiet the listening class had been.

The teacher had asked the other children to study their example well. She'd used her stick to point out Emilia's dirty hands and nails. How, she'd asked them, could a girl with hands like that be allowed to touch their books? She'd make them so dirty that even the best students wouldn't be able to read a word. Then the teacher had wrinkled her brow and scratched her head, as if Emilia was some problem that could not be understood. She'd poked at the torn hem of Emilia's best skirt with her stick. Then she'd raised it and clapped her hand over her mouth in horror, because Emilia hadn't been wearing shoes. She'd puckered up her lips, taken a step back and sniffed. Holding her nose, with her little finger arched up, she'd turned to her students. Had *they*, also, noticed a new and 'unRomanian' smell in their nice clean class?

Laughter had rippled along the rows. Emilia hadn't been sure what sort of joke this was, so she'd laughed too, at first. The big girl had laughed so much she'd wept. The teacher'd prodded Emilia's blackened feet with her stick and this had made her jump. The other children had erupted with delight.

'This little gypsy,' the teacher'd cried, 'had better learn to wash and mend before she tries to come to *our* school!'

Next, Emilia remembered that the old woman had asked her class if they agreed with her, and when they'd all roared 'yes!' she'd let herself smile, just a very little bit. The children had howled and bayed, like dogs in a pack. The teacher had used her stick to wave them on, and showed them where to point. They'd all stabbed the thick air with their grubby fingers, and they'd laughed at Emilia until the tears ran down their faces like sweat. Emilia had looked along the rows of desks. She'd seen their bulging eyes and their swollen, wide-stretched lips. When she'd glanced at the girls in the front row, she'd seen right down their throats.

Now, as she recalled their contorted faces, she was reminded of wilted flowers, torn up then dropped along a scorching road. The laughter had finally ended when the teacher hit a desk with her stick. Like beasts before an upraised arm, the children had cowered, then fallen quiet. The teacher had smoothed back her white hair and refastened a dangling grip. Then, snatching at Emilia's collar again, she'd dragged her to a place at the back, where the biggest boys all sat.

Months later, when her mother had been sweeping in the square and she'd been drawing in the mud, the young teacher had hurried past, then stopped and turned back. She'd talked about returning to the school. She'd said that she'd been disappointed to learn that Emilia hadn't carried on. Emilia'd pretended not to recognise her. She hadn't even looked up. She'd rubbed her foot to and fro over the drawing and she hadn't stopped until she'd been sure the teacher had gone.

Now, she stretched her arms above her head and looked at the picture she'd just done. Then she hid the book under the sofa and returned to the window overlooking the street. Somewhere out there, a black wind whined, and rolled an empty can to and fro. It was evening again, and cars were parked on both sides of the road. A cyclist with a winking red light was bending over his handlebars and swerving from side to side as he struggled against the wind. There was no sign of the girl in the red jacket, nor of her family coming home. While the street became quieter in the evening, the building she was in was always noisier than before. She imagined the other residents coming in from the cold and blowing on their fingers after they'd turned on their lights. She could hear them turning on their televisions and listening to music as they moved about, calling to each other, putting plates on a table and starting to warm up their food. They'd be more cheerful because they'd escaped the wind. As she listened, she heard a child start to cry and next door, maybe, someone was stirring something round and round with a scratchy metal spoon. Outside the wind snuffled against the window and whined, and the can still rolled about.

As she listened she remembered another windy evening when she'd also been looking onto a street. It had been at the end of the next winter in Bucharest. In her house another child was being born. Elizabeta had refused to go into the hospital, so was giving birth secretly, at home. Their district was full of rumours of what happened to gypsy babies in hospitals, so she was taking no risks. The house had been full of women who were gypsies like themselves, and had come to help. Emilia remembered sitting on the windy step outside, shivering and listening to the sounds of birth. Zoltan was with her, but he was busy playing with a stray pup and a bit of string. The women had been calling her to come and look, but she'd refused. She'd never been interested in babies and births. The whole thing disgusted her so much, she hadn't wanted to learn.

Instead, she'd crouched over the box on her lap and

carefully raised its lid. Inside, was her collection of picked-up papers that she'd begun the night she'd hidden the napkin and the banknote under that piece of wood. She'd been collecting interesting pieces of paper ever since. Originally she'd kept them all together, underneath her bed. Then she'd found an empty box outside a big hotel. It was perfect and unmarked and she'd run the length of the street to get to it first. There was a folded piece of thin white paper inside and the writing on the red lid was in gold. To begin with, the box had smelt of something sweet and there'd been a dusting of sugar in its cracks. By the time it was half full with her collection of papers, that smell had faded and as she'd sat on the step, she hadn't been able to smell it at all.

She'd built the collection up by hanging around grocery stores and kiosks in the main streets. Those were the places where rich people bought things and often tossed the wrappings down. Summer had always been better for collecting than winter. The sun brought the tourists who'd lingered in the streets and bought things to take back home. Winter meant fewer tourists. It also meant that anything dropped was soon spoilt by mud. But she'd collected steadily, pouncing on things that previously she'd have rejected as too small, or not useful enough, to pick up. She'd had her favourites and she'd looked at those again and again. One was a piece of petal-thin purple tissue. It had been around a bouquet of dried-up flowers that she'd spotted in a bin. She'd also loved the gold and silver foils from inside packs of foreign cigarettes.

Her mother was scornful but she hadn't interfered. Whenever she'd been angry with Emilia, she'd called the collection 'that stinking rubbish', and threatened to burn the lot. Sometimes she'd complained to her neighbours about the shame of having a daughter who was either stupid or mad, but Emilia hadn't cared. Once, she'd tried to explain to her mother that these pieces of paper were beautiful and precious, like gold. When Elizabeta had laughed at her, she hadn't tried again. Yet in the evenings she'd often sat by herself, with the box on her knees. Sometimes, she'd spent hours smoothing the creases away, especially from the foils. At other times, she'd arranged the papers into patterns and pictures on the floor. She'd also memorised their marks and lines and copied them in her own pictures. She'd hoped to find so many different shades of colours that eventually she'd have been able to arrange them in overlapping bands like a rainbow's magic arc. Often, she'd been so absorbed by the papers that when she'd put her hands amongst them, she'd dreamed that she was in some better, brighter place.

And that was what she'd been doing on the evening of the baby's birth. She hadn't taken the papers from the box because as soon as she'd opened the lid, the wind had got amongst them and threatened to scatter them down the street. The women had come out to the step and pinched her cheeks, and teased her, as they'd tried to persuade her to come inside. They'd told her that her turn would come. Once she was married, they'd joked, there would be no escape from birth. She'd opened the lid of the box and slipped her hands inside. She'd felt the touch of the papers on her skin and she'd ignored the women. She'd imagined a thousand shades of red instead.

She hadn't wanted to think about the baby. Babies didn't

interest her and the thought of marriage had always made her feel uncomfortable and odd. When the child was finally born, Emilia had been revolted by the way it smelt and by its wrinkled, hairy skin. She'd preferred her papers. Their smells excited her, like the smell of incense in the church or the street smell of a coming summer storm. When the women had handed the baby boy to her, she'd kissed him, guiltily, and hoped that no one had noticed her pity and disgust.

It must have been late when her parents finally returned to the hostel. Emilia had already fallen asleep, but she was woken by the sound of the key in the lock, then by Zoltan, coughing in the night. When she got up the next morning it was clear that he was ill. He was refusing to leave his bed and had hunched himself up with his face in the pillow. His gruff voice emerged as a croak. Elizabeta and Daniel stood on either side of his bed. They talked about finding medicines or a doctor, but they did not know how. When Zoltan coughed, the mound of bedclothes heaved and he burrowed deeper in. Elizabeta pulled them from his grasp and then he squinted back at her through swollen, tear-stained eyes. He coughed again, then couldn't stop. It looked as if he was trying to spit his tongue out of his mouth.

Emilia turned away and stared into the street. Few traces of snow remained on the roofs of houses but outside it looked bitterly cold. Below her, people were hurrying along with their heads down and their faces muffled against the biting wind. When she went back into the bedroom, Zoltan was being sick. His forehead glistened with sweat and his spine stuck out like a bent reed. There was no alternative: Elizabeta must go out and beg. Daniel would go with her, to make sure she was safe. Then, with money in their hands, they could approach a doctor or buy strong medicine to drive away the cough.

When they'd gone, Emilia sat beside Zoltan on his bed. She was sorry for him but didn't know what to do. She touched his shoulder awkwardly, but he jerked his arm to keep her off.

'Perhaps they'll bring you back one of those huge chocolates that you saw the other day.' She hoped the thought might cheer him up. He lay still for a moment, with his face buried in the pillow, then he turned onto his back.

'D'you think they will?' His voice was a raw squeak, but he must have liked her idea because after she'd nodded, he shut his eyes and seemed to sleep.

Emilia went to the window and rested her head against the glass until another spasm of coughing brought her back. He muttered something else about chocolate, then settled down to sleep. When Emilia returned to the window, she saw the black-haired girl standing on the bottom step, staring up. Her hair fell from her upturned face like a sleek black wing. Her breath hung in the frozen air like a plume of smoke. Her red jacket was zipped up to her chin, but her wrists and neck stuck out and she looked very cold. When their eyes met, the girl stepped back onto the pavement to get a better view. Then waved.

Picture 4

A Basket of Red Plums

Instantly, Emilia ducked out of sight below the window ledge. She felt as if a hand had grabbed her throat and was squeezing it, so that she couldn't breathe. She wanted to wave back, but she couldn't even move. She bit into the skin around her thumbnail to make herself do something, but when she finally forced herself to peer over the sill, the black-haired girl had gone. Once more, Emilia struggled with the painted-over catch. Although she knew she was too late, she was still desperate to raise the window and shout out. She used all her strength but couldn't shift it at all. She clenched her knuckles and drew her arm back but wasn't brave enough to knock. She'd become such a coward that she didn't even dare bang on the glass.

She turned away. She despised herself, and hated whatever it was that held her back. A few weeks ago, in England, she had been a girl whom people liked and wanted to know. She'd had her photograph in the local newspaper and been described as a Young Romanian Artist. Her framed pictures had been hanging on the walls of the English school. Total strangers had been interested in what she was doing and had made offers of help.

And now? Now she'd become a cringing coward who ducked out of sight when someone waved. She was so useless, she hadn't dared wave back.

'Emilia?' Zoltan called from the other room. 'Emilia, won't that chocolate be too *big* to get in?' He'd pushed back the covers and his restless glance ran round the yellow walls of the room. He was frowning.

'I don't know.' She shrugged. She'd been thinking about herself, not him, and she hadn't understood what he'd meant.

'*If* it's the biggest chocolate in the world, like Dad said, how'll they get it *in*?' Tears were glittering in his eyes as he crawled down the bed towards her. When he coughed, he wiped his mouth on her wrist. His lips were burning hot.

'Don't worry about that. They'll . . .' She couldn't think of a reply so she smoothed back his damp curls instead.

'*Wha-at*?' He whined and scowled. 'What'll they *do*?'

When she remained silent, he gave her a shove. Then he lunged at her with his heel, before tangling himself in his covers and rocking to and fro. She returned to the window and noticed that the mist was rolling back down the street. Outside, the edges of the buildings were being eaten away. In the bedroom, Zoltan was coughing and choking on his phlegm. Suddenly, desperately, she wanted to escape. She wanted to leave these yellow rooms and be that other girl who was able to walk down the vanishing street to some other, unseen place where she could be free.

On the main road, beyond the tree, the cars and buses had all turned on their lights. They were dimmed by mist, but Emilia knew that they were still crawling towards destinations and sights that she might never see.

'I know!' Zoltan called out. When she went in, he was already sitting up in bed and smiling. 'I know what they'll do! I've remembered what I forgot!' He spat. 'They can use a *hammer*, can't they, or an *axe*. That's how they'll smash my chocolate up!' He lay back on the pillow and let Emilia straighten the sheets. 'Isn't it lucky that I'm so smart? Because *you'd* never have thought of that, would you, Emi?' His anger had disappeared. He was smiling, and when she'd given him another drink, he closed his eyes and slept. She stayed beside him, studying his face, and as she did so, she suddenly had an idea about the picture that she could draw next.

This time it would be a small picture, on a single page. It would be brilliantly coloured and so realistic that when you first looked at it you'd expect to be able to reach out and touch what she'd drawn. She reckoned that if she worked quickly she could finish it before Zoltan woke. He was already drawing deeper, steadier breaths. Silently willing him to sleep on, she went to get the book.

She was remembering the end of the next summer in Bucharest. It was after the new baby was born, and the city had been dry and dirty and hot. Her parents had unexpectedly decided to make a trip. She'd been surprised and excited. She'd never travelled outside Bucharest. Her parents had both been born in the city, and though she'd heard them talking about the countryside, she'd never seen it herself. She'd only known the city's streets, so she'd been amazed when she'd first seen fields and views from the windows of the bus. She'd been so used to the smoky air and stained concrete of Bucharest that when the hills and forests had spread before her, she'd felt like a guest at someone else's feast. She'd pressed her face to the jolting glass and could have looked forever at the thousand shades of green. It had been a long, hot journey to the mountains and neither Zoltan nor the baby Nicolae had kept quiet. One or other of them had been continually in her arms, whimpering or wriggling and getting in her way.

She couldn't now remember the name of the place they'd visited, but it had been a whole day's journey away. A man whom her father had addressed as uncle had been waiting for the bus at the side of a deserted road. He was one of Daniel's relatives and he also came from Bucharest. When the authorities had bulldozed one of the old quarters of the town he'd lost his house and his trade, so had come here instead. He and his family were basket-makers, but his wife had died soon after the move and his children had married and drifted back to the town. He had stayed on, practising his craft, and was making a not too bad living from it, he'd said. In summer, he sold his baskets to the tourists passing along the main road, and in winter he sold baskets to the farmers and traders who were still around.

He'd settled in an abandoned house by a stream. Some of the rooms had tumbled down, but it hadn't mattered because at the time of their visit the weather was still dry and warm. Emilia had thought that this piece of land by a stream was the most beautiful place she'd ever seen. It lay amongst quiet hills, and in the distance mountains rose into the sky. There were tumbling wild flowers and thick patches of rushes and reeds grew on the banks of the stream. In the parched, uncultivated fields, the uncut grass

59

was pale and tall and thin. And wherever she was, from the early morning to the first shadows of evening, she'd heard birds sing.

On one such evening, Emilia had slipped away from the grown-ups. They'd been sitting around a fire and talking over family matters. She hadn't been interested, so she'd crept away and brushed through the rustling stems of grass to the hedge at the far side of a field. This was where she'd seen a tree of ripened plums. Some had fallen to the ground, but more hung overhead. In the evening light they'd shone like great glass jewels. She'd tucked up her skirt, kicked off her slippers and begun to climb. There'd been few trees left in their part of Bucharest. During the last few winters, when fuel was so short, most of the remaining trees had been cut down, so it was ages since she'd climbed. She'd felt giddy with excitement as she'd put her bare foot against the bark and swung herself off the ground. When she'd found a branch firm enough to stand on, she'd wedged herself into a fork. Then, she'd reached up through the dry edged leaves and held the soft weight of the plums in the hollow of her hand.

Now, as she leant over the book and drew the shapes of those plums, and coloured them in, she remembered the taste of their golden, parting flesh, the feel of their hidden stones on her teeth, and the sticky pink stains that had run down her wrists and arms.

On that evening, while she'd been picking plums, a red sun had been setting behind the distant mountain peaks. She'd balanced there, between the branches, with the sweet taste on her tongue, and she'd watched the sun's slow fall. Through the leaves, she'd seen a sky that was purple and orange and gold. The sun had lit whatever it touched like a breath blown on smouldering coal. She'd realised how different the countryside was from the town, where the skies were grey with smoke, and nothing fresh or green grew at all. She'd rested her head against the trunk and stared up into the sky. The only sound filtering through the leaves had been the rippling songs of birds. She'd bitten into another plum and wondered what sort of person she'd have been if this view, and those colours, had always been hers. Would she still have wanted to draw?

She'd been so absorbed in these thoughts that she hadn't heard the old man approach. She hadn't realised that he was standing under the tree until he'd thrust a basket through the branches, and spoken to her.

'Here,' he'd said, 'you can fill it up with the fruit.'

She'd caught hold of the handle, then straightened her back and stared at the sky again. High above her, a small brown bird fluttered as it sang. She hadn't looked down, although she'd known that the man was there, waiting below. Slowly, she'd picked another plum and laid it in.

'This is not Bucharest,' he'd said, 'but I'm a good man. And in summer, you could pick plums and listen to my larks, because they always sing.' He'd stretched up through the leaves. His old man's hand, with mottled skin like brittle bark was close to her bare foot, and she would have moved if she could. Instead, she'd pushed her hair off her hot face and laughed. Her plaits had caught on twigs and partly pulled undone.

'And this is still a trade,' he'd continued, reaching up further and tapping the basket with his nail.

She knew it was one he'd made. She'd already recognised

the intricate pattern that he'd woven into its gentle, swelling shape. It had reminded her of a nest: she'd imagined that the plums were crimson eggs, and for a moment she'd pictured fantastic birds chipping their way through the shells and flying off on brilliant, flame red wings.

'Well, what do you think of that?'

She hadn't known what to say, so she'd bitten into another plum. She knew that basket-making was a good craft. And he must have earned a reasonable amount of money because she'd noticed that there'd been meat for this man and her father at meals, whereas they'd almost never eaten meat at home, in Bucharest. She'd watched the man at his work as well. She'd seen the cane softening in the stream and she'd squatted in the shade of an old wall as he'd selected the lengths that he needed, sometimes splitting them, sometimes forcing them in and out. She'd admired the skill with which his hard, brown hands had made the baskets grow.

He'd stopped tapping the basket and when his fingers touched her ankle she'd screamed and swung herself onto a higher branch.

He'd laughed, and in that instant she'd suddenly understood why her family had come.

Yet she could have stayed on in that place. She could have enjoyed learning how to cut and weave the canes, and on summer evenings she could have enjoyed walking down here through the drying grasses and listening to the larks.

He'd been amused by her fear and he'd laughed again as he'd pulled a branch aside and told her that he wasn't angry. He could wait. He was a widower, as she knew, and one of his granddaughters was about her age, so he understood how young girls felt. And he'd already told her parents that he was prepared to wait. Anyway, he wouldn't have wanted so young a bride to be too keen. She'd hung her head. He'd called her his little lark. He'd whispered through the drying leaves that he knew that she was shy, but he'd always liked a woman who was quiet. He'd heard the gossip that she was soft in the head, and liked to draw instead of work. He didn't mind. He could teach her everything she needed to know. If she was good with her hands, that was even better: she'd soon learn his craft. But there was no hurry. She was still young and he was a patient man. He was content to wait, but in the end he'd cage his little lark.

Now, she looked up from the small, bright picture that she'd drawn. The coloured plums lay in the drawn basket exactly as she'd picked them from the tree. She licked the tip of her finger and smoothed it over them to give their skins a better sheen. Then she ran a crayon round the handle of the basket again, following the exact pattern of the canes. She was pleased. This was a *good* picture and this was all she wanted to set down from that evening. She didn't want to draw his thin brown neck and melancholy eyes or his old man's mouth of broken, yellowed teeth.

One day, maybe, but not yet.

Instead, she bent over the picture again. She wanted to remember the colours and the scents of the fruits and to get them perfectly right. Meticulously, she touched in a freshly broken end of stalk and she used one of her own hairs to mark the tiny dots of pink and gold and green.

She remembered how she'd remained in the tree, long after she'd heard the man walk away. Then, when the sun had set, she'd jumped down and run back to her parents, stumbling in the dark and stubbing her toes on stones and dried up clods and ruts.

The man had not been there and her father hadn't answered when she'd asked him why they'd come. He'd tapped his hat over his eyes and stared into the fire.

'Mum?'

Her mother had been sitting apart, leaning against the wall of the house. Emilia couldn't see the expression on her face, but as she'd sat beside her, she'd heard the sounds of the baby sucking on her mother's breast.

'Mum? Is it true? Is this why we've come? So that I can be married to that man?'

'How can I know?' Her mother's voice had been steady in the dark. 'You'll have to ask your father. He's *his* relative, not mine. But he's made us a good offer because he thinks a great deal of you. You can be sure of that.'

'I *won't* marry him.' Emilia's reply had been sharp.

'You'll do what I think best!' Her father's voice had been sharper.

'Emilia.' Her mother had bent over the baby. She was fingering his head and Emilia had heard the sound of her nail on his scalp, scratching something off. 'You could do worse than him. And,' she'd lowered her voice, 'old men are more faithful, and less trouble than someone young. So –'

'I won't!'

'Oh won't you? Do you think anybody *else* will want you?' This time her mother's voice was hard.

'No!' Emilia'd shouted back. 'I don't care about that! I don't *want* anyone to want me!' It had been true. She'd never wanted to marry even though she'd always known

64

that that was what girls did. Some went to men who were old. Others married boys their own age. A few unlucky ones went to other children, to little boys who had no hair on their upper lip and who still played with homemade cars. Gizella, from next door, had been married twice before she was grown-up. First, she'd fallen in love with a local boy and they'd run away, but his mother had never liked Gizella and so she'd soon come back. Emilia had been to that wedding and seen the presents and the nightdress and the silky bridal bed decorated with plastic flowers and fluffy children's toys. Gizella had been dressed like a real princess. She'd looked so different as a bride that Emilia hadn't recognised her at first. And later, even though her baby had died, and she'd fled that home where her young husband had beaten her while her mother-in-law looked on, Gizella'd still talked dreamily about the wedding ceremony. She'd still insisted that her marriage day was the best day in her life. Emilia had listened to these stories, but she'd known that she never wanted such a day herself.

So that evening, as they'd sat near the fire, she'd heard the old man's step and studied him when he'd emerged from the shadows with the basket of plums in his hand. He'd resembled her father and was no different from other men she knew. He was shabbier, maybe, and definitely old, but she hadn't cared about that. She'd just known that she didn't want to marry him or anyone. She hadn't known what she did want, but she'd been certain that it wasn't that.

In the silence, her father had cleared his throat and tipped back his hat as if about to speak, but at that moment the baby had been sick. Little Nico had screamed in the dark and arched his back. When he'd opened his mouth, all the milk had shot out. She still remembered her disgust. When she'd taken the baby from her mother he'd been limp and hot. She'd dipped a rag in the stream and tried to clean him up, but he'd been sticky to touch and had smelled of mouldy cheese. Fretfully, he'd turned his bald head this way and that. Once, his mouth had touched her chest and he'd tried to suck. Horrified, she'd held him at arm's length and kept him as far from her body as she could.

'His first wife was your father's cousin,' her mother'd remarked when Emilia'd handed Nico back. 'And I never heard *her* complain about him. Nor did anyone else, because I've asked around, Emilia. Of course I have. He's known to be a kind man and that's good in a husband. It really is.'

'I don't – '

'Don't *what*? Eh? I'll tell you something for nothing, my girl. Do you think anybody else will want to marry you, with your odd ways? If you think young men want wives who draw pictures and keep rubbish in a box, then you'd better think again!'

'I don't want anybody to want me.' Emilia'd repeated herself as firmly as she could.

'Don't be so stupid!' Her mother had laughed out loud. 'Anyway, you can't always stay with us!'

'Why not?'

'Because – ' her mother'd looked down at the baby in her arms.

'Because,' her father'd interrupted, 'because, if you don't marry, you can't become a mother, can you? You can't have a child of your own.'

'I don't want a child. I want – '

'What? What do you mean by that? Every woman wants a child of her own. Even *you* can't be as stupid as that!' Elizabeta's patience had gone. 'If you don't marry, what else is there to do? Anyway, you're young. You don't know what you want. Young people never do. But when the time comes, you'll be pleased to be a bride and proud to wear your plaits like married women do. And you'll be grateful that he'll take you at all. Do you think people haven't noticed you, playing in the dust and sitting about when there's work to be done? What decent woman with a household to run wants a daughter-in-law like you? You just be grateful that his mother is long dead.'

The fire had burnt down. The man, who'd been listening at a distance, had walked over to where they sat.

'I've said I'll wait, Elizabeta, so for the moment that's enough.' He'd set the basket of plums beside Emilia's feet. 'Even the sweetest plum is sour, if you pick it too soon.'

Emilia had pulled a face at the imagined tartness of the fruit and he'd laughed his old man's laugh, in the shadows of the night.

Later, something had woken her up. They'd been sleeping in the house, so she'd stepped carefully over her mother and Zoltan and gone outside. The unexpected midnight cold had made her gasp as she'd drawn in a breath, but she'd stayed there in the startling whiteness of the moonlight and looked at the sky above.

'I knew you'd come.' The man had reached out from the shadows by the wall and touched her cheek and tangled hair. Then he'd moved his hand down her neck and touched her breast. She hadn't moved. 'There, there, my little bird,' he'd murmured as he stroked her flesh. 'Isn't that nice? Eh? Eh?'

She'd looked down at his hand. His nails had been as rough as broken sticks. He'd hesitated. Indifferently, she'd turned her head aside although she'd sensed that he was open-mouthed, and smiling in the dark. His breath had been hot while hers had been like ice in her throat. He'd glanced towards the house where her parents were asleep. She'd stepped away. He'd coughed.

She'd strolled away from him and crossed the silent field and never once looked back. When she'd put her hand on the trunk of the tree it had felt moist and black. She'd found a foothold and scrambled up. Then she'd parted the sleeping leaves and reached through, to grasp a silvered plum hanging overhead. The skin had been cold as she'd bitten in, but underneath, the flesh still held the warmth and sweetness of the red, red sun. Distantly, like a beast in the night, she'd heard the baby cry, but she hadn't gone back. She'd stayed where she was amongst the branches in the sky and slept or dozed.

'Emilia? What are you doing?' Now Zoltan pushed his chin into her neck. He must have woken and slipped out of bed, because he was pushing her arm aside, trying to see what she'd drawn. 'Let me *look*, Emi. Please?' His cheeks were creased with sleep. His hair stood up on end. 'Wow, Emi! Where did you get that book?' He was pulling it from under her elbow, and trying to get it free.

'I found it.' She held on. 'But don't tell Mum and Dad. Please.'

'Why not?' He licked his lips and scowled. 'You're not allowed to draw, Emi. That's what they said. And they told me to watch you, because they said that if you hadn't drawn those horrible pictures of us in Bucharest, people in England wouldn't have hated us, and then we wouldn't have had to leave. That's what they said. So it's your fault we had to go, and it's your fault I'm not in England still, playing football for my school!'

He pinched the soft skin inside her wrist, trying to force her to give up the book, but another bout of coughing made him stop. When he'd wiped his mouth and got his breath back, he began again.

'People liked *me* in England. It was *you* they hated, you ugly baldy head!'

She concentrated on keeping hold of the book.

'My teacher said I was the best striker they'd ever had! And she wanted me in her school, because the children in *my* class liked me a lot. Nobody tried to cut *my* hair off! It was *you* they hated. You stupid baldy head! And I'll tell Mum and Dad that you've been drawing, as soon as they get back. Unless – '

'Unless what?'

'Unless you let me look.' He'd got hold of the cover and was pulling so hard she was afraid he'd rip it off. She let go and he fell with a thump. She watched as he flipped through.

'Is that all it is?' he frowned. 'I thought – '

'What?'

'I thought you were doing those pictures you did in England. You know, the ones everybody talked about, the ones that showed the fires.' He sniffed. 'Anyway, this last picture's stupid. Who wants to look at *fruit*?' He was turning the picture this way and that.

'Don't you know what it is?'

Zoltan shook his head.

'Don't you remember that place in the country? We went there after Nico was born. And there was a man who made baskets and lived by a stream? Well, this is one of those baskets, and these are the plums I picked.'

'Didn't I pick any?' Zoltan wrinkled his nose.

'I don't think so, but you built a dam across the stream and Dad caught fish.'

'I don't remember. I think you're making it up and I'll still tell them what you've been doing, as soon as they come back!'

'Please – '

Then, they both looked up. Someone had knocked on their door. Emilia tried to snatch the book back, but Zoltan was too quick. He ran to his bed, pushed the book under the covers and climbed in on top.

'Hello?' It wasn't their parents. It was the girl.

This time, Emilia knew who was knocking. And this time she wanted to speak.

'You can't!' Zoltan grabbed her skirt as she moved towards the door. 'You're not allowed to. Dad said. He said I was to watch you didn't speak to anyone at all.'

'Hello? You are in there?' The girl's voice came through the locked door.

This time Emilia didn't try to push Zoltan off. Instead, she struggled to the door with him clinging to her leg.

'It is I, Zeynep Kara. Like before.'

Then, they heard the sound of something torn. Outside something rustled, then, as they watched, a corner of paper appeared beneath the yellow door. Zoltan squatted down.

He smiled in amazement as a torn piece of paper came through, and he prodded it with his finger as if it were alive. Someone had marked it with words. Emilia tried to understand but Zoltan snatched the paper and ran to the window overlooking the street.

'Lin-den. Lindenstr-stra-sse-3. Lindenstrasse 3! Look!' He was pointing to the street as he yelled. 'See? Lindenstrasse 3. Isn't that what it says?'

She pressed her face to the glass. He was right. The same words were on a sign on the white wall opposite. Suddenly she understood. *This* was where they *were*. This was an address, and the girl outside was telling them that she lived here too. She pointed to the other two words on the paper and Zoltan read them out: 'Zey-nep-Ka-ra.' Then he read them again and grinned. He'd learnt to read much better than she had, even though he was younger. She'd tried so hard and failed. Her parents had said that it was natural, because she was a girl, but she'd envied Zoltan all the same.

'Hello?' The girl outside the door was speaking again. 'I am Zeynep. Who you are, in there?'

'I'm Zoltan. Zoltan Radu! And I'm *ill*!' In his excitement, he'd forgotten that he and Emilia were supposed to keep themselves apart.

'Hello Zoltan! I can come in? Please?'

'Yes!' He was already rattling the door when Emilia shouted no. The single word stuck to her throat and tongue so she shouted it again.

'No?' The girl sounded surprised. 'Why I can't come in?'

'Because . . .' Emilia pressed her lips to the yellow edge. From the other side the door handle moved up and down.

'Ah! That is why! You are locked in?'

'Quick!' Zoltan screamed from the window before Emilia could answer. 'Quick, they're coming back. I can see them in the street. Make her go away, Emi, quick. If they see her they'll be angry again!'

'Please?' Suddenly, Emilia found she could speak. 'You go. Please? My mother and my father, they are coming back. Please, Zeynep, you are my friend, you *go* away from here. Please?'

'All right. I'll go. But I promise you, I'm coming back.'

'Emi?' Zoltan crept close. 'Please, Emi, promise not to tell them that I said she could come in.'

Emilia nodded. She was listening for the girl's swift footfall and the clang of the lift door.

'Please Emi,' Zoltan begged, 'don't tell them that I spoke.'

Picture 5
Fathers and Sons

Their parents took longer than usual to unlock the yellow door. Emilia could hear them outside, fumbling with rustling plastic bags and bottles or jars that chinked. If they had seen the girl, Zeynep Kara, in the corridor, they didn't mention it when they stepped inside. However, it was clear to Emilia that they had other, better things on their mind. They were smiling and both looked more cheerful than they'd been for days. Daniel kicked the door shut with the heel of his boot, and set two bulging bags on the floor. One tipped over so that oranges and apples and a jar of jam rolled out. Zoltan grinned and clapped his hands. He knelt beside the bags and began digging amongst the packets of rice and pasta like a dog after a bone. Elizabeta must have done a good morning's work, despite the mist.

'Where's the *special* thing for me?' Zoltan sat back on his heels. He was holding jam in one hand and a bar of bright blue soap in the other.

'It's all for you, my little prince,' his father laughed.

Zoltan coughed and continued to search. He'd learnt about shopping in England. Over there, everyone had shopped, even when they were poor. On Saturdays, the English people had all gone to the shops and bought and bought. The girls in Emilia's class had all seemed to have money of their own. At weekends they'd gone to the shops and bought new clothes and make-up and music tapes for themselves. They'd also bought presents for friends. They'd given each other gifts of shampoo, and jewellery, and extraordinary coloured varnishes which they'd painted on one another's nails during breaks. Even the younger children in Zoltan's class had bought toys and sweets and little picture cards, which they swapped and bought and sold. He'd happily joined in. After football, shopping had been Zoltan's favourite way to spend his time. Once he'd arrived in England he'd enthusiastically started to copy English ways. He'd raced around the huge, brightly lit shops, picking objects up and asking endlessly why he couldn't just have them, as well. Emilia had been embarrassed by his behaviour and hadn't wanted to take him out. She'd been ashamed of his greed. Now, as she saw his disappointment, she was sorry for him, and wished she could have helped.

'Haven't you got any medicine for *me*, for my *throat*?' He was brushing away a tear.

Elizabeta didn't answer. She was humming as she packed their purchases into the little cupboard under the sink. Daniel had stretched out on the sofa. Now he called his wife.

'Haven't you?' Zoltan followed his mother and watched her pulling off his father's boots.

'Haven't I *what*?' Daniel sat up and belched. Emilia could smell the beer.

'Haven't you . . . got . . .' Cautiously, Zoltan touched his father's arm. In the kitchen, onions were hissing and bubbling in hot fat.

'Haven't you . . .' Zoltan persisted. This time he stroked his father's cheek, trying to stop him falling asleep. When Daniel opened one eye Zoltan stepped back and coughed.

'Haven't you . . .' he spluttered.

'*What*?' Daniel's roar filled the room. Zoltan's lips trembled. Elizabeta came to the door with a piece of raw meat in her hand.

'Haven't you got the medicine for his throat?' Emilia's hand flew to her mouth, but it was too late. The words had slipped out. Now, she couldn't put them back.

'You!' Daniel swivelled round and pointed at her. His finger stabbed the yellow air. 'You stupid girl! You shut your lying mouth. Don't ever try and interfere with us!'

Zoltan's face was bright red. He began to cough, but Daniel had already turned his back on Emilia and was feeling through his pockets.

'Here.' He held something out. 'Here, take it. This is all for you.' A tiny, silver-wrapped bar of chocolate lay on Daniel's palm. 'Isn't *this* what you wanted? And isn't this ten times better than any foreign medicine? Eh? Did you think I'd forget?'

Zoltan stared as if unable to believe that the chocolate was so small. Then he frowned.

'It's not the one I wanted. I wanted the big . . .' his voice was weak.

'What? What did you say?' Daniel's voice was low.

'It's . . . it's . . .' Zoltan could not get his words out.

'It's *all* they had!' Daniel stared intently at his son.

'Was it . . . was it . . . all they had?' Zoltan rubbed his fists into his eyes and sniffed.

'Yes.' Daniel lay back on the sofa. He tipped his hat over his brow and folded his arms across his chest, as if about to sleep. 'What do you think your mother and I've been doing all day? Sitting about? Oh no, not us! We've been searching for *this*! I promise you, my little prince, because of this terrible weather and the mist, there was no chocolate in any shop in town. It was just like Bucharest. The shelves were as empty as your sister's head.' He was smiling at his own joke beneath the brim of his hat. 'But when I told the shop people about you, they said they'd have another look. "My son, Zoltan, is ill," I said. And as soon as the manager heard that, he made the shop girls have another look. Then they searched properly and found *this* especially for you, they said. And, this chocolate has medicine in it. It's made for children with sore throats. It's much better than ordinary medicine. That's what they said. But next week, if this mist clears, they may get a new delivery of the big bars again. And if they do . . . if they . . . do . . .' Daniel began to snore.

'Oh.' Zoltan unpeeled the foil. 'I didn't know that.' He put the whole chocolate in his mouth and began to suck.

Elizabeta returned to the kitchen. Daniel continued to snore contentedly beneath the brim of his hat. Emilia watched. He had surprised her, as he always did. She was afraid of him, but despite that, he was the one she loved. He wasn't like other people. He might shout and drink too much, but unlike her mother, he'd always fascinated her with his new ideas. He thought of things that other people never did. He imagined things as well. It wasn't exactly lying: it was more that he talked about how things should have been, but weren't. How else could he have told the story about the special chocolate and the empty shops? And how else could he have taken them from their street in Bucharest, and brought them across half the world, to a place like this? It had been his idea. Emilia knew that her mother could not have done that.

If Elizabeta had had her way, they'd never have left their home. Her mother would still have been sweeping mud and dust. No matter how bad her life had been, she would never have given it up and left. That was not Elizabeta's way. She expected their lives to be hard and difficult. She believed that it was their fate. Life had always been unfair to Romanian gypsies, and she was convinced that it would never change.

She couldn't imagine that anything could be different from the way it had always been. But Daniel could, and did. Usually he kept his thoughts to himself, but when he did speak, Emilia was aware of masses of ideas whirling around in his head. Back in Bucharest she had actually witnessed the moment when one of his ideas had taken shape. She'd seen her father imagine a different future for them all and suddenly decide that they must all leave Bucharest. It had happened after Nico's funeral, when the mourners had finally gone. She'd woken in the night and seen her father looking out of the window and describing things that were not there to be seen. He hadn't been lying, he'd been imagining their escape from all the dirt and pain and death.

Now, she studied him as he lay on the sofa. He was a small man, and plump. He was breathing noisily and his round stomach rose and fell above his loosened belt. As he settled into a deeper sleep, his mouth slackened. His chin was unshaven, and his collar was open. She could see the red striped bootlace around his neck. There was nothing original about his appearance. The difference was that he saw things in his mind, much as she imagined pictures in her head. And, as she watched him sleeping on the sofa, she was aware of the seed of an idea for a new picture beginning to take root in her mind.

In the kitchen, Elizabeta was frying meat. The smell of smoking fat mingled with the hot spices and drifted through the flat. As Emilia sat by herself breathing them in, Zoltan crept up.

'Emi.' He glanced over his shoulder to where their father slept. 'Emi, if you like, you can have *this*, for your own.' The foil from the chocolate lay in his hand like a crumpled silver leaf. 'You could start a new collection, couldn't you, like you had before?' He was so close she could smell the chocolate on his breath and see a brown stain on his lip.

'Yes. Thanks a lot.' She mouthed the words while Zoltan pushed his head of curls into her cheek and rubbed against her like a cat.

The next morning the mist had turned to rain, so their parents couldn't go out, and another day passed before Emilia could begin the picture she'd thought of the evening before. But the morning after was fine, so they left early and Emilia was glad. Elizabeta was going to work the neighbouring street along. Zoltan was feeling better, and had wanted to go too. When they wouldn't take him, he'd stamped back to bed and sulked. Then he refused to give the book to Emilia. At first he said it wasn't in his bed. Then he pretended it had gone.

'Mum found it,' he crowed, 'when she made my bed.'

'She couldn't have – ' Emilia was panic-stricken. If her mother had discovered the pictures, she would have torn them up.

'She did!' Zoltan grinned. He pulled the covers up to his chin and kicked, to keep her off.

Within minutes he was bored with the joke. He produced the book from under the bedclothes but held it just out of reach.

'Why aren't there any pictures of *me*?' he whined.

'Because . . .' she couldn't think.

'I'll give it back if you promise to draw *me*. Me, and no one else!'

'All right. But how about . . . you and Dad?'

'Me and Dad? OK. But lots of *me*. I want to be there *most*. And you've got to let me watch.'

She sat beside him on the bed and shaded in a newborn baby's dented skull and wrinkled, fuzzy skin.

'Is *that* me?' Zoltan pressed his chin into her arm.

She shook her head and drew a tiny, crumpled ear and a baby's fleshy lips against her mother's breast. Zoltan sniggered and clapped his hand over his mouth.

'That's not me. I never . . .'

'No. It's not you. Not yet. It's Nicolae. Don't you remember him?'

Zoltan shook his head. He grumbled about not being in the picture but as she continued drawing, he became quiet and watched. The baby, Nicolae, had never been strong. The neighbours had blamed his ill health on the choice of name. They said it was asking for trouble to have named a child after a President who'd been shot. Elizabeta had been upset and changed the name to Nico but it hadn't helped. The child had never been healthy and had always cried too much.

Now, Emilia sketched Nico's face again. In this second drawing he was older, and should have been sitting up, people said. When they'd returned from that trip to the mountains, Nico was worse. Neighbours had suggested remedies. One brought round the remains of a medicine that had done her small son good, but nothing worked. Elizabeta had muttered about bad luck. She feared the child was cursed.

As Emilia began a third sketch, which showed their trip to the local hospital with the sick child, Zoltan suddenly recognised himself.

'There!' He pointed to the figure of a little black-haired boy. 'That's me, isn't it? In my other boots.' She nodded and worked on. Zoltan grinned.

She remembered that the hospital orderly had been reluctant to let them in and they had all got very cold waiting outside. A doctor in a soiled white coat had left them in the freezing waiting room until the last. Then he'd barely looked.

'You people and your sick babies,' he'd sighed, 'what do you expect?' It had been so cold in the clinic that he was stamping his feet.

Now, she drew Nico's lolling head.

The doctor had looked over and frowned as he'd watched her mother trying to balance Nico on her lap in an attempt to get him to sit up. Zoltan, who had been standing beside his father, had looked on and had been unusually quiet. In the opposite corner of the deserted waiting room, the orderly had tossed down his cigarette butt and begun sweeping up. Daniel had got to his feet and taken off his hat.

'Please sir,' he'd begged, staring at the doctor's shoes and turning his hat round and round in his hands. 'Please sir, please look.'

Now, Emilia marked in the black hairs she'd seen on the doctor's wrist as he'd pushed something metal down into Nico's throat.

'What do you expect?' he'd repeated with a frown. He'd shaken his head quite sympathetically, then shrugged and straightened up.

'Your child is very ill,' he'd said.

Emilia used a red biro for the drops of Nico's blood. She remembered that the doctor had polished them from the tip of the instrument with the sleeve of his coat. Then he'd glanced from the metal thing to the paper where the orderly had written their address.

'Your child is ill, but what do you expect, when you live in a filthy district like that? The air down there, so close to those factories, really isn't any good.' He'd lifted the baby's limp arm, then sighed as it fell back. As he'd turned to go, Elizabeta had grabbed at the hem of his white coat. He'd tried to pull away.

'Maybe,' he'd muttered, still trying to drag his coat from her grip, 'maybe something could be done . . . like . . .'

'Like?' Elizabeta hadn't let go. The orderly had looked up.

'I mean, if you people bothered to buy decent food, like – '

'Like?'

The orderly had stopped sweeping and begun to walk across.

81

'Like . . . like *eggs*!' the doctor had shouted, finally getting free.

When they'd left the hospital it had already been dark outside. She remembered how the night air had smelt of frost and smoke. No streetlights were ever lit in that part of Bucharest and as Emilia'd felt her way along that night, she'd known her hands would be as black as soot. Daniel had taken Elizabeta and the baby home but he'd sent Emilia and Zoltan out again, to work. It was the first time Emilia'd begged at night.

'Help me, for the love of God,' she'd whispered, holding out her hand to the crowds waiting for a bus. 'Help me. It is for my baby brother who is ill. The doctor says he needs an egg . . .'

They'd shuffled their way up and down the endless evening queues, but the night had been so black that she hadn't even seen the faces of the people who all said no. She had held tight to Zoltan and moved on, trying again and again, but it had been hopeless. Respectable people whose own children hardly ever ate eggs had laughed at her or told her what gypsy rubbish like herself should do.

Now she glanced at Zoltan. He was staring at her sketches with a puzzled look on his face. She was glad that he didn't seem to remember either that dreadful night, or the expression on their mother's face when Emilia'd confessed that she hadn't earned any money at all. When the baby had died, Emilia'd accepted that she was to blame. She knew that she should have tried harder, or stayed out longer. Somehow, she should have earned the money for an egg and saved her baby brother's life.

A neighbour had lent her father cash for the funeral

expenses. Another had helped to make the coffin out of wood he'd stolen from a fence the night before.

'Is that *me* again?' Now, Zoltan leant across and pointed to the figure of a small boy watching the men working to make the planks smooth.

'Yes.' She'd drawn him as she remembered him, watching the men sawing up the planks and hammering in the straightened nails. He'd run about, playing with the curled shavings and sticking his fingers into knots in the wood that had oozed drops of resin like honey in a comb.

Now, in the sixth sketch, Emilia drew the two candles that had burnt at either end of the coffin. Their flames had flickered and swung and given her a final view of Nico's face, before her father'd hammered down the lid. At the last minute, Elizabeta had snatched the baby back. She'd blown into his mouth and claimed that he wasn't dead. She'd screamed that he was only sleeping more soundly than before.

At the wake, Emilia'd hidden herself in the darkest corner of their crowded room. She'd watched the priest pile up his plate, and she'd longed for the mourners to leave so that they might be on their own. If she'd been alone, she could have chosen the best papers from her collection and made something for the dead child. Instead, she had to watch as the priest picked up another piece of meat and popped it into his mouth, just as her father filled another glass with beer. Daniel had spoken of Nicolae confusedly and at such length that she'd thought he'd never stop. Finally, he'd proposed a toast.

'To the health of my remaining child. May God grant this child long life and strength!' The words had been spoken through tears as Daniel had swayed on his feet. Her eyes had watered too. She'd rubbed away the sting of smoke, but when she'd blinked, she'd seen Zoltan in his father's arms, being held aloft, so that his curls had touched the roof. Nobody had even glanced towards the corner where she'd sat.

'But *this* son,' Daniel's hands had lingered in Zoltan's curls, 'this son they shall not have! Because . . .' He'd stepped away from the table and tipped back his hat.

'Because?' the priest had prompted.

'Because . . .' her father had looked round the room at the friends and neighbours and relatives who were all crammed in.

'Because?' the priest had asked again, in a voice like oil. Daniel had hesitated. A hush had fallen over the room. Everyone had avoided one another's eyes. The old President of Romania might have been dead, but everyone knew that his secret police were alive and well, and might even be amongst the mourners, listening carefully to what was being said.

Her father had set his son down. When he'd straightened up, his eyes had met the priest's. His lips had remained open as if he'd been about to say more, but he hadn't uttered another word. He'd shut his mouth and wiped his hands across as if there had been something sticky that had been caught there and that he must clean away.

'The only place safer than silence is the grave.' That's what Daniel had always said before, but on that night, he'd only rubbed his hand across his lips, and poured himself another beer. He must have remembered his own words and decided to be safe. Around him, the voices of the other mourners had rolled back over his awkward silence, and swiftly covered it up.

'Here!' Daintily, the priest had felt amongst the pieces of roast meat on his plate.

'Here, take it, my child.' He'd smiled at Zoltan and held out a curve of glistening fat. 'Here,' he'd beckoned again, and Emilia'd watched as her brother made his way through the guests. He'd grinned shyly, and she hadn't known if it was pleasure, or fear, that had made him open his mouth so wide. He'd snapped at the dangling piece like a hungry dog and when people had laughed, he'd blushed. He'd forgotten that he was forbidden to eat food from someone else's plate, because it was unclean. He'd pushed past the wall of legs and knees and backs and plunged his face into his mother's skirt. Elizabeta hadn't noticed what he'd done. She'd continued rocking to and fro and had stroked the curls on Zoltan's neck as the tears ran down her cheeks.

Later that night, when the mourners had finally gone, Emilia had woken to see Daniel pushing aside the curtain that divided their single room into two. He'd plucked Zoltan from where he'd been sleeping, curled up against Emilia's side.

'See?' He'd taken his son to the window and shaken him quite roughly. 'Look! Do you see *that*?'

Emilia, watching through half-closed eyes, had seen her father pointing through the window into the impenetrable black. Zoltan had whimpered in his father's arms and tried to sleep.

'See?' Daniel had repeated, shaking his son and catching hold of his chin again to make him look. 'Can't you see

85

that, over there? *That's* where I'll take you, as soon as I can. That's where we'll go. And over there, you'll live like a prince. But if we stay here, you'll have no life at all. Over there, any man can be great.'

Now, she sketched in her father's profile with smoky shades of grey. She shadowed the twist of his moustache against his cheek and the pointed collar of his shirt. Then she drew Zoltan's trailing hand and his drooping head of curls that had been resting against his father's neck.

'Over there,' Daniel had continued, 'even I can be a man.'

She'd pretended to be asleep when her father had laid the child back in. But later that night, when she'd been certain no one else was awake, she'd slipped from the bed to examine what he'd seen. The window had been partly boarded up. Children had broken it months before, and Daniel had been unable to find glass. So, as winter had approached, he'd nailed pieces of wood over the gap instead. She'd stood where he'd stood, and she'd looked through the bit that was left and it had been just as she'd suspected: there'd been no view at all. It had been too dark to see across the street. But even if there'd been streetlights, there'd still have been nothing to see, because a large block of flats had been started, then abandoned, directly opposite them on the other side of the narrow street. This block had cut off their view as effectively as a prison wall. Her father hadn't seen some distant, better place. He'd imagined it in his head.

She'd climbed back into bed, and as she'd curled herself around Zoltan she'd realised that Daniel had been doing what she did all the time. He'd been imagining something that was more real to him than the black street that he'd seen. He'd replaced it with an idea that had taken a shape in his head.

Now she remembered how she'd turned to Zoltan and wriggled close. Their heads had touched on the pillow and she'd breathed in his sleepy smell. He'd stretched and sighed and she'd realised that her brother was her one chance. If her father had decided to take Zoltan to some better place so that he could become a great man, then she could follow Zoltan's progress and help. Zoltan's future was now her chance of escape. Carefully, so as not to wake him up, she'd put her arm across his chest. From that moment, she'd decided to love her brother more and to do whatever was necessary to keep him safe.

'Is that me too?' Now Zoltan was pointing to her final picture of him as a child in Bucharest. In her last sketch she'd drawn him playing football with other boys outside their house. She'd also drawn herself and Gizella, watching from the step. The boys hadn't had a ball, but were kicking around a dried-up lemon which they'd often used instead. In her picture, Zoltan was in the foreground. His foot was poised, and he was ready to shoot.

'Emi?' He touched her hand.

'What?'

'Draw me shooting a goal! Please?'

'All right. Why not?' She quickly altered the little figure to one who'd just struck home the shot. Zoltan punched the air and shouted 'yes!' just as he'd done in England when he'd driven a good goal in. Then he scrambled out of bed and ran to the window.

'Over there, Emi, behind those buildings, I've seen a park. Dad promised he'd take me, as soon as I'm well again. He promised to buy me more chocolate and he said I could sit on the seat and look at the ducks on the pond. He said I could watch the other children playing football on the grass.' Zoltan paused and pressed his face against the glass. 'But I don't *want* to do that.'

'Why not?'

'Because I want it to be like it is in *your* picture! I want to *play* with the children and I want to score a goal.'

'Then you will.'

'But I won't!' he wailed. 'Dad says it isn't safe. He says I mustn't play. He says I can only *watch*!'

Emilia got up and put an arm round his shoulder, but before she could speak she was distracted by the sound of a car driving fast down the street. Its brakes squealed as it stopped in front of their building. They saw two men leap out. Then the air was filled with the crash of breaking glass. The car's engine roared. More glass shattered and fell down like ice from a roof. The men got back in. The car raced for the main road. It slid round the corner by the tree, darted amongst the traffic, and then was gone.

Below them, people were spilling out of the surrounding houses and running up and down the road. Emilia couldn't move. A moment before, one of the men in the car had looked back. He'd stared directly at the window where she stood and as their eyes had met, he'd winked at her and drawn his finger right across his throat.

Picture 6
A Portrait of the Priest's Wife in her New Clothes

That night a half-familiar noise woke Emilia up. It wasn't the crash of more breaking glass. This time it was a soft sound, like paper torn across. She might have turned over and gone back to sleep, if it hadn't reminded her of something, and if the night hadn't been so hot. As she lay there and tried to work out what it was, her skin burnt and when she licked her lips, they were dry and cracked. Now that she was fully awake, she decided to get up and find a drink. When she extended her foot, the air in the room felt wonderfully cool, and she was about to push the rest of the covers off, when she heard it again. It was a soft, swishing sound that she seemed to have heard before. If she hadn't felt so hot, she was sure she could have remembered when. Yet it wasn't only thirst that was muddling her head. Now that she was sitting up, she felt distinctly odd. She wanted to lie down again and she longed for someone to lay a wet cloth across her head. When she swallowed, her spit scorched her throat like smoke. It was so hot in the room that it could have been a stifling summer night in Bucharest. There, the day's heat and dust had sunk down on the city after dark, coating it like ash, so that no air moved.

She rubbed her hand amongst the damp tufts of hair on the nape of her neck. Sweat was trickling down her back. Then she remembered when she'd heard that sound before. It had been on another airless summer night in Bucharest, and, soft as the noise had been, it had also woken her up. Without switching on the light, Emilia felt her way to the bathroom, and turned on the cold tap. As she splashed her face and neck she heard it again. Then, sitting on the edge of the bath, in the dark, she began to remember back.

After Nico's death, her father had stopped trading in scrap and had gone into business with his brother instead. Secretly, they'd crossed and re-crossed the borders between Romania and the surrounding countries, buying and selling anything that they could trade. Daniel had often stayed away for days on end, but the brothers were clearly doing well. The roll of foreign money that he counted secretly at night had finally begun to grow. Every few months their rooms had been stacked with sacks and boxes of new goods and as word of a delivery got round, people used to gather near their door. At first, Daniel had dealt in cheap plastic ware. He'd sold dishes and bowls decorated with flowers, and glass jars with cheerful coloured tops. Then, she remembered cases of knives and forks and shiny coffee spoons. Once, he'd arrived with sets of saucepans with extraordinary glass lids. Those had been very popular. People had queued along the street and the priest's wife had bought two sets.

Sometimes Daniel had brought back foreign clothes. There'd been suitcases of blue jeans and lots of T-shirts with flowers and sparkling pictures embroidered on the front. She also remembered a sack of woolly hats and brightly coloured, stripy gloves which stretched to fit any size of hand. There'd been jars of hazelnut and chocolate spread which the neighbours had bought and smeared on their children's bread. Zoltan had cried with disappointment when he'd seen that, but his father hadn't allowed him even the smallest taste. Daniel had not let them keep anything for themselves. Every single thing that came into the house had been turned into foreign cash.

When the brothers began to deal in more expensive goods, like cameras and television sets, their neighbours could no longer afford to buy. Then, people had turned their backs on the Radus and whispered that this new business of theirs only proved what everybody had always suspected: that these gypsies were nothing but thieves. They said that it was not possible, or right, for poor folk like the Radus to suddenly be rich. Where was their money coming from, if it wasn't being stolen from the Romanians themselves?

One night Daniel had been attacked as he walked home from church. A group of local men had kicked him black and blue and cracked his ribs. It was a lesson, they'd said. Since the old president's death, the gypsies had been getting above themselves and were too uppity by half. They needed to learn their place. The police had taken no action when Daniel complained. The priest had declared that street fights were nothing to do with him. Maybe, he was heard to have said, a little beating here and there wasn't

91

such a bad thing. It could help to sort out the gypsy problem before anyone got killed.

The priest had been wrong. News came in from other districts that the gypsies living there had been burnt out of their homes by angry mobs. Daniel and his brother stopped doing business from their houses and Emilia often heard them predicting that more violence was to come. Shortly after the news of the first fires on the outskirts of Bucharest, Daniel's brother and his family suddenly packed up their things and left for the west. Daniel had continued to trade alone and by the third summer after Nico's death, his secret rolls of foreign banknotes had grown to three. He'd hidden them under the floorboards in the part of the room where Emilia and Zoltan slept. The whole family had known that the money was there, but they never mentioned it aloud, even between themselves. Nevertheless, Emilia had known that her parents feared thieves, and that was the first thing she'd thought of when an unfamiliar sound had woken her, on a hot summer night in Bucharest.

It had been very early. The room had been in shadow and not yet coloured by the coming light. Emilia'd half opened her eyes and looked through her lashes because she'd been too scared to move her head. She'd expected to see robbers crouched above the opened floorboards, and for a moment she'd been confused: why would thieves be tearing the money up? Then she'd remembered the Secret Police: that was the sort of senseless thing people said the Secret Police did.

So, with her heart beating against her ribs like a caged bird's wing, she'd gradually raised her head and peered over Zoltan's sleeping back. It hadn't been a thief. Nor was it

Daniel, counting how much money he'd got. It had been her mother who'd been kneeling in the corner, with Emilia's paper collection tipped out in a heap. A shaft of strengthening light had crept through the unboarded half of the window and lit her mother up. Emilia had watched as her mother systematically ripped each piece of the collection apart. Their eyes had met when Elizabeta looked up.

'How could you do this to me?' Her mother had held up the beautiful blue banknote that Emilia had kept back. 'Have you no shame? How could you steal from your own family like this?' She'd stood up and waved the note in Emilia's face. 'You're evil, Emilia, that's what you are. You're a sly, tricky girl and no daughter of mine!' Elizabeta had suddenly stamped down the edges of the box.

Emilia hadn't said a word. Silently, she'd got up and pushed the bits and scraps together with her toe. Her collection had been utterly ruined and she'd felt as if her heart might break.

'Here!' Her mother had held out the shovel. 'Bring them here then, to light the stove.' Her voice had been less angry. 'At least they can be some use! That's why I looked at them, Emilia, I needed more paper to light the stove. That's when I saw this note. How could you, Emilia? How could you steal from us, like that?' Her mother had wiped away a tear. 'How could I have a daughter who's a *thief*?' She'd shaken her head. 'But I won't tell your father. He'd be so upset, he'd – ' She'd retied her scarf without finishing her words. 'So, be a good girl now. I've got the money safe, so you can sweep the rest of this rubbish up for the fire, while I get more wood.'

Now, Emilia gripped the edge of the bath. She remembered that she hadn't been good and done as her mother had asked. Instead, she'd swept the remains of her precious papers over the step and out into the street with a single swing of the broom. Her mother had whirled round and slapped her face, but she hadn't cared. She'd watched the torn scraps flutter down the street and settle in the dirt. And she'd wondered, as she'd often wondered before, if she truly was her mother's daughter after all.

Now, she opened the bathroom door and approached the kitchen on her burning feet. There was a line of light under the yellow door. But this time it wasn't her mother who looked up from the floor. It was Zoltan. He was kneeling in the middle of the pile of newspapers and polythene bags from under the sink. Emilia had made him jump.

'What are you doing?' she asked.

'Nothing!' He was crawling away from her. 'Nothing, honestly Emi. It's only *rubbish* I'm looking at. But that chocolate Dad bought was *so* small that I wondered if there was another one, sort of tangled up amongst the bags. I want there to be a chocolate, Emi, one he forgot . . .'

'Is there?'

'No! There isn't *anything*. It's just stupid papers and rubbish like this.' He threw a torn paper bag onto the pile, and yawned. 'It isn't fair. Because he *promised* me, Emi. Like he *always* does . . .' Zoltan yawned again. 'He promised me that he'd get me that very big one. But he *didn't*. He didn't get me anything special, just that stupid little one that was gone as soon as I put it in my mouth.' He kicked at the pile of papers before trailing back to bed. Emilia tidied up, then drank more water to try and cool her throbbing head.

When she next woke, the flat was quiet but full of light.

Someone had opened the curtains and sunshine was streaming in. The yellow walls were more dazzling than ever and hurt her eyes when she looked at them. She lay there, licking her parched lips and listening to the morning sounds of the other people in the building, getting up. Her parents must have gone out very early, without speaking to her, though she had vague memories of her father peering down at her before they'd left. Zoltan must have recovered sufficiently to go with them, because there were no signs of him around. Once again she was alone. She took a deep breath and made herself cross the heaving floor to the window. Each time she blinked, her eyes stung, as if the hard-edged winter sun had scraped them raw. She wanted a drink, but was too tired to get it, so she stayed slumped in the chair as the yellow walls pulsed to and fro.

She must have dozed off again, because suddenly she was dreaming about her mother. She awoke confused about where she was. She thought she'd heard the sounds of Elizabeta sweeping the street, but when she'd rubbed her eyes, and rested her forehead on the windowpane, she saw the girl, Zeynep Kara, amongst a group of people standing in the road. They weren't speaking, and one or two had their arms round each other, as if they were scared. They were staring at the area in front of the hotel, which was now blocked off. Men and women in uniforms were ducking under the barriers and hurrying about. Other people were taking photographs or talking into mobile phones.

Directly below her, a black man in orange overalls stopped sweeping and wiped the sweat from his face. Then he put the broom aside and began to shovel up a large heap of broken glass. He worked steadily and the sound of the glass shards raining down into the metal bin reminded Emilia of waves breaking amongst pebbles on an icy winter beach.

Now, Emilia realised that this was the damage that those men had done the previous evening. They'd smashed the windows along the front of the hostel before disappearing in the car. The noise that had woken her now was the sound of the man in the street, clearing up. She made herself look through the bright light into the crowd. No, neither her mother nor any of her family was there, but the girl, Zeynep Kara, still was. She was wearing the same blue jeans and plum red jacket and her hands were tucked into the cuffs as if she was cold. Zeynep was watching the man in orange shovelling up the broken glass, but suddenly she looked up. Her black hair swung back from her face, and when their eyes met, the girl smiled, then withdrew her hand from her cuffs and waved.

This time, Emilia waved back.

Immediately something sour and disgusting flooded her throat. She clamped her hand over her mouth, clawed her way to the bathroom and was repeatedly and miserably sick. When she'd washed her face and mouth, and gone back, a few onlookers still stood in the road, but Zeynep had gone. Emilia could have wept. Once again she'd messed things up and missed her chance. No wonder her parents always left her behind: she was a fool and a coward who never got things right.

Nevertheless, she was surprised by the extent of the damage to the building and also surprised that her parents hadn't mentioned it when they'd come in. All that broken glass would have been hard to miss, and it must have reminded them of what had happened before. So maybe that was it: maybe they'd wanted to forget. Maybe they feared recalling the flames and the shouting and the crack of splintering glass. Maybe they were afraid to remember, just as she was afraid to forget.

Slowly, trying not to jar her head, she reached under the sofa and found the book. She turned to a fresh page. Her first pictures of the Romanian attacks on the gypsy quarters of Bucharest had been drawn when she was at the school in England. There, she'd tried to show everything in great detail: the burnt-out buildings, the collapsed roofs and the heaps of belongings that the gypsies had saved before the flames took hold. In England she'd used charcoal for the blackened windows and doorways that even on the morning after the fires had still oozed smoke like rotten, stinking breath. She'd sketched every detail of the twisted metal limbs of stools, dusted with flaking ash, and the curious remains of plastic basins and bowls that had melted and dripped onto other surfaces like pools of dirty wax.

The English people had liked those pictures a lot. At first they hadn't believed she'd drawn them herself. Then they'd doubted that life in the gypsy quarter could have been as dangerous as that. But in the end, they'd watched her draw in silence and accepted the pictures as her work alone. Lots of her pictures had been framed and some of the teachers had arranged an exhibition in the school. Her pictures of those fires and attacks had been hung on the walls, and her name, Emilia Radu, had been printed in black letters on small white cards underneath. And she'd been happy. She'd felt like the heroine of an old story she'd once heard, about a girl brought back to life after a jealous aunt had cursed her, and cast her into a sort of sleeping death. But her happiness hadn't lasted. As the weeks went by, some of the people in that English town had begun to hate her and her family, just as some of the Romanians had hated them in Bucharest. When her parents had become aware of this hatred Elizabeta blamed it on Emilia's pictures. She'd said that this was all Emilia's fault. The pictures of them escaping from the fires had made the gypsies look so desperate and filthy that it was not surprising that English people shouted at them in the street.

Secretly, Emilia had sometimes wondered if her mother might be right. So this time she decided not to draw another picture of the blazing homes. Instead, she planned to tell the story with a portrait of the priest's wife, all dressed up.

It had been very hot, on that summer evening in Bucharest. She'd been sitting on the front step with the neighbour's daughter, Gizella, and a couple of Gizella's friends. Once, when they'd stopped gossiping and looked up, they'd seen the priest and his wife approaching from the other end of the street. At first they'd suppressed their laughter. Even Gizella, who'd been married twice and wasn't frightened of anything, had waited until the priest and his wife had strolled past, before she'd begun to laugh. Then they'd all exploded, rolling around on the step with their hands over their mouths, trying to stifle their giggles. Each time one of them succeeded, someone else had set them off. The priest's wife must have heard because she'd stopped in the middle of the empty road and looked back. The silky stuff of her new blouse and skirt, had stuck to her flesh, 'like flies on crap' Gizella had snorted behind her fist. Under her arms and round her waist the material had been dark with sweat. The priest had clutched at his wife's arm and tried to urge her on, but she'd refused to budge. When the girls had seen her fend him off with a jab of her elbow, they'd fallen about helplessly and laughed till they'd wept all over again. The priest's wife was a huge woman, with calves and thighs like posts. As they'd watched, she'd turned herself round slowly, like a bus, forced to back.

'Look at her!' Gizella had screamed into Emilia's ear. 'Do you see what that greedyguts is wearing? Like a great fat sow, dressed up!'

Emilia had giggled and drawn a quick caricature in the dust. Now, as she drew the scene in the book, she remembered how her finger had moved round and round on the warm stone step as she'd created the mountainous curves of those soft, fleshy hips. The priest's wife had been walking in high-heeled shoes, so her hips had shaken and tumbled against each other, like ripe fruit in a bag. Her solemn eyes had been as brown as the kidneys in a butcher's shop and her pale, smooth cheeks had been delicately veined, with threads of violet and red, exactly like the secret mounds of waxy fat which form a kidney's bed. Yet she'd been magnificent, in her way. Her beautiful hair had been as sleek as poured cream, her neck as round and firm as polished stone. She'd stood there scrutinising them before she'd pointed them out to the priest. He'd glanced unhappily at the girls, then mopped the sweat from his cheeks and chin before patting his wife's plump white hand as he'd tried to encourage her to take no notice.

Emilia had often heard gossip about the priest's wife. Women asked each other how that woman had grown so enormous when there was so little nourishing food about, although every child in their street already knew the answer to that! They knew that each night, before she went to bed, the priest's wife drank a wineglass full of warm gypsy blood. The blood had been drained from the bodies of gypsy babies, which explained why gypsy babies were so often sick. And that was why the gypsies only took their children into hospital as a last resort. As soon as the parents' backs were turned, the doctors picked out their sharpest knives and pulled the curtains tightly round the little cots. Stone-faced nurses held up enamel bowls to catch the blood, while the greedy doctors went to work. That's what the local children said, and Gizella, whose baby son had died in the hospital, agreed. She hadn't seen this happening, but she'd heard the rumours and when her baby had been so sick, the nurses had kept her out of the cubicle where her child had lain.

'Anyway, who does she think she is?' one of the other girls had muttered under her breath. 'The President's wife?'

But they weren't only jealous of her ample, rolling flesh. They hated the priest's wife because the new clothes she'd been wearing, including the high-heeled shoes and the diamond-patterned stockings, had not been hers to have. Everybody knew that these clothes had come out of one of the boxes of free charity goods delivered by foreigners to the mental asylum on the hill. News of the arrival of these foreigners and their lorry load of gifts had run through their district like a flood. Everyone had raced up the hill to claim their share. The priest had taken charge of the distribution, to prevent a riot, he'd said. He'd locked himself in with the boxes, while the mad people and everyone else had howled outside the door. His wife had joined him and together they'd decided which families in his parish deserved these gifts. The gypsies had got nothing, except what they'd managed to snatch when the lorry doors were first unlocked. When some of the foreigners had protested that the clothes weren't intended for local people, the priest had explained to them that there was no point giving good clothes to the asylum inmates, because they were all mad. They'd only soil the garments or rip them from each other's backs.

Emilia hadn't gone to the asylum on the hill. Elizabeta had run with the crowd, but Emilia had been unsure. She'd heard that some of the asylum inmates were gypsy children. They'd been left there, to be looked after for a short time, when food was really scarce, but when their parents had come back for them, they'd been told that their children had died. She'd never been sure if she really believed this story, but it had scared her a lot. Even before she'd refused to marry the old man, her mother had often called her mad and sometimes, when her mother had been particularly angry with her, Elizabeta had threatened to 'leave her on the hill'.

So on that evening, as they'd sat on the step, Gizella had nudged Emilia again, and she'd looked up. A rush of gritty wind had been gusting down the street. It had blown the dust over her picture on the step. It had also whisked up the edge of the priest's wife's skirt. Emilia had only seen the black elastic wound round the woman's thighs to keep the stockings in their place, but Gizella'd snorted that she'd seen pink lace on the priest's wife's foreign pants! When they'd heard that, the girls had collapsed into a heap and laughed together until they'd wept.

Now, bending over the portrait that she'd drawn, Emilia pulled the elastic so tight that the thick flesh bulged over the top.

'Greedy pig!' Gizella had muttered as the woman had pulled down her skirt.

Emilia hadn't agreed: no animal had ever looked at her with the hatred she'd seen in the priest's wife's face. And later, when the fires were taking hold, Emilia had realised that no animal would have stayed as close to the heat of the terrible flames as the priest's wife had. Because that was what she'd done two weeks later.

One evening, the church bells had tolled unexpectedly and a crowd had gathered at the end of their street. Some had howled abuse at the gypsies, others had told them to pack up and leave Bucharest as soon as they could. Then the crowd had thrown stones. Later, nobody could remember who had lit the first match, but as the shouting increased, they'd all noticed the smell of petrol in the air. Suddenly, both ends of their street had begun to burn at once.

The priest's wife had positioned herself in the middle, by the abandoned block of flats. Emilia had noticed her leaning there and she'd thought the woman was tired or resting her heavy legs. She hadn't been wearing her new clothes, but had been carrying a piece of cardboard torn from one of the charity boxes instead. At first, she'd used it to shield her eyes, but when a couple of houses were well alight and the heat had begun to spread, she'd fanned herself, and kept away the smoke and smuts. She hadn't seemed afraid and hadn't moved when the roof timbers of the next house gave way and a huge tongue of flame had rushed up into the night. Others had scattered when the street filled with sparks, but the priest's wife had flicked something from her arm and stayed where she was. She'd watched as the gypsies formed a chain and passed their buckets from hand to hand, but she hadn't helped. As the fires had increased in strength, she'd fanned herself more energetically and watched the gypsies being driven back.

The priest's wife had watched the drama from beginning to end, and had still been there, leaning against the wall and fanning herself, when the gypsies had gathered up their screaming children and run away. Emilia knew that no animal would have done that. They would have feared the flames and heat, but the priest's wife had never even looked scared. She'd watched the destruction with a depth of hate in her brown eyes that no animal could ever have had.

Immediately after those fires, the Radu family had left Bucharest. They'd moved in with relatives two hours' journey out of town. By then, Daniel had completed most of his plans for leaving, and Emilia knew that he'd already paid the first instalment of money to the traffickers for their secret journey to the west. His brother had also sent a message from England that he was ready to help them whenever they arrived.

As the prospect of leaving drew nearer, Elizabeta had become increasingly sad. Emilia, by contrast, had barely been able to hide her joy. The coming journey was what she'd been waiting for. When they'd returned to their house, the day after the fires, and had stepped through the stumps of the black charred door, Elizabeta had wept, but Emilia had wanted to laugh. At last, they were free to go. Their life had now been so destroyed that there was nothing left to save and nothing to hold them back. The ties had been burnt through and were all turned to ash. When Emilia'd blurted out something like that, her mother had whirled round in the ashes and shouted through tears that Emilia was a wicked, selfish daughter, with no natural feelings at all. Then she'd slapped her cheek. Didn't she realise, her mother'd screamed, that people would be the same wherever they went? Didn't Emilia understand that being a gypsy meant being hated for life? It would always be like this, wherever they went, because it was part of their fate.

Emilia hadn't replied. She'd trodden a pattern into the ash, then left the ruined house. She hadn't believed her mother and that night she'd fallen asleep silently repeating her lucky words 'helloplease' just as she always had.

Now, as she looked at her portrait of the priest's wife, and remembered what had happened in England, she wondered if her mother's earlier words had been right.

Was it part of her fate to be hated, wherever she went?

Outside, the workman had finished clearing up. The crowd of onlookers had gone. The street was quiet, but in the gutter a missed fragment of glass glittered and winked like something coming to life in a strengthening winter sun.

Picture 7

An Eye in the Dark

Emilia had woken with a start. The sun had gone. The sofa was in shadow and Zoltan was bending over her. He was so close that she could see her face reflected in the pupil of his eye.

'They told me to have a look.' He was sniffing and licking his lips.

'Did they?' Even that whisper scratched her throat.

'Yes! Dad said I'd got to.' Zoltan was still bundled up in the black padded anorak his father had bought him in England. It had always been too big. Now it hid his hands completely. His black woolly hat was pulled down over his ears and he was peering from beneath it like a young rat looking out of its hole. 'Dad said I'd got to see if you were still so hot.' He extracted a hand and laid his palm on her cheek. His touch was sticky and she smelt something chocolatey and sweet.

'Ouch!' he laughed and blew on his fingers, then raced off to his parents. 'She's *ever* so hot. I think she'll blow up! Why don't you go and look?'

Now Emilia could hear them talking in the hall. She

rubbed her hands over her face, propped herself up on one elbow, and swallowed with care. Her lips felt like crumpled tissue paper. Her throat was raw. She must have slept for hours, after finishing the picture of the priest's wife, because it was evening now and clearly her family had only just got back. In the hall, Zoltan was talking loudly and stamping his feet.

'She isn't ill,' he protested, 'she's just *hot*. Or not as ill as *me*. *I* was very ill, you said. But I think she'll blow up, so go and feel her head.'

But they didn't approach her and she was glad, because she couldn't remember how carefully she'd hidden the book.

She lay there, listening to the sounds from the kitchen. Elizabeta was filling the kettle, taking crockery from a shelf and opening the fridge. Zoltan came back and turned the television on. He increased the volume and began to leap about. Emilia shut her eyes but the music gnawed at her head. When she next looked up, her father was watching her from under the brim of his hat. Their eyes met. Abruptly he zipped up his jacket and left the room. He shouted that he wouldn't be long, and he told Elizabeta to carry on preparing his meal. Emilia heard the yellow door click shut. Then he was gone. She imagined him walking quickly down the street and turning the corner by the illuminated tree. Was he meeting someone? Did he want more cigarettes? Or did he just need to escape from the sight of her, and walk through the dark night streets by himself?

The pop group on the television was playing more shrilly. Zoltan, who still wore his jacket, jumped and danced to their beat. Elizabeta came to the doorway with a knife still in her hand and watched. She smiled when Zoltan struck the table like a drum. His rhythm was fast and good. In the kitchen, a saucepan came to the boil, and the yellow room was filled with steam and the thick smell of cooking meat.

Then someone banged on their door. Elizabeta dropped the knife and backed away. Zoltan, who hadn't heard the knock, shouted at her to stay and watch. Outside, it sounded as if someone was pounding the door with their fists. Then a man began to speak, calling out words that could barely be heard through the music, let alone be understood.

'What shall I do?' Elizabeta was staring at the door. Her hands were clamped over her mouth.

'Nothing!' Emilia rasped as loud as she could. She was terrified. Suppose Zeynep was outside, smiling, and expecting to come in?

'What if it's *them*?' Elizabeta turned directly to Emilia for the first time in days. 'What if it's *those men* again? Whatever shall I do?'

'What men?'

'*Those men!* I don't know who they are, but they came last night and smashed all the windows near the street. Your father says they're trying to drive out foreigners like us. "Savages" he called them, and I agree. But what if it's men like that, waiting outside our door, wanting to get in?'

She backed into the sofa and sat down heavily on its edge. Her shoulders shook with fear. Then, the handle turned. Elizabeta screamed and hid her face. Emilia crawled to the end of the sofa. As she watched their door begin to move, she remembered that Daniel hadn't turned the key.

'Zoltan!' Elizabeta's second scream devoured the other noise. 'Zoltan! Come here, quick!'

'Wha-at?' He stopped mid-dance, zapped off the TV sound and pulled a face. 'What? You've made me miss a bit!'

Then he shrieked.

'Thank you.' A tall, thin black man was standing in the open doorway and smiling. He was holding the hand of a tiny girl wearing a flowered dress and shiny, buckled shoes. 'Thank you,' he repeated. 'I am Michael, from next door. I am speaking to Mr Radu, downstairs. Thank you, that you turn your television off. My wife is ill. I want that she can sleep.' He smiled again, and hovered at the door as if expecting one of them to speak. The little girl stared at them and swayed on legs as thin as twigs. When none of them replied the man shrugged awkwardly and turned to go, then turned back, spinning the child round, like a pretty, decorated top.

'You are ill, too?' Now, he was speaking to Emilia, who leant against the wall. 'Perhaps it is the flu, like my wife has, though she will sleep now, a little bit. But . . . I can help *you*?'

'No!' She looked down. Without meaning to, she'd met his eye when he'd first spoken to her, and when he'd smiled, she knew she'd smiled back.

'I'm a doctor, from Ni – ' He was stepping forward as though he meant to come inside.

'No!' Zoltan ran at him. 'Leave us alone! You go away from us!'

Emilia saw the surprise on the man's face. He stepped back into the corridor so suddenly that the child stumbled

108

and fell. Zoltan slammed the yellow door, then reached under his anorak and pulled out his key. Hastily, he turned it in the lock.

'Thank God for my brave son.' Elizabeta crossed herself. 'What would I have done without you?' She opened her arms, as if expecting Zoltan to rush in. He didn't. He scowled and fiddled with the remote, zapping the sound of the television on and off.

'What could that savage have wanted?' Elizabeta composed herself. She straightened her scarf and pushed back her long plaits.

'I dunno.' Zoltan shrugged and wiped his nose on his overhanging cuff. It left a trail there, like a snail's silver slime.

'Fancy walking into my home like that!' Elizabeta continued. 'Savages, that's what these people are, and probably thieves. Your father will be so angry when he hears.'

'Don't tell!' Zoltan dropped the remote and flung his arms around his mother's waist. He was butting her with his head. 'Please, Mum,' he begged, 'don't tell him about the unlocked door. Please? Please don't tell him I forgot.'

Watching them, Emilia realised that she was the only one who'd understood why their neighbour had knocked on their door.

'How could you have forgotten that? You *know* your father says we mustn't let anyone in.' Elizabeta frowned as she ran her fingers through Zoltan's curls. 'He says we've got to keep that door locked all the time. It's the only safe thing to do, in a place like this, that is full of murderers and men like that! "Keep that door locked and don't speak to anyone." That's what your father told you, so I can't think

109

why you forgot, especially when you knew the windows were smashed last night. But I won't tell him. I don't want any more upsets.' She wiped the tears from her cheeks with the back of her hand and rubbed her chest. 'It's bad for my heart. It's bad enough having to live beside someone as black as that, without them trying to put their filthy feet on my floor! I always *knew* we shouldn't have come away. But nobody ever listens to me. Your father was determined to leave Bucharest.'

She was trying to get away from Zoltan, but he burrowed against her and sniffed.

'Your father said we had to leave for *your* sake, so that you could grow up. But I've never believed that. And I didn't want to leave my home. And,' she looked over at Emilia, 'I never wanted to leave England once we'd settled in. At least *there*, they gave us a flat. It was difficult living there, but it wasn't as bad as *this*. And we wouldn't have had to leave *that* flat, if it wasn't for *you*, madam!' She turned on Emilia. 'If *you* hadn't behaved so shamefully in England, running away from home to live with people who weren't like us, and letting all our secrets out! If you hadn't done that, and if you hadn't painted those dreadful pictures and brought us such disgrace, we could have been there still, living in our flat!'

'See?' Zoltan stuck his tongue out at Emilia. 'It's all *your* fault, you "stupidbitch".'

When Elizabeta returned to the kitchen, Emilia climbed back onto the sofa and pulled the covers over her head. She'd never understood what those English words meant, but Yasmina had explained that although some people used them all the time, the words were still rude, and an insult. In Yasmina's family, no one spoke like that.

'If it wasn't for *you* – ' Zoltan had followed Emilia to the sofa. Now, he snatched the covers out of her grip – 'I'd have been captain of my school team! That's what my football teacher said. He said I was the best striker they'd ever had!'

'I know,' Emilia whispered, 'you were very good.'

It was true. In England, when she'd collected him from school, she'd often watched the playground game and seen him score lots of goals.

'I was "wicked" at football. That's what everybody said. I was good, wasn't I?' His anger had eased.

'Yes, and you will be again. They must play football here – '

'They *do*!' He crouched down and put his head on the pillow beside hers. 'I told you, I've seen boys, Emi, lots of boys playing football in the park . . .'

'Well, there you are.' Once again he was so close that she could see her reflection in his eyes: there was her mouth, her nose, her chin, her cut-off hair all sticking out.

'I've seen a football place near the swings.' His lashes were brushing her cheek.

'There you are,' she whispered. 'Show them what you can do.'

He smiled, then leapt up and stamped his foot.

'I can't!'

'Why not?'

'Because Father says I'm not allowed to! He says it isn't safe! He says I've got to sit on the bench with him, and watch! And *watching's* stupid. I want to play!'

She tried to speak but choked on the phlegm in her throat.

'I – '

'What?' He stared sulkily. '*What?* Why don't you speak?'

'I want . . . a drink. "Please"?'

'If I get one,' he glanced over his shoulder towards the kitchen, 'you've got to promise to come to the park. And promise you'll let me play football, even if it isn't safe.'

When she'd nodded, he ran into the kitchen and dashed back, slopping water from a dripping glass.

'When?' he urged, leaning so close that he jogged her elbow and she spilt more down her front. 'Will you take me to the park tomorrow?'

She was nodding when they heard their father re-enter the flat. Instantly, Zoltan moved away and started looking for the remote.

Daniel unzipped his leather jacket and threw it on a chair. As he did so, two lemons fell from a pocket and rolled across the floor. Zoltan pounced and picked them up. As Emilia smelt their scent she was seized by a sudden desire to escape from the rooms. She wanted to discover what sort of place this was, where you could walk down a street and find fresh lemons in the middle of a winter night.

'Give the lemons to your mother.' Daniel switched on the television and took the remote out of Zoltan's hand. 'The juice is to be mixed with salt. And – ' he'd settled himself with his back to the sofa. 'And tell your mother to make her drink it.' He jerked his head towards Emilia. 'For her sore throat.'

Emilia winced. When she'd swallowed it the liquid had burnt like flames licking through rotten wood. Her mother had folded her arms and watched in silence. When Emilia had finished, her mother held out her hand for the empty cup, then went.

Later, in the bathroom, Emilia splashed water over her

face and examined herself in the mirror. Her eyes were dark-ringed. Her mouth and nose were blotched with red. She hadn't been outside for days, so her skin was pale and her freckles had almost gone. No wonder the man at the door had noticed that she was ill. She touched her hair which was beginning to grow back. Sometimes, she thought she could have got used to short hair, if only her parents hadn't minded so much, and if Zoltan hadn't teased her all the time. Apart from the cold, the main difference was that the loss of her plaits sometimes made her head feel unsteady. If she moved quickly, she felt as if her skull and brains were floating away. Otherwise, maybe her hair didn't look so bad.

She'd never resembled the rest of her family, anyway. Her hair was fair and her eyes were not an honest brown, like theirs, but an indefinite, watery blue. In Romania, some people had admired her, but her mother had always pursed her lips and frowned before muttering that she'd never understood how her daughter had got 'shifty eyes' like that. One of Daniel's sisters had been fair, but Elizabeta never remembered this. Instead, she'd continually grumbled about her daughter's looks. Emilia's hair had been 'colourless', her body was 'stick-like' and her eyes were 'as treacherous as the sea'. Sometimes Elizabeta had muttered that Emilia's unusual appearance was a sign of bad luck.

Now, Emilia polished the bathroom mirror with her sleeve. They hadn't owned a mirror in Bucharest. In those days, if she'd wanted to look at herself, she'd gone in to Gizella's mother, next door. Here, there were mirrors everywhere. She remembered how the girls in England had carried tiny mirrors in their pockets and constantly repaired their make-up, or fiddled with their hair or dabbed stuff on their spots. Then she remembered how they'd run their ink-stained fingers up and down her plaits.

'Go on, Emi,' they'd urged, tweaking the ends, 'show us how long your hair really is. Please?' When she'd pulled off the rubber bands, they'd been amazed to see her hair fall below her waist. They'd fished out brushes and combs from their bags. At first, she'd been horrified and disgusted to be touched by strangers, but she'd got used to it and soon hadn't minded at all. She'd liked the smell of their hairsprays and scents and she'd enjoyed the touch of their hands on her cheeks. Sometimes she'd noticed boys watching them, but she hadn't cared. It was the girls she'd loved. And Sam. 'You can't be a *real* gypsy, Emi. Not really. Not with hair like that,' the girls had protested, as they'd brushed out the long strands. 'Gypsies are dark, aren't they? So, shouldn't your hair be black?' She'd never known how to reply, so had giggled and shrugged, but she'd often wondered if life would've been simpler if her eyes had been brown, and her hair as thick and black as Elizabeta's own.

Later that evening, her mother brought her a bowl of soup. 'Your father says you must eat . . .'

Emilia nodded and tore off a small piece of bread and dipped it in.

'Because . . .' Elizabeta folded her arms, 'because we may have to move on.'

Emilia forced herself to swallow although the cooling fat coated her tongue like wax.

'And if you're not well, or not strong enough, your father says we may have to leave you – '

'No!'

'Only for a day or two. But I'm surprised you care.'

'Please – '

'It's not definite and I'm only telling you what he said.' Her mother was looking at her curiously. 'So *eat*! Why won't you ever eat and do as you're told? If you really wanted to come with us, you'd be trying to get well and finishing it all up! Or is there something wrong with my soup, because it isn't like their English soup used to be?'

Emilia shook her head.

'Anyway,' Elizabeta's voice was as sharp as a knife, 'I'm surprised you want to come with us. I thought you wanted to live with *them*, now, and not amongst *gypsies*, like us.'

'No! I only wanted – '

But Elizabeta had walked away.

Emilia reached down and put the bowl on the floor. Further under the sofa lay the book. Now, the thought of either moving on, or being left behind, filled her with dread. It was like being pushed into fast-flowing water, when you knew you couldn't swim. And when they moved on, more possessions would be lost. In the turmoil of packing up, she might forget the book. Yet, if they moved on without her, she'd have nothing. Nothing at all. There'd be nothing to cling to, except the pictures that she'd drawn in someone else's book.

'Yuk!' Zoltan, who'd come for the bowl, tipped it, and pulled a face. 'They said you had to finish it.' The white fat had set across the surface like early morning ice.

'They said – '

'I know what they said!' Emilia retorted. 'They said I had to eat it up!'

He stared. Nowadays, she never answered back.

'I'm not eating it! I've drunk their lemon juice, but that soup makes me sick. So, tip it away, Zoltan. Please?'

'Where? They might find out. But . . . but what'll you give me, if I do?'

'My knife?'

'What! The penknife you found in England? You mean you'd give me *that*?'

She nodded. He snatched it from the palm of her hand, and jabbed the blade into the arm of the sofa.

'Wow!' He fingered the cuts. 'That's brilliant. Thanks a lot.' He was clicking the blades in and out. Then he stopped and looked up. 'Emi? D'you know what Mum and Dad told the people they met this afternoon?'

She shook her head.

'Well, we met this family that Dad knew in Bucharest, and they told them that you're a bit stupid, a bit soft in the head. And now I think it's *true*! Fancy you giving me a valuable knife like this. You must be a bit stupid, mustn't you? Or mad!'

That night, when the others were in bed, Emilia reached under the sofa and pulled out the book. An eye in the dark, with her face reflected in it: that was the picture to draw next. And the reflection of her face could not be the reflection that she'd seen in the bathroom mirror today. It would have to be a reflection of her old face, the face she'd had when she'd climbed into the lorry that would take them away from Romania, to some distant, better place.

After the fires, they'd continued to stay with their relatives outside Bucharest, and each day had brought more bad news. All over Romania, gypsies were being attacked. A little boy sleeping in a haystack after lunch had been burnt alive when villagers torched the rick. Two young gypsy men accused of stealing tiles off a roof weren't put on trial, but were beaten so badly that their teeth and jaws were smashed, and now one couldn't talk. Every day had brought new horrors and everyone had been afraid. Gypsies who weren't leaving Romania hadn't known what to do or where to go to be safe. Daniel, however, had made his plans and within a month of the fires she and Zoltan had been sitting on a pile of rocks beside a mountain road, watching for the lorry that would take them away.

They'd been waiting for three days. Another group of gypsies was travelling with them and food and water had already begun to run short. There'd also been arguments over the delay. Daniel had explained that the lorry was coming from Istanbul and would take a time. He knew the route well because his business had repeatedly taken him along it in recent years. There were mountains to cross and by the end of the summer the roads were often cracked and broken up. In Bulgaria and Romania, diesel was always hard to find. But the lorry would come, he'd promised. They only had to wait. So they had waited, sweltering under the low, autumn sun, and shivering in mountain nights that were cold and damp. They had settled among the ruins of a deserted village, but it hadn't given them any help. They had all been anxious and some thought they'd been betrayed.

Very few vehicles had passed them. The pick-up point had been chosen because it was isolated, but also gave a clear view of the valley below. Each time they'd heard an engine labouring up the hill, the adults had hidden themselves, leaving Emilia and Zoltan and another boy to keep watch. Neither the local Romanians nor the police would see anything suspicious about gypsy kids sitting by the road. People had always called the gypsies layabouts and they expected gypsy children to be the same. So that was why Emilia and Zoltan had been sent to sit on the pile of stones and keep watch.

Emilia remembered observing a farmer who'd been following an ox and plough across a field in the valley below. From her vantage point, they'd looked like tiny, stumbling beetles and the dusty earth had drifted up around them like smoke. Behind her, the adults had huddled in groups. One woman's voice had wafted through the heat. The ruined village had once been *her* village, and it had held both Romanian and gypsy homes. The woman's family had been metal workers, and they'd all got along with their neighbours until the day the old President, Ceausescu, had decided that he didn't want old-fashioned villages like theirs. They were an eyesore, he'd said, and a disgrace in his modern country. He'd ordered the village to be pulled down and replaced by modern flats. Two bulldozers had taken forever to climb the mountain road. Then, in less than a day, they'd knocked down every single building. The villagers had carried away what they could save, but when that was done, they had only been able to stand around and watch the destruction of their homes.

Afterwards the local Romanians had begun to mutter that the gypsies were to blame. If they hadn't started being so troublesome and made a fuss about their rights, Ceausescu would never have known there was a village on that hill. It hadn't even been a special village, the woman had said, only very old. Its carved wooden houses had been built from forests that were now cut down. Their church had been old, hundreds of years old, some experts had said. Its icons had been dark with age, but nobody had minded that. They had still been beautiful and not everything could be new, could it? After all, it had been their home, and it would have remained their home if the gypsies had kept their lying mouths shut. That's what other people had muttered as the bulldozers smashed the buildings to the ground. Such gossip about the gypsies hadn't been true of course, but nobody had cared about that. There'd been fights. A couple of gypsies were taken into police custody and had almost been beaten to death, but it hadn't helped because by then the old village had already gone.

The Romanian villagers had moved down into the valley but the gypsies had slowly drifted back. They hadn't rebuilt anything, but had lived amongst the ruins and carried on with their work, lighting their fires from the fallen timbers and beating out their copper pots. Their former neighbours accused them of living like beasts. They'd begun to claim that the gypsies had turned the Romanians out of their homes intentionally, so they could occupy the village for themselves. 'But it wasn't like that,' the woman had protested, her murmur dwindling to tears. 'We never wanted anything from them. We weren't their enemies. We only wanted to be left alone and not attacked.'

The woman had cried, and Elizabeta had joined in, but Emilia had suspected that their tears weren't only for their ruined homes and lives. They were also weeping for themselves, because they hadn't wanted to leave.

'Don't you think it's a good thing to go away?' Emilia'd asked Zoltan, but he hadn't replied. He'd only been inter-

119

ested in seeing the lorry before she did. He hadn't seemed to understand that they were going away forever, because he'd often asked her when they were coming back.

In the end, Zoltan had seen the lorry first. He'd leapt up and yelled. Behind them, the adults had come out of hiding and watched. At the last moment, however, they almost hadn't gone. Her father had been negotiating with the driver. They'd shaken hands on the deal, and had been smoking a last cigarette while the others gathered up their bags. An old coach, roaring down the hill from higher up, had swung round the bend on the wrong side of the road. The driver had swerved when he'd seen their lorry directly in front. The coach brakes had screamed, the wheels had flung up showers of stones and earth. The group of gypsies, who had been about to climb into the lorry, had scattered, dropping their bags and stumbling over the rocks in their panic to get clear. Only Emilia hadn't moved. She'd had one foot on the back of the lorry but she hadn't let go. As the coach had hurtled towards her she'd swung herself up. She'd been dreaming of that moment for so long that she wasn't going to let anything stand in her way.

It had been dark inside the lorry, but she hadn't been afraid. Stacks of fruit boxes formed a wall from floor to ceiling, but she'd known that the driver had left a gap. Slowly she'd felt her way through. She'd wedged herself in a corner, wrapped her skirt round her toes and rested her chin on her knees. She'd heard the people outside protesting about their escape from the coach. She'd smiled to herself, and breathed in the scents of oranges and lemon leaves and resin from the freshly split pinewood. She'd felt her heart beating under her skin, and she'd hugged her knees more tightly as she'd waited for the others to stop fussing and to climb in. A warmth that she'd never felt before had flowed from the soles of her feet to her cheeks: this, at last, was it. This was her escape.

As she'd waited in her corner, she'd remembered a cartoon she'd seen on a neighbour's television. It had told the story of a family of brothers and sisters whose parents had died, leaving them alone on their farm. An uncle and aunt had moved in to look after them, but the children soon became suspicious that these relatives didn't really want to help them at all. The children had been so unhappy. Their uncle had forced them to work outside from dawn till dusk, while he and his wife drank beer and ate roast meat before falling asleep in two armchairs on either side of the glowing fire.

Then, one of the girls, who always wore the red jumper her own mother had knitted for her, had overheard the wicked pair plotting to seize the farm as their own. The next evening, their uncle had grinned his treacherous grin, and told the children that tomorrow he was taking them deep into the forest, to pick wild strawberries for their tea. The little girl had opened her little pink mouth and reminded him that strawberries didn't grow deep in the forest, but he'd only grinned more broadly, and revealed the blackened stumps of his teeth. So the little girl had stayed up all that night, unravelling her red jersey, and winding the wool into a big red ball. The next morning, as their uncle led them out of the farm, she'd quickly tied one end of the red wool to the gatepost. As he'd led them further and further from the sunlit meadows, and deeper and deeper into the shadows of the forest, the little girl had unwound the ball of wool.

121

Naturally, the children hadn't found any strawberries because the black pines let nothing grow. The youngest brother had cried. The wicked uncle had grinned and as night crept under the pines one by one, the children had cried themselves to sleep. When they'd woken their uncle had vanished, so all the other children cried again. Only the little girl hadn't, even though she'd been shivering with cold. She'd shaken the pine needles from her skirt and held up the other end of the ball of wool. 'Follow me!' she'd shouted. And they had. They'd wiped the teardrops from their cheeks and followed her and step by step they'd found their way firstly to the meadows and then to the farm itself.

When Emilia'd first watched the film, she'd enjoyed it, but as she'd sat in the lorry, she'd found herself thinking more deeply about the ending at the farm gate and she'd suddenly realised that the little girl had made a fatal mistake. She should never have taken her brothers and sisters back to the farm. She should have led them straight past the gate because as soon as they returned the wicked uncle would have started his wicked deeds all over again. They should have abandoned their farm and run on down that road as fast and as far as they could. Like her, they should have escaped.

When the lorry doors had finally been slammed shut Emilia had remembered the red-haired girl from the square in Bucharest. She'd felt as if that girl had handed her the invisible end of an invisible ball of wool. So, when the lorry wheels had started to move over the road, Emilia had felt as if she too was finally winding in her own ball of red wool.

Soon after they'd started, Zoltan had begun asking when they would arrive. He'd complained that his legs were numb, and that he was feeling sick. Emilia'd pulled him onto her lap and given him sips from her bottle of water, until he'd fallen asleep. Inside the lorry it had grown hotter and hotter. Elizabeta had continually compared their position to being buried alive, but the other women had begged her to be quiet.

To begin with, Emilia had smelt the unfamiliar sourness of other people's sweat and each time the lorry had jolted or the driver had braked, she'd heard the gasp of other people's anxious, drawn-in breath. Slowly, and with Zoltan still asleep in her arms, she'd worked herself over to a thin line of light. As she did so, her hand had touched someone else's body, and she'd drawn sharply back.

'Go on,' an old voice had said in the dark. 'Go on: have a last look at your own land, my dear. It's a beautiful sight, and one you mustn't forget.' She'd felt a rush of cold air as she'd put her eye to the crack.

'Can you see?' the old man had asked.

'Yes,' she'd lied, although the lorry had been travelling so fast that she hadn't seen a thing. She had smelt the old man very close, and when she'd looked up, over Zoltan's nodding head, towards his face, she'd known that he'd been weeping, so she'd lied again. 'Yes, I can see it all and you're right: it is the most beautiful country in the world, just like you said.'

And that was when she'd seen the reflection of her face, in his eye, in the dark. And she'd hugged the sleeping Zoltan close and gazed at her own excited face in the old man's eye.

Now, she concentrated on drawing what she'd seen. Delicately she laid a crimson net of veins over the smeared white of his old eye. Then she drew herself as she'd been then, reflected in his eye. She drew her sunburnt forehead that had been as smooth as handled gold. She touched in her freckles that were like spots dabbed on the belly of a fish. She drew her plaits falling below her waist and one of them, she remembered, had been pulled undone. Dust had shadowed her cheek and her eager, opened lips had revealed the moist pink tip of her tongue.

Now, she sat up and stretched. She was stiff and cold and her head ached from bending over the book. She held the picture at arm's length: and there she was, just as she had been on that day, smiling excitedly and happily, amid the old man's fear and grief. Happiness and excitement had sustained her on that long journey across countries whose names she'd never known. It had helped her withstand the dreadful intimacy of strange people whom she'd never met before. It had quenched her thirst, and made her indifferent to the sudden swarms of little flies that had erupted all around. And on the final sea crossing, when the lorry had pitched and rolled and they had feared for their lives, the same hot rush of excitement had convinced her that if she could just cling on, and endure it, everything would be all right in the end.

Somehow, she'd never stopped believing that when the red thread was finally wound in and the lorry doors finally opened, she would jump down into some other, better place.

Picture 8

A Landscape with Autumn Leaves

A couple of mornings later Zoltan wandered into the front room. When he pulled back the curtains, he let out a shout.

Emilia'd been awake for some time. She'd heard the murmur of her parents' low voices in the kitchen, then she'd heard them go out. They hadn't spoken to her before they left but she hadn't minded. She was feeling better, and had remained under the covers in the darkened room, planning the next picture in her head.

'What is it?' Now she opened her eyes at his shout.

'Get up! Come and look what's happened in the night.' Zoltan was still in his pyjamas, his face puffy with sleep.

Outside, a wave of red swastikas had been sprayed onto the white wall opposite. Some of the paint had run down, and spattered like blood. Emilia watched as people going to work glanced up and frowned, then hurried on. She remembered the shape of those marks from England, though she'd never understood exactly what they meant.

'*He* had those marks on his knuckles,' Zoltan remarked as they looked out. He was breathing on a patch of glass and misting it up. 'And on his neck. Only *his* marks were blue, sort of, and not as big as those.'

'Who's "he"? What d'you mean?' Emilia was surprised that Zoltan had recognised the swastikas. In England, she'd seen lots of them, scratched or sprayed on doors and walls around where they'd lived. School friends, like Yasmina and Katy, had made her understand that they were something forbidden and bad. And once, when someone had scrawled one over the washbasins in school, Yasmina had reported it, and a teacher had come straight down and scrubbed it off herself. But Emilia had still not learnt what they *meant*.

'*Who* had those marks on his knuckles and neck?' Emilia repeated.

'No one I *know*,' Zoltan shrugged as he traced a swastika onto the steamed up glass. 'It was just that man who spat at Mum. *That's* where he had them.' He pointed to his own neck and then to his knuckles.

'And he spat at Mum? How disgusting! When was this?'

'Yesterday. That's why we came back early and Mum couldn't finish work.'

Now Emilia remembered that they had returned unexpectedly, after lunch. Elizabeta had gone straight to the bathroom to wash and then hadn't gone back to beg. Now, Zoltan explained what had happened.

It had been another cold day, but the sun had shone, and there'd been quite a few people out on the streets. Zoltan hadn't enjoyed it: his feet had ached too much. He'd complained to his parents about his freezing toes. His green plastic boots had let the cold in and had turned his feet to ice. Elizabeta had told him not to fuss. It'd only been a moderately successful morning's work, so Daniel had decided to return to a shopping centre where they'd done well a few days ago. He'd remembered a space outside a café, with seats and boxes of frozen winter plants. On bright days, he'd noticed crowds lingering there to talk. He'd told Elizabeta to beg as usual, and he'd kept watch for her, from inside, while he was having a beer. Zoltan had asked to go into the warm with his father, but they hadn't let him. He'd told his mother that he was fed up with following her around, but she hadn't listened. She'd squeezed his arm, and reminded him that she always earned more when he was with her. If she did well, she'd promised him another chocolate as a treat. He'd sulked, and kept turning round to stare at the café window where his father sat.

Zoltan had noticed a couple of big men in jeans and black leather boots who were leaning back on one of the seats, with their long legs stretched out. They'd been laughing and drinking from cans. Suddenly, they'd gone quiet, and when Zoltan had turned round to see what they were doing, he'd realised that they were both watching him. They'd got up and begun to stroll over. As their huge legs swung to and fro, they'd reached into the pockets of their jeans as if they were looking for change. Once they were close, he'd realised that they were young, more boys than men, with shaved heads and pink soft skin. Then he'd noticed the marks on their necks. At first he'd thought it was dirt but when they'd come closer still, Zoltan had seen that the marks were like crosses, but bent at the end. Elizabeta had also looked up. They'd smiled, and said something to her. Then they'd spat in her face. She hadn't said a word, and if any of the passing shoppers had noticed, they hadn't stopped or intervened. Zoltan had watched his mother wipe off the gobs of spit, then throw her soiled scarf down. The men had laughed, and moved off. Zoltan had run to the café to fetch his father, who'd said that they must go home at once, so that Elizabeta could wash, and make herself clean.

'And these . . . these *boys*, had they got the same sort of bent cross marks on their *hands*?' Emilia looked at the wall.

'Yes. But Dad said it would be all right.' Zoltan shrugged. 'He was angry, but he said she needn't worry *too* much, because it *would* wash off.' Now Zoltan pointed to the marks on the wall and sniggered. 'Anyway, it would serve her right if it *had* been red paint!'

'That's a horrid thing to say!'

'It isn't horrid,' Zoltan shouted back. 'It's *her* fault. If she wasn't always begging, people wouldn't *spit*. Anyway, I hate her because she's always making me do things I don't want to do, like *begging*. I hate begging now, because it's different here. It's – oh! Quick, Emi! Come and look at this!'

The girl in the red jacket had reappeared below them in the street. This time, Zeynep Kara wasn't walking away. She was standing on the opposite pavement, with her hands pushed into her pockets. She was staring up at the marks on the wall. As they watched, she stepped closer, and took a can from one of her pockets. Then she stretched up, and sprayed a red line from the bent over tip of one of the swastikas, and joined it to its centre, so that it resembled the petal of a flower. She repeated this action three more times, then stepped back to examine her transformation of the swastika into a red-petalled bloom. She glanced over her shoulder, then reached up again, and sprayed on a stem and leaves. Finally, with a series of quick strokes, she added spikes of red grass, so that the flower was growing from the ground.

'Wow!' Zoltan excitedly banged on the glass.

Zeynep reacted as if she'd been hit. The can dropped from her hand and clattered across the pavement. She was running so fast that she'd disappeared round the corner, at the far end of the street, before the can had rolled into the gutter. Emilia and Zoltan watched in astonishment.

'Wow!' Zoltan was impressed. 'I didn't know girls could run like that, I bet you couldn't! Could you, Emi? Could you run like that?'

Emilia shook her head. Then she closed her eyes and bit into a ridge of softened skin. She imagined herself running down that street. She imagined them running together, she and that girl, Zeynep. They'd be running shoulder-to-shoulder, with the winter wind snatching away their breath. And when they'd escaped round the corner, they'd collapse into each other's arms, laughing and crying together, because that was what ordinary girls did.

When she opened her eyes, she was sure that the yellow walls had edged in on her. Suddenly, she was revolted by their colour and wanted to be free of the thick yellow light and outside, in the grey street, with the wind in her face. She wanted to run as far and as fast as she could. It didn't matter where she ran to, and she didn't even care if she was running away.

'Emi . . .' Zoltan was dragging on her arm, 'I'm bored. Will you play –?'

'No!'

'But . . .' He was so surprised by her anger that he didn't know what to say.

'If you want to go and play, then *go*!' she shouted. 'You've got the *key*, haven't you? I know you have, because I've seen it. So *go*, if you like! Unlock the door and *go*. Go and play in that park. I don't care. And, I won't tell. So just *go*, can't you, and – '

'I'll tell Mum.' He sniffed and touched the key that hung round his neck.

'I don't care!'

'I *will* . . .'

She wasn't listening. She'd already put the book on the table and begun to work. She'd been planning this picture of her first moments in England ever since she'd been ill in bed. She'd decided on a landscape study, which would show her first impressions of the land to which she'd come. She'd planned a detailed drawing of the countryside, with its wet, golden leaves and red berried hedges winding quietly down both sides of that quiet country lane. Now, as she looked at the empty page, she changed her mind. The picture must still record the new landscape, but within it she would draw a series of smaller sketches recording what had happened when they'd finally arrived.

On that day, in the autumn, when the lorry's engine had finally been switched off, they'd continued crouching like beasts in a lair as they'd listened to the sound of the driver dragging back the bolts. At first, nobody had moved: the doors hadn't been opened since they'd left. No one had known what this meant. She'd been the first of their group to stand up, and the first to clamber down. She'd been shut in the moving lorry for so long that she'd staggered as she'd taken her first steps on the wet grass verge. She'd felt as giddy as if she was still on the move. For a moment, she hadn't known if she was standing still, or if the ground beneath her feet was rolling on. Outside, it had been quiet, but the roar of the wheels rolling over the road had continued to howl in her head. She'd blinked, and shaded her eyes against the brilliance of the low afternoon light. The air had been so fresh it had snatched away her breath, and she'd had to cough, to get it back. Her ankles and legs had felt old and stiff, but her hot, sweaty feet were deliciously cooled as her slippers slid through the wet grass. She'd moved away from the lorry, and looked up and down a lane, and she'd been overwhelmed.

In Bucharest, she'd often imagined what this moment would be like, but she'd never pictured it like this. She'd always thought that they would arrive on the edge of a big, bustling square. She'd expected to see lots of people, and they would have been smartly dressed in new coats and jackets lined with soft white fur. The square had always been shining with the glittering shop windows, and as she'd stepped down from the lorry into the crowds she'd been carried away by them like a raindrop falling into a running stream.

Whenever her father had talked about their new life he had always believed it would be in a foreign town. When he'd spoken to his brother, before they'd left, the two had arranged to meet at a special lay-by on a main road out of town. Now it appeared that Daniel had got it wrong. They'd reached this other, distant place, but there was no lay-by, and no main road and no sign of a town. At first, Emilia hadn't been worried: this was more beautiful than anything she'd imagined in her head. She'd tilted her face to feel the warmth of a different side of the sun and she'd accepted that this was what she'd been waiting for. This was where Zoltan could grow up to be a man, and this was where her own life could begin. It was her country now. These autumn hedgerows, where spiders' jewelled webs hung and swung and sparkled along the road, were hers.

'Well, here we are.' The driver'd smiled at her, as if he understood. He was a Turkish gypsy, from Istanbul, and she knew from her father that he had already helped several groups leave Romania in this way. He'd yawned and stretched his arms above his head. Then he'd lit another cigarette. Emilia'd remembered her family, and looked back.

Elizabeta had been standing on the tailboard, with her hand over her mouth, staring at the deserted countryside in horror and distress. She'd been born and brought up in Bucharest, and had assumed that they'd be coming to another town, with flats and streets and shops. She'd been appalled to see ploughed fields and empty hills, so she'd stood there, dazed with exhaustion and fear, slowly shaking her head.

Emilia had looked along the silent country lane and been unafraid. She'd seen the low sun shining on the banks of tangled roots, fat berries and golden, autumn leaves. It must have just stopped raining, because every twig, stem and thorn glistened and dripped. Stormclouds hung over far off hills, but high above her, in an opening patch of blue, a bird had fluttered as it sang.

Now, she remembered how she'd stepped off the wet grass onto the smooth, black surface of the road. On both

132

sides of the lane, a green land rolled away from the hedges and up into distant clumps of darker trees. The fields stretched and sparkled and gleamed. She'd felt as if they'd been waiting for her: as if they'd been lying unappreciated until she came and brought them back to life. While she'd been gazing around, her father had jumped down from the back of the lorry. He'd begun to walk up and down the lane. She'd followed him. Her heart had pounded so loudly, she'd covered it with her hand, in case he'd overheard. The rest of the group had stayed close to the lorry, as if afraid to go beyond. Her father'd tapped down his hat and frowned. She'd felt as if she'd stepped onto the surface of a star, but when she'd turned to him, she'd decided to keep quiet.

'Well, folks,' the driver had glanced at his watch. 'This is it! This is as far as I go, and now I've got to be off.' He'd rubbed his hands briskly. 'And remember, if anyone asks you *how* you got here, you say: "by bus".'

She remembered the sound of their whispers: 'bybusby-busbybus'.

Daniel had looked worried. He'd peered up and down the lane again. This was not what he'd agreed. The deal he'd struck in Istanbul was that they should be met. The driver had jumped back into the lorry and begun to toss out the rest of their bags. Emilia'd gone to help, but she'd been so embarrassed by the smell of the dirt they'd left behind that she'd stepped back. Her father had begun examining a small map which his contacts in Istanbul had drawn. He'd held it out to the driver, protesting that this was not the drop-off point: this was *nowhere*, and they were lost. According to his map, the drop-off point was along a main road, in the lay-by, where there was a phone. The driver had scowled. He'd kept on throwing out their stuff.

Emilia'd moved further away. She was afraid that he might notice that they'd smashed open a couple of his crates of fruit. They'd been so desperately thirsty that they'd squeezed the juice from the lemons straight into their mouths. Some of the others had been so hungry they'd eaten the fruit and the skins. If the driver asked *her* about it, she'd decided to own up. She'd felt guilty stealing his fruit, because she'd known that it was wrong. But the driver hadn't asked her. He'd been too busy kicking the litter of fruit skins and splintered wood onto the grass verge, on top of all their other filth. Then she'd realised that he didn't care what happened to them. He'd delivered them, and now he only wanted to get away as fast as he could.

When he'd finished clearing up, he'd bolted the lorry doors. They'd protested. They'd begged him not to leave. Her mother had followed him to the cab. She'd accused him of abandoning helpless women and children, but he'd pointed to his ear and shrugged, as if he'd suddenly gone deaf. The old man, the one who'd wanted Emilia to have a last look at her land, had stood in front of the bonnet, holding up his arms. As the lorry had edged forward, he'd been forced to step back, and as the wheels bumped over the verge, he'd stumbled to one side and fallen against the hedge. When the lorry'd disappeared round the bend, the lane had been very quiet. The adults had huddled together in the middle of the empty road. They'd talked in low voices, and had kept glancing over their shoulders, as if afraid of being overheard. Zoltan and the other boy had jumped from puddle to puddle, and splashed. Elizabeta had been rubbing her hands to and fro across her folded arms, as if she'd suddenly felt cold. Emilia had shut her eyes and tilted her head back, so that the sun fell full on her face. High above her, little fork-tailed birds swooped down from the edges of a cloud, and sang.

Suddenly a shining red car had swung round the bend towards them. Rainwater had spun from its slithering wheels as it braked. The group in the road had screamed, and scattered like leaves in a gust. Zoltan had tumbled into the ditch. The car had been small, but full of passengers, who'd wound down their windows and stared. The beat of their music had filled the air. A tall girl, as thin and short-haired as a man, had opened her door and got out. Her open mouth and white face had registered her shock. Emilia'd seen that she was young, perhaps not much older than herself. The girl had spoken, then sucked in her bottom lip. Zoltan had got up. His knees were muddy. He'd fingered a new scratch on his cheek and then looked at the smear of blood. The driver of the car had reached out, and touched the tall girl's arm. She'd leant towards him, a crescent of her skin appearing below her T-shirt like a pale slice of fruit. She'd said something else to the group by the roadside, and smiled, but they'd looked away at the sight of her flesh. None of them had smiled back. If she'd known what to say, Emilia would have spoken up, but as she'd opened her mouth to try 'hello' she'd seen the girl's smile fade. The driver pulled her back into the car. As it had driven slowly past, Emilia'd seen the girl bend over and kiss the young man on his lips. The other people in the back had craned round once more, and had a final look.

After the car had disappeared round the next bend, the

adults had begun to shout at each other. Some believed that they were about to be betrayed: that tall girl was a half-naked slut who would come straight back, bringing the police. If they didn't hurry, and make their escape, they'd be caught between these high hedges like animals in a trap. It was Daniel's fault, they said. If he'd made better arrangements, they wouldn't have been turned off the lorry like that. He was responsible for the mess. Daniel had raised his fists, and stepped back as another younger man raised his. After so many days of silence, hidden in the lorry, they'd seemed about to explode. Emilia had listened, but she hadn't spoken. She'd known there was no point. They'd never have paid attention to her, even though she'd realised they were wrong. She'd noticed the expression on the tall girl's face. That girl and her friends had meant no harm. They wouldn't be going to the police. They'd been curious, that was all, and scared, because the wheels of their car might not have stopped in time.

Then, somewhere not so far away, a dog had barked. The other family had picked up their bags. When they'd heard voices as well, this other family had begun to walk in the opposite direction as fast as they could. When the voices and the barking became louder, they'd run. Emilia had seen the old man limping after them and calling them to wait.

Daniel only hesitated for a second. Then he'd stuffed the map back in his jacket, grabbed Zoltan's hand and begun to walk straight towards the sounds. Zoltan had tried to splash in a puddle, but Daniel had dragged him on. He'd shouted over his shoulder that they mustn't look guilty or afraid: running away was always suspicious. It was the worst thing to do. So Emilia and her mother had picked up their bags.

Emilia had smiled to herself: this wasn't Romania, so there was no reason to feel guilty or scared. There were no secret police in these places, or that's what her father had always said.

They'd paused at the next field and looked through the bars of a gate. Three children were running towards them. A small brown dog had leapt and barked around their feet. They'd been coming down a track which seemed to go round the edge of the field. It continued above the children, and finally disappeared under huge, grey-barked trees that leant towards each other like the pillars of an ancient arch. Then Emilia'd noticed two more children further up the track. They'd been laughing and tossing about great armfuls of copper leaves that had shone like brown waves breaking on a beaten copper shore. Daniel had struggled with the latch on the gate. Two women, dressed in trousers and men's thick boots, had been talking loudly as they'd waded through the leaves. As they'd come nearer, Emilia had noticed that one of them was carrying a bunch of twigs. She smiled to herself as she sketched them in: on that first day, she'd thought those sticks were for a fire. Later, she'd realised that English women didn't warm their houses or cook with fires. They actually decorated their rooms with twigs and sticks like that. The women had continued talking, but as they'd approached the gate they'd fallen quiet. The smallest child had run back to them and pushed himself between. In the silence that followed, Emilia knew that they'd all noticed her plastic slippers, and her wet, bare feet.

' "Bybusbybus?" ' Zoltan, who'd been resting his chin on a bar of the gate, had suddenly called out.

The two women had looked at each other. Zoltan's voice had never been a child's voice, but always deep and gruff. When he'd spoken, the other children had giggled and grinned.

' "Bybus! Bybus!" ' Zoltan had grinned back.

'You want to catch *a bus*?' The English woman, with the bunch of twigs, had spoken slowly, and smiled.

At the time, none of the Radus had understood a word, but the women hadn't given up. They'd pointed back up the track in the direction they'd come from, and moved their cupped hands up and down as though drawing hills in the air. Emilia'd watched closely, then, as they'd repeated it, she'd thought *she'd* understood: these women were advising them to follow the track under the trees, and to carry on, over the top of the hill. Somehow, amongst all the unknown sounds that the women were making, she'd caught and clung on to the repeated sound of 'bus'. When she was certain she'd understood, she pushed back her plaits and smiled. She'd stepped forward, and started to pull on the latch. One of the children had come over and shown her how to uncouple the two iron rings that were holding it shut.

She'd hurried through as soon as the gate was opened, and she'd been halfway up the track before she'd heard her father calling her back. Distantly, she'd also been aware of her parents arguing. Elizabeta hadn't liked the look of the track. It would be filthy and muddy up there, and once they'd left the road, she was afraid they'd be hopelessly lost. Emilia had only paused for a moment. When she'd looked back, she'd seen her father taking his hat off and scratching the back of his neck. He looked unshaven and exhausted

138

and still stared at his map. So she'd pressed on, and pretended that she hadn't heard his shout.

Then, she'd run. Her legs were awkward, after so long in the lorry, and her breath came in gasps, but she hadn't stopped. The bags had swung and banged, and the leaves had rustled and slid, but from somewhere she'd found a deeper, darker breath and with that she'd reached the safety of the trees. Then she'd dropped the bags and leant against one of the trunks. She'd stared up at the arch above. When she'd caught her breath, she'd looked down at the leaves which covered her feet. Then she'd looked up at the dappled light filtering through the branches, and at the sky above. She'd touched the bark, and it had felt like roughened skin. A breeze had blown through the faraway twigs, high overhead, and a few more leaves had fluttered down, and settled on the rest. When she'd looked back, her parents were still staring at the map.

Faintly, she caught the distant sounds of the children and their dog. Then she'd lifted up her red skirt, which dragged, and waded beneath the canopy of branches. She'd felt the cool leaves swish and eddy as they'd flowed across her feet. When she'd emerged from the tunnel of trees, she'd been on a sunlit hillside, so she'd struggled on until she'd reached the top. Below her, on the other side of the hill, she'd seen a big road, so she'd flung herself down on the grass and lay there, panting, until the others caught her up.

Zoltan had got there first. He'd been scarlet-faced. He'd looked at her, then at the road, and run back to his parents, shouting that it was all right: they weren't lost. He'd seen a big road and a town.

Now, she darkened the curve of the tarmac road they'd

seen from the hill. Then she added the rows of tiny houses and a distant flash of water that she later learnt was the sea.

The beginnings of that town had been further off than they'd thought. It had taken them two hours to reach the edge of that road. By then, it had been dark. Emilia'd been so tired that she'd nodded off as she'd walked. They'd taken turns carrying Zoltan, and after they'd climbed through a wire fence and scrambled down an embankment to the edge of the road, they'd been too exhausted to decide what to do next. They hadn't known whether to cross the road, or even, which way to turn. There was no lay-by, and no phone. They'd stood at the side of the road, as the lights of the cars and lorries flashed by them like flames streaking down sticks of wood. Emilia had heard her mother begin to cry. She'd sobbed that they *never* should have come. If she'd had *her* way, they'd have been safely asleep, in their house in Bucharest, instead of *here*, and lost. Emilia had opened her mouth, but her father had spoken first and told Elizabeta to be quiet. He'd promised to find a phone, as soon as it was light. She wasn't to worry about the future: he'd got them here, hadn't he? And what was a night in the open to them? And who said they wouldn't be safe? As soon as he'd phoned to his brother, everything would be sorted out.

'And tonight?' her mother had asked, through tears.

'Tonight – ' A coach had roared past on the road. It had been too close, and they'd all leapt back. The rushing, gritty air had snatched Daniel's words from his lips and scattered them in the night. Glancing through the orange glow from the lamps, which quivered overhead, Emilia'd seen something like fear on her father's face.

140

'*Tonight*?' her mother'd asked again.

Her father had not answered.

'*Tonight*,' Emilia had interrupted, 'we should go back to that wood. If we stay *here*, we'll be spotted. *There*, we can sleep under those trees.' She'd expected her father to tell her to be quiet. But he hadn't. He'd nodded and tapped down his hat.

Her mother'd objected that the wood was too far away, but her father had begun to climb back up the bank. As they'd climbed, he'd shouted at them to hurry, as if some nasty thing from the road had been snapping at their heels, and jumping up.

Her mother had been right too: the wood was too far away. Halfway there, they'd settled for the shelter of a hedge. Once Emilia had closed her eyes, she'd imagined that she was lying on that bed of copper leaves, and that the branches of those trees were sheltering her above. She must've dreamed that it was sunny, in the night, because she thought she'd looked up through the grey branches and seen sky that was blue and bright. She'd dream that, while her parents and Zoltan were asleep, she'd worked herself free of them, bit by bit. When she'd stood up, the leaves had dropped from her, like a snake's sloughed-off skin. She'd also dreamt that she'd stretched out her arms and sound-lessly stepped through the dappled light into the dazzling hillside sun. There, she'd run. Someone had opened an old door, or an old iron gate, so she'd kept on running, and there'd been nothing in her way, like wire, to hold her back. She'd run down the hill, then down the bank, then along a road and she'd taken her place amongst the stream of vehicles, as if it had been the most natural thing in the world. She'd noticed that other people were also running amongst the cars, and nobody had made them stop. She'd run faster than most. Once, several little red-haired girls had looked out of a taxi and laughed. She'd kept on running, and now and again, she'd skipped. Then she'd flown. Her plaits had been streaming out behind her in the wind. She'd fluttered her forked tail and sung like a lark, and her arms had been covered with coloured feathers and when she'd stroked them, they'd rippled like reeds.

'You asleep, Emi?' Zoltan was pulling at her sleeve. She blinked. She'd been dreaming and he'd woken her up.

'Emi, *don't sleep*. It's not fair, if you sleep when I'm bored.'

She rubbed her eyes. She'd fallen asleep on top of the new picture. Now, she was uncertain about when she'd had the dream.

'Emi-ii?' Zoltan was dangling the key on its string. '*You* can have the key, if you like. I don't want to go out by myself.'

They were staring at each other. Then he went to the window and pointed to the wall.

'Anyway, your flowers are better than *that*.'

Outside, on the wall the red flower still bloomed in the sun.

'Do *you* want to go out?' he asked swinging the key to and fro. 'Or are you afraid that people'll laugh at your hair?'

'No! It's just . . .' It was just that as soon as she thought about stepping outside, something grabbed her throat, and held on.

'Please, Emi?' He touched her hand. 'Let's go out. I didn't mean it, about your hair. I mean . . . I mean . . . now it's growing, it's not so bad . . .'

142

'Emi?'

The grip on her throat had tightened. Now she couldn't speak.

Instead, she hid the book under the sofa, felt for her pens, then joined Zoltan by the door. She wanted to ask him when their parents would return, but couldn't, because of the hand at her throat.

Zoltan unlocked the door. She put her head outside, and looked up and down the corridor, as though preparing to cross a road. There was nobody about, so she stepped outside. Zoltan double-locked the door behind them. As they walked to the lift, she smelt strange cooking, and the oily odours of sweat in unwashed clothes. She could hear people behind their brightly painted doors. Somewhere, another baby was crying, and through one half-opened door, she heard men's voices and smelt the smoke from cigarettes. She bit off a sliver of new skin. She was half-waiting for someone to rush out and scream at her.

The lobby was still full of men. She took a gulp of breath, grabbed Zoltan's arm, and followed him through. She couldn't believe she was doing it. Five minutes ago, she'd been locked in the yellow room. Now, she put another finger in her mouth and tore at a larger piece of skin, to prove that this wasn't a dream. When Zoltan opened the front door, she gasped. The air was fresh. She hesitated on the top of the steps and gripped the wet black rail.

'Come on!' Zoltan was jumping about on the pavement below. She went down a couple of steps as clumsily as if she'd forgotten how to walk. Rain ran off the rail and down her wrist. Something banged and pulsed in her ears like a drum. In front of her, the empty street was as vast as a winter sea.

'Come *on*!' Zoltan was balancing on the edge of the kerb, rocking to and fro. 'Come on! Be quick!'

She ran at him, snatched his hand, and kept on running straight across the road.

Picture 9
Drawn on the Wall

'Go *on*,' Zoltan hissed when they got to the other side. 'Draw something, quick!'

Once again, Emilia couldn't move. Fear, or whatever it was, had bounded after her, and hooked its rough hand back around her throat. She tried to move towards the wall, but it held on tight and its hot, smoky breath covered her face.

'Hurry!' Zoltan stamped his foot. 'Draw something Emi, before it's too late.'

She stared up at the white wall. In the low winter sun, it was too bright.

'Go *on*!' Zoltan butted her with his head.

She put her fingers in her mouth. The space was too large, too white. She'd never drawn on anything like this before. In Bucharest, her pictures had been on the paving slabs in the public square, but they always been hidden by dust and mud. This expanse of wall terrified her. Yet she wanted to stay and draw, and would have started, if the old fear hadn't dug its claws in so tightly.

'Go *on*,' Zoltan gave her another shove.

145

Fear was choking her as effectively as smoke.

'Ple-ease?' Zoltan stopped pushing. 'Please, Emi? Before it's too late . . . ?' He reached up and touched her hand, pulling it from her mouth. His animal eyes were soft and brown. His black curls fell across her wrist. His breath was sweet.

Oddly, she remembered Nico. She saw his baby face again, all spoilt and marked and cold. His stilled eyes had been half shut and glazed with something like sour milk. She'd been fascinated and disgusted by the way he'd looked. Now, as she looked at Zoltan, she remembered the smell of the other child's death. Suddenly, anger made her blaze up as if her fever had returned. Her skin was so hot that the hand at her throat melted away and she could breathe.

'Emi?'

'Yes?' She gulped in the air and was somehow less afraid. She began to feel in the pocket of her red skirt for her thickest pens.

'Draw something, Emi. Please?'

She stepped closer and made her first mark on the wall. Close to, the surface was pitted and cracked and not as white as she'd thought.

'If you like, Emi, if you need a good idea, you could draw . . . *me* . . . Please?' Zoltan's eyes sought hers.

She was startled. She'd never seen him plead like that, not even when he'd been begging in the street. Above them the swastika flowers bloomed on the wall. Why shouldn't she draw him? He could be running across those flowers and heading in a goal. She reached up to sketch in goalposts, at the far end of a pitch. Then she drew Zoltan, as she'd seen him so many times in England, tearing over Zeynep's flowers and spikes of grass, and shooting in a spectacular goal. She drew a goalkeeper, leaping but just missing the shot. Beside her on the pavement Zoltan gasped.

He was so close, her elbow banged his forehead. This time, however, he didn't hit back or complain. He only sniffed. She was working quickly, drawing in his flying limbs and his tangled curls blown back. She drew his smile of triumph and realised that she was happy too. Now that her arm had adjusted to the size and texture of the wall she drew with more confidence than before. She added another player, a defender, who was watching Zoltan's winning kick. Then she drew several other kids sitting astride a wall. They were waving their arms and cheering Zoltan on. She changed pens and drew a tree, then outlined the blocks of flats that had overlooked the park.

'Hey!'

Emilia froze. It wasn't her brother's voice. She leapt back onto Zoltan's foot. He squealed like an animal hit. Then she grabbed his arm and ran, dragging him back across the road and up the hostel steps. He was protesting, but she clung to him with a strength she didn't know she had. She didn't release him until they reached the yellow door.

'Hurry!' She screamed at him as he fumbled with the key. 'Hurry up!'

Further down the corridor, someone opened another door and watched.

'Hurry!' She screamed again, not caring who heard. When he dropped the key, she snatched it from round his neck and opened the door herself. She double-locked it as soon as they were in, but her heart still beat too fast and she felt a nerve in her cheek beginning to twitch. She couldn't help flattening herself against the door, desperate to keep it shut, although nobody was outside.

'Why did you do *that*?' Zoltan was inspecting the mark she'd made on his wrist.

'I . . .' She couldn't answer so they stared at each other in the yellow light.

She hated herself for what she'd done. How could she have been so stupid? How could she have taken that risk, not with herself, but with *him*, when she'd *vowed* to keep him safe? Why had she unlocked the door and gone into the street, when she knew it was dangerous and when her parents had told her never to do such a thing? They'd threatened to abandon her if she disobeyed them again. So why had she done it? Why had she taken the risk? Ridiculously, she sensed tears forming somewhere in her head. She bit off another piece of skin but it was no use. The tears ran down her cheeks.

'Why did you *run*?' Zoltan asked again.

'I . . .' She was still leaning against the locked door, as if that would have kept them safe.

'You're *so* stupid, Emi,' Zoltan frowned. 'She only wanted to say "*hello*".'

'Who? What d'you mean?'

'That *girl*, of course. See?' He went to the window and pointed to the street.

'Who?' Emilia made herself leave the door.

'See?' Zoltan jabbed his elbow into her ribs.

'Oh . . .'

He was right: Zeynep was standing by the wall, looking at what she'd drawn.

'*And* you stamped on my foot.'

'I'm sorry. I was . . . frightened.'

'Why? I wasn't frightened.'

On the opposite side of the street Zeynep had turned her back on the picture and was looking up at their window. When their eyes met, Zeynep pointed to the picture on the wall behind her, then up at them. Her lips were moving, but Emilia couldn't hear what she said. As Zeynep turned to and fro, her hair shone and swung, and her fine brows arched against her forehead like a small bird's curved wing.

'Go on!' Zoltan urged. 'Quick!'

'How? What?'

'*Answer*, you idiot. Nod! Say the English "yes" like everyone does!'

'But . . .'

'Nod, Emi, quick!'

So she did.

'See?' Zoltan shouted triumphantly. Below them, in the street, Zeynep was smiling a warm, wide smile like a burst of sun.

'See? I was right, wasn't I?' Zoltan crowed. 'She was asking if *you'd* drawn that picture!' He was still jumping about.

'How did you know that?'

'I – ' he pulled a face and shrugged. 'I just did.'

Outside, Zeynep waved and Zoltan waved back.

'D'you think she'll come up and talk to us again?' he asked.

'No!' Emilia quickly shook her head. She didn't want that to happen because it would make her life even more complicated. Yet she was restless all morning, listening for Zeynep's knock.

In the afternoon Zoltan watched a cowboy film on the television but it was only when the light was beginning to fade that Emilia settled down to draw. She glanced out of the window at her picture on the wall, then turned to a fresh page and began the outlines for another drawing, on another wall. The idea for the picture had imposed itself so suddenly that within moments she was totally absorbed.

This other wall had been made of concrete, not painted brick, and when she'd first seen it, a white cat had been crouching on top. Rain had been running down the concrete face and on over the litter of patterns and words that people had sprayed or scratched or painted across it. This wall had been one of the first things she'd seen when she'd climbed out of her uncle's van, in England.

After that first night, when they'd slept under the hedge, Daniel had got up with the dawn and returned to the main road. Emilia and Zoltan had stayed with their mother out of sight. Her father had walked a long way before he'd found a petrol station with a phone. Then, he'd been lucky. One of his pocketfuls of foreign coins had fitted the slot, and he'd been able to tap in the numbers and get through to his brother. Nevertheless, it'd taken the rest of the morning for his brother to find the right filling station, and when Emilia had eventually heard voices that she recognised, she'd realised that her uncle had brought his whole family to welcome them to their new home. She'd been overwhelmed. Her cousins had changed in the two years since she'd seen them. They'd become strangers and she hadn't known what to say. Once they were all in the van, her uncle had insisted on driving them around for what had seemed like hours, so that Daniel and Zoltan, who were sitting in the front beside him, could enjoy a good view.

There'd been no windows in the back of the van where Emilia sat and it had been crowded and hot. Her aunt had never stopped talking. She'd described the pleasures of their new life endlessly. Things in England were the best she'd ever known, she said, and somewhere in the dark beside her, Emilia had sensed that her cousins were nodding their heads. In their flat, clean water streamed from the taps day and night. The electricity had never gone off, not even once. And they had a telephone and a colour television, because *everybody* did. They also had an oven and a fridge, and last summer, when it had been so hot, they'd made ice-cubes from the boxes of coloured fruit juices that you could buy in any shop. Then, on hot evenings, they'd sat on their balcony on the tenth floor, sucking these frozen sweets, and listening to music, and watching the traffic and the people in the streets far below. Life in Bucharest had never been like that. After telling them this, her aunt had lowered her voice and confessed that sometimes, in this new life, she felt like a film star, in a film.

Elizabeta had refused to be impressed. She hadn't lowered her voice as she'd reminded her sister-in-law that she'd never wanted to leave their home in Bucharest. What had been good enough for her parents, and for their parents before them, was good enough for her. But Daniel was different, she'd sighed. He'd always been a discontented man. He'd insisted that they leave Romania and she'd only agreed because of Zoltan. Elizabeta had shaken her head wearily and admitted that it might be right for the boy to have a chance, but if she had her way, they wouldn't be

151

staying long: maybe for a year or two, or five, at the most. Then they'd return.

There'd been a moment of silence in the van. It was obvious that their relatives disagreed. Elizabeta had coughed, then wondered if so much electricity in one flat was a healthy thing. And about that water, she'd asked. How did they *know* it was clean? The gypsy way of telling what was truly clean was a special gift which those who weren't gypsies would never have, despite their wealth.

Emilia's aunt had exchanged glances with her daughters. Then she'd described the shops. She didn't *want* all the things on display, she'd explained. She wasn't a greedy person, like that. It was just such a pleasure to go into the shops with everyone else, and look. The van had grown hotter and her aunt's voice had run on like warm oil in a pan. Emilia had rested her head back for a moment, but must have fallen deeply asleep.

She'd only woken when the van stopped. Once again, she'd clambered out into puddles and the sparkle of rain. This time, however, they were no longer in the country. As she'd stepped down, Emilia'd heard town noises and smelt wet streets and cars. When she'd looked around she could have laughed with delight. The place where they'd stopped had actually looked like places she'd known in Bucharest! She'd glanced at her mother to see if she was equally pleased, but Elizabeta had been standing with folded arms. She'd been staring at the ground.

They'd been in some sort of car park, with tall buildings all around. Emilia had looked up at the towering blocks of flats, where lines of washing dripped and flapped on balconies darkened by rain. The scene had reminded her of some of the newer parts of Bucharest. She and her mother had occasionally worked in areas like this, although the money had never been as good as the money they'd earned in the square. Her family had never lived in a modern block, but it was what most gypsy families dreamed of doing when they'd finally saved up the cash.

As she'd looked curiously around, her uncle had explained that he had business with friends over the road and he'd suggested that Daniel go with him. He'd told the rest of them to look around. This area, he'd said, was likely to be their home. Lots of foreigners had been settled here and there were other gypsy families about. Her aunt had nodded and pointed out the steeple of a church. Her flat was nearby, and from her tenth floor she had a breathtaking view. On a clear day, they could even see the sea and the port.

The two men had walked away and her aunt had resumed talking. Emilia'd yawned and rubbed her eyes. Although she'd wanted to look around, she was so tired that she could have slept standing up. She'd tried to stay awake by concentrating on a white cat which she'd noticed picking its way through the puddles. It was easily the biggest cat she'd ever seen and it had a large piece of fried fish clamped tightly between its jaws. As she'd watched, a bit of the flesh fell off and revealed the cooked white backbone underneath. The sky overhead had been darkening and, as the cat stalked past, Emilia had noticed its odd reflection amongst stormclouds, in a large puddle on the ground.

A sudden scream had made them all jump. Emilia's father and uncle must have heard it as well because she'd seen them hesitate, then turn back. A big, red-faced woman, who was half-dressed, appeared to be splashing through the car park puddles to get to them. She'd waved her arms as if she'd been driving cattle, but there'd been none about. Then she'd screamed again, as loudly as she could. As she'd approached, Emilia'd noticed that her white shins were bare and splattered with rain and mud. At the same moment, a gust of wind had blown through the car park and slapped the wet hem of Emilia's best red skirt against her legs. She'd shivered with cold.

She'd also felt sorry for the screaming woman, who wore no skirt. She'd pitied her and wondered how it must feel to be so upset that you forgot how to dress. She'd decided that the woman was mad and this too had reminded her of Bucharest. There, the streets had been home to all sorts of desperate people. If their families turned them out, they'd stayed on the streets until the authorities cleared them off. As Emilia watched, the woman had lifted up her vest and revealed her belly as she scratched herself. Instantly, Emilia had remembered the asylum on the hill. People had said that the asylum inmates behaved like that. They screamed and howled and tore off their clothes. Sometimes they'd been seen running naked in the snow. She'd also heard that the stoves in the asylum were never lit because the authorities said that mad people couldn't feel the cold. So she'd stared at the woman who'd only worn underwear, and she'd noticed that she didn't look cold. Then she'd felt ashamed of staring so rudely and she'd studied the cat instead.

Gizella, who'd watched films on her second husband's television, had reported that foreign people allowed unclean animals, like cats, to live in their houses. They treated these creatures as if they were children, letting them eat from china plates and sleep on the ends of their beds. Emilia hadn't entirely believed Gizella. Everybody knew that cats cleaned themselves by licking their fur. This meant that they put their own filth back inside their bodies, which was disgusting as well as forbidden for gypsies. Even little gypsy children knew that. Emilia had always been revolted by the thought of such foul habits, and she'd avoided cats or thrown stones to keep them away. That evening, however, as she'd looked at the cat, she'd been surprised by how plump and soft it was. It had reminded her of a silky bridal pillow, decorated with frills and bits of lace. She'd noticed the cat's shiny collar and realised that someone must have gently parted the white fur to fasten the collar round its neck. So, someone must have loved that creature, and fed it well, or it wouldn't have grown so enormous. As she'd watched the cat, she'd suspected that Gizella had been telling the truth after all. Briefly, she'd pictured that cat curled up on her own bed. Then, she'd been sickened by the thought and her stomach had heaved. She'd put her hand over her mouth and retched.

When a dog had barked close by, she'd moved away from the van. When it barked again, the cat had hissed, then puffed itself up so that a spike of wet fur rose along its back like a fin. A sharp rattle of barking, like stones in a can, had finally sent the cat streaking towards the wall. It had leapt up, with the fish still in its mouth. Now, Emilia shivered as she remembered the sound of its claws on the concrete edge. The cat had squinted down from the top, then swished its tail and begun to creep along. And that's when she'd first noticed the things drawn on the wall.

The barking had got louder and when Emilia'd looked

round for a stone, she'd realised that the van was in the centre of a gathering crowd. Rain was falling more heavily. A young woman with a pushchair, who'd been standing under the lamp, had pulled a plastic cover over her child, but neither she nor anyone else had moved away.

Then Emilia had noticed a man who had been standing near the screaming woman. He'd moved and planted himself in front of the van, with his short, thick legs apart and his hands behind his back. She'd watched them exchange a few words, then the woman had resumed shouting and the man hadn't tried to make her quiet. He'd held his head to one side and rocked on his heels as his eyes had darted between the gypsies by the van, and the crowd gathered around. He hadn't looked angry. In fact, he'd been half smiling, as though standing out there in the rain was his idea of fun. As she'd watched, the crowd had parted and revealed another, taller man. He was struggling to hold back the barking dog which had been twisting and choking on the end of a bit of green string.

Emilia had become aware of her father and uncle edging back towards the van. They'd been moving like old men, shuffling and looking at the ground. The crowd had grown. People had appeared from nowhere. They'd emerged from the wet, black shadows and had stood bare headed in the rain. The woman with no skirt had continued to shout and scream and the tall man had kicked the dog which snarled and bared its teeth as it writhed this way and that and struggled to break free. Then an old man had stepped from the crowd and shaken his fist in Daniel's face. Her father had flinched and Emilia'd seen fear in his face. Then she'd hurriedly looked away.

156

She'd tipped back her head so that cool rain could fall on her face and above her a big white bird had called into the darkening, gusting sky. Now she drew its stretched-out neck and open yellow beak. As the shouting around her had increased, she'd concentrated on the bird's flight and avoided looking at anything else. She'd watched the bird swoop down on the dropped bit of fish, then sail up, silenced now, but flapping hard against the wind. Finally, it had disappeared round the corner of the block of flats, which she was now carefully sketching in.

Her pen was racing over the page as she recreated the double band of rectangular windows that had run from top to bottom of the block. She added the jutting balconies that had stuck out like old men's teeth. Some had been stacked with furniture and boxes. Another had carried piles of plastic crates. On several, lines of wet washing had swung and sagged and dripped. She'd noticed a man in a light shirt leaning over one of the balcony rails. He'd looked as though he was watching what was happening to them in the car park below. Now, she drew him in as well.

She remembered how the edges of the wind had sliced across her face, and how her feet and legs had ached with tiredness and cold. When she'd glanced down, she'd realised that she was standing in water. She'd wanted to get away from the barking dog, but hadn't looked where she was going, so had stepped right into the puddle. She'd soaked the hem of her red skirt right through.

She still hadn't understood why the woman was shouting, but as soon as she'd realised that her father was scared, she'd begun to feel frightened too. She'd glanced back at the crowd and noticed that none of them were staring at the mad woman. They were all staring at her family and her.

In Bucharest people hadn't stared. There, everyone had known about gypsies and though most people hadn't liked them, they hadn't taken much notice of them either. Some Romanians had regularly shouted abuse and she'd been used to it. She'd either ducked or run off to avoid an angry fist or curse. Her mother had taught her to expect this and had told her to curse her tormentors back. So, as she'd grown older, she often had. Her father had been less tolerant. He'd believed that life for gypsies like them, in Romania, would only get worse. That was why he'd wanted to leave. But here, in this distant place, where no one knew about them, Emilia hadn't understood why they'd been met by such an angry crowd.

Now, as she recalled that evening with increasing clarity, she added more and more detail to the picture. When people in the English school had asked her how she remembered all the parts of the buildings so accurately, she'd never known what to say. She hadn't been able to explain that once she'd seen a building, it was somehow fixed in her head. She still didn't know how this happened, but she could remember the lines of a building as easily as other people remembered tunes. And today, when her pen had touched the paper, the lines and patterns of this picture had flowed from it like a song.

Buildings had been the first things that she'd copied and while she was in Romania, she hadn't drawn anything else. People had always scared her. She'd also heard adults say that making pictures of other men and women was a shameful thing to do, and she'd agreed with them. There had been something secret and unreliable about a person's constantly changing shapes, and it had made her feel anxious and unsafe. In England, however, those feelings had changed. People had admired her intricate drawings of buildings, especially her pictures of Ceausescu's palace, but they'd expected her to draw other things as well. They'd encouraged her to draw children and then grown-ups and then, anything and everything that caught her eye. She'd drawn portraits and had felt excited by them, rather than ashamed. And, as she'd used more and more colour, she'd begun to believe that her dreams could come true.

But on that first evening, in that English town, she hadn't thought about colours, although she'd been aware of the faces in the crowd darkening, as the storm clouds had gathered overhead. The only thing that she'd thought about had been her desire to get away from the noise and the men and the dog. That was why she'd edged away and gone deeper into the puddle. Then, as she'd stood there with her feet in the water she'd seen something shining beneath the widening ripples. Without thinking about it, she'd scooped it from the water and slipped it into her pocket. At the same moment a howl from the crowd had made her spin around. She'd thought her heart would stop, but when she'd faced the crowd again, she had realised that no one had been interested in her.

They'd all been watching the thickset man, who had moved to the front of her uncle's van. They'd seen the hammer behind his back and they'd yelled. He'd waved it in the air. They'd yelled again and when he'd swung it down and smashed the windscreen in, they'd roared. Emilia's aunt had screamed. The crowd had jeered. Daniel had started forward, but his brother had held him back. The man with the hammer had sauntered to the rear of the van and smashed those windows in as well. Each time the glass had exploded, another roar had escaped from the crowd. The white cat had fled along the wall, finally dropping the fish as it leapt through a small window that someone had hurriedly opened from inside. Emilia's aunt had covered her mouth with her scarf and stared in horror at the ruined van. Her daughters had run to her and taken hold of her hands. Daniel had shielded his head with his arms.

At first, Emilia hadn't realised that the men and women in black uniforms were police. She'd noticed some vehicles with flashing lights, but she hadn't expected her uncle to hurry towards them and to look relieved. In Bucharest, the gypsies had always stayed as far from the police as they could. Now, she remembered how one policeman had appeared to be nodding sympathetically, as he'd listened to what her uncle said. Another had had his arms round the mad woman and was keeping her away from the crowd.

As she'd watched, Emilia had seen a light come on behind the window through which the white cat had jumped. A bare bulb had blazed in the gloom, and then she'd noticed someone standing in the room. A hand had pulled apart some bits of net curtain and an old face had pressed itself against the glass. Emilia'd seen an old woman in a very large hat, holding the cat in her arms like a baby. She'd been rocking it to and fro. Then it must've struggled, or perhaps she'd grown tired, because, as Emilia'd stared, she'd seen the old woman set the animal gently down. Together, they'd peered out, side by side, through the rain-spattered glass. The old woman's mouth had been moving, as if there'd been something to tell, and the cat could have been listening, because she'd seen it stretching up and rubbing its head against the old woman's cheek.

Vividly, ridiculously, Emilia'd imagined the cat asleep in the old woman's bed.

'Why are you *smiling*?' Zoltan had broken free from his mother's grip and had splashed through the puddle towards her, in his green plastic boots. 'Why did you *laugh*?' he'd asked again.

'Did I?' Emilia hadn't realised that she had.

'*Why*?' Zoltan had stamped his boot. He'd looked exhausted and angry and he'd begun to push her about. 'Why did you *laugh*, when they've broken my uncle's van?'

She'd shrugged her shoulders.

But she must have laughed, because the old woman at the window had suddenly waved at her and laughed too.

'*Why-y*?' Zoltan had pushed her again. When she hadn't replied, he had stamped in the water, then rammed his head into the small of her back and begun to drive her towards the van.

The crowd had not diminished, despite the rain. One policeman was still standing with the woman with no skirt, but, as she looked about her, Emilia had noticed that other women were also dressed like that. And they couldn't all be mad. She'd glanced at her mother, whose long skirt swept the ground. Then she'd noticed the expression on her mother's face. She'd realised that it was the same as the expression on the face of the woman with no skirt. It had never been the expression of madness. It had just been everyday fear and hate.

Somewhere, thunder had cracked across the sky and

when the rain had begun to fall on them as thickly as water that's been tipped, the crowd had finally dissolved away. Soon, only the shouting woman and the man with the dog remained, and both were quieter than they'd been before. Emilia had watched the police help her aunt and cousins into their larger van. Elizabeta had been persuaded to get in as well, but as soon as she'd climbed up she must have changed her mind, because she wouldn't sit down. When she'd tried to get out, she'd tripped on the hem of her skirt and would have fallen, if one of the policemen hadn't leapt forward and held her up. Outside in the rain, the other woman had seen this and laughed.

'Go *on*!' Step by step, Zoltan had been forcing Emilia out of the puddle and towards the van. When their father'd called them, Zoltan had left her, and run back by himself.

'Emilia!' her father'd called again. 'Hurry up! Your uncle knows the police. He says we must go with them, but it'll be all right.'

At the sound of his voice, she'd closed her eyes, put her fingers in her mouth and bitten through her skin. She'd wanted something impossible to happen, and she'd wanted it so badly that she'd almost believed it would. She'd wanted them to forget her and drive off. She'd wanted to hear the doors of the police van slam shut, and see it speed out of the car park, even if it had meant that she'd never see them again. And she hadn't been afraid. Not really. In spite of the angry woman, and the dog, and the hateful, crashing glass that still glittered on the ground, she hadn't been afraid. And she'd known exactly what to do: as soon as they'd gone, she'd have run like lightning. She'd have streaked across the car park, and banged on that little window, where the bare bulb still shone. She'd have banged and banged, and wouldn't have needed to explain herself because the old woman who'd waved and smiled would've understood that she was a girl who needed help. And that old woman would have opened her front door and taken her in. Once she was inside, and out of the rain, the white cat would have crept over and rubbed itself against her cold feet, and made them warm again. And then . . .

'Emilia!' Her father had called sharply. When she'd opened her eyes, a young policewoman had already been coming towards her, and she'd realised that she'd left it too late to escape.

She'd looked back, as they were being driven away but she hadn't been able to see the old woman and the cat. The last thing she'd seen had been the concrete wall and that had been where she'd first noticed the bent crosses. Someone had sprayed and daubed and scratched them all over that wall, just as someone had marked them over the white wall outside.

Now she looked down at what she'd drawn. This ninth picture was more or less finished and she was pleased with it. But before she signed her name in the corner she quickly added a sketch of two women whose faces were contorted with fear and hate.

Picture 10

Group Portrait, with Sam

'No!' Elizabeta shouted back. 'He doesn't *have* to go!' She snatched at Zoltan, and would have held him close, if he hadn't wriggled free.

'He *does!*' Daniel pulled off his boots himself, and flung them into the corner of the hall. They'd only just come in, but had started shouting as soon as they'd shut the door. 'I've already *told* you! The manager said he has to *go!* He told me that if *we* want to stay here, the children *have* to go to school!'

Her parents had been quarrelling about school ever since the day before, and Emilia suspected that this was why they hadn't noticed her picture of Zoltan on the wall outside. Their arguments had started when Daniel had taken a letter down to the hostel manager and asked him what it said. The young man had explained that it was an official letter from the local school board. It was requesting more information about Zoltan and Emilia, so that they could both start at suitable schools. Daniel had been upset. He'd made it clear that he didn't want this, but the longhaired young man in the office had not understood. 'Why shouldn't your children go to school?' he'd demanded. 'Other asylum seekers' children go.'

Daniel hadn't replied. He was still too ashamed of what had happened in England, and Emilia knew that he could never have mentioned it to anyone else, because of the disgrace. She could imagine the scene in the office between the two men, because she'd witnessed such scenes before. People would repeatedly try to persuade her father to explain his thoughts to them, but he never did. He'd tap his hat over his brow, then stare straight through the person questioning him, as though they were not there. In the end, the questioner gave up. It had been like that with the hostel manager. Finally, the young man had shrugged irritably and handed the school letter back to Daniel. Then he'd swivelled round in his chair and begun dealing with someone else's problems instead.

'Well,' Elizabeta bent down and picked up the cowboy boots, 'go and *tell* that young fellow what he wants to hear. Tell him that, yes, our son will go to school. But not yet. What's the rush? What does it matter if he goes today, or not? Any way, the boy's been ill. So go and tell that to the young man.' She put her hands on her hips and shook her head. 'What's more, do you think they want our sick child in their school? *Never.* So, tell *that* to the young man with the long hair. It's the best answer – '

'*Best!*' Daniel roared at her. 'How can you know what's *best*?'

'Because – ' she hissed. 'Because I *knew* what was best before. I *knew* it would be like this over here, didn't I? I never wanted to leave Bucharest. Did I? Eh? But did you listen? Eh?'

They were staring at each other with a look of dislike on both their faces that Emilia had never seen before.

'Eh?'

Daniel turned away, but Elizabeta wouldn't let him go.

'You didn't even hear my words.' She tossed back her plaits. 'I knew what was best *then*, just as I know now! Bucharest wasn't perfect, but it was better than this! At least there, nobody tried to take our son away and put him in a school! At least our daughter – '

'Don't!' Daniel jabbed his finger in her face.

'Don't what?' She didn't step back.

'Don't *ever*,' his noise filled the room, 'ever mention that girl again!'

Emilia saw his spit on her mother's cheek, but his fury was cut short by the sound of knocking. In the momentary silence, as their parents glared at each other, Zoltan kicked the yellow wall.

'I'm *not* ill,' he shouted, 'so why can't I go to school?'

Someone knocked again. This time, they all realised that it wasn't someone objecting to the noise. There was actually somebody outside, knocking on their door.

'If it's *him*, if it's that idiot with woman's hair,' Daniel muttered, 'still going on about the school – '

'Ssh.' Elizabeta put her finger to her lips. 'Pretend we're not in.'

Nobody moved. Emilia watched the anger drain from her parents' faces. Now, they only looked scared.

'Hello?' The voice outside was soft. 'Hello? You are in?'

Emilia recognised Zeynep at once. It was what she'd feared: this girl, finally at their door, wanting to be friendly, and wanting to talk. Daniel was looking at Elizabeta. When she nodded, he unlocked the door.

'Hello,' the girl's voice slid in.

'What?' Daniel put his eye to the gap. 'What you want here?' He was shouting although the girl was so near. Emilia bit into her skin.

'I am wanting, please,' Zeynep's voice was softer still, 'the book – '

'Book?' Daniel repeated and glanced at Elizabeta. She frowned and shook her head.

'What *book*?' He snarled through the crack, before flinging the door open, and shouting the question as loudly as he could. 'What book?'

'Please – ' Zeynep stepped back.

'Go away! No book here!'

Emilia shut her eyes. The door slammed and then she heard the sound of Zeynep hurrying away.

'What did she want?' Elizabeta asked. 'Was it about the school?'

'Yes,' Daniel lit a cigarette. 'But I told her didn't I? I said "no school!"'

Elizabeta nodded and went into the kitchen to prepare their food. Daniel sat down on the sofa and flicked through the TV programmes until he found a match.

'Come!' He beckoned to Zoltan. 'Come here, my son.' He was patting the space beside him. 'You like football, so come and watch it with me.'

Zoltan sat stiffly at the other end of the sofa. His father pulled him close. They watched the screen in silence as the players chased the ball over the bright green pitch. When the pan of meat was boiling on the stove, Elizabeta came back into the room.

'That girl,' she had to raise her voice over the sounds of the match, 'what did she *say* about the school?'

'Nothing!' Daniel stared irritably at the match. 'Nothing at all.' On the screen, a football hit the crossbar but missed the goal. The crowd roared.

'But she must have wanted something.' Elizabeta persisted. 'Or *said* something. Or . . . has she been here before?'

Zoltan blinked rapidly and coughed.

'I told you! It was nothing!' Daniel zapped up the sound. 'Just some girl at the wrong door!'

Zoltan choked but Elizabeta didn't return to the kitchen. She stayed where she was and stared. When Emilia looked up, her mother's eyes were fixed on her.

Later that evening, when Elizabeta had gone to bed and Daniel was sleeping in front of the flickering screen, Zoltan sidled up to the window where Emilia was sitting by herself. Without saying a word, they parted the curtains and rested their heads side by side on the cold glass. When the curtains had dropped back, they were hidden from the room. For the last couple of evenings Emilia had been drawing the curtains across early, to prevent her parents noticing the picture outside. Now, as she and Zoltan stared into the night, she could see that her drawings were still there on the white wall.

'It wasn't true, was it, that she asked about school?' Zoltan whispered with his lips against her cheek.

Emilia shook her head.

'And I'm *not* ill, am I? Not any more. So, I can go to school, can't I?' His breath had misted up the glass.

She put an arm round him and he sniffed. Somewhere, someone was playing music and further down the street, someone in another house turned on their light so that it fell through their windows in golden blocks onto the wet black road.

'Emi, why did that girl ask about a book?'

In the room, on the other side of the curtains, Daniel snored.

'D'you think she meant your *secret* book, where you're drawing those pictures about our life?'

'No!' Emilia shook her head so vigorously that her skin squeaked on the glass. It was the question she'd dreaded, the one she hadn't wanted to even think about . . .

'That's good,' Zoltan pressed closer, 'because you won't have to give the book back, will you, Emi, not if it isn't hers . . . And you can make more pictures, can't you, Emi? Please?' He was drawing something with his finger on the misted-over glass.

'Do you think,' he continued, 'you could *draw* a picture of the school for me? If I promise not to tell . . .' He pushed his cold nose into her cheek. 'You could draw me the best school in the world, where they play football all day.' He laughed. 'And I won't tell them, Emi. I won't tell them *anything*, ever again. Not *now*.'

That night, when she was sure that everyone was asleep, Emilia went into the bathroom and locked the door. She took the book from under her jumper and held it up to the bright light. She needed to compare the words in the book with the words that Zeynep had written on the scrap of paper she'd pushed under their door. If this was Zeynep's book, as she now secretly feared, she was likely to find the name Zeynep Kara written somewhere inside.

When she'd started going to the school in England, she'd been amazed that everybody wrote their names on things they said were theirs. Pupils marked their books and their bags. They even sewed nametapes into the backs of their clothes. Some had written their names inside their shoes. Later, Emilia had learnt that the teachers expected everybody to do that, and were cross if they found things unmarked. Yasmina had written her name in her diary. As soon as they'd become friends, she'd shown Emilia two words in coloured letters in the middle of the first page. It was her name: Yasmina Habib. Underneath it were more words, which made up Yasmina's address.

Now, Emilia checked the first page of the diary again. She knew she was no good with letters and words. Nevertheless, nothing resembled the Z of Zeynep, although one or two words seemed to have Kara's K. She was disappointed at first. Then, guiltily, she was pleased. If she'd found Zeynep's name, she would have had to give the book back. So long as she didn't find that name, it was safe.

She looked through the pages once again and convinced herself that Zeynep could not have been asking for the book. It must have belonged to someone else, quite unknown, who had hidden their book under the table and then gone away. In places like this, where strangers came and went, lots of things must get left behind and since the book couldn't be returned to its rightful owner, she could truthfully say it was hers.

She rested it on the edge of the bath and began to write in her name: Emilia Radu, just as they'd shown her in the English school.

'E-mi-li-a Ra-du . . .'

As she checked the letters again, she remembered the comic sound of the English teacher attempting to say her name on her first day in school.

'Emi – ' The teacher'd tried again.

'Emi-Emi-Emi.' Each time she'd repeated it, an echo had rippled round the classroom. That first time, Emilia had still been standing at the front of the class. She had glanced down at her new diamond-patterned socks, then up into the far corner of the room. She'd been concentrating on a corner where the wall met the ceiling, and where something wasn't straight. She'd blinked, and stared at the spot, as she'd waited for the laughter to begin.

It had been a wet and windy morning on her first day in school. She'd worn new red shoes, and diamond-patterned socks, and, as she'd stood there, in front of the class, waiting for the laughter to begin, she'd been glad that at least her clothes weren't muddy or old.

But this time, no one had laughed at her. All they'd done was give her a new name: Emi.

The evening before, her uncle and aunt had visited and explained about the school. Her cousins had been attending their school for about two years, so they knew exactly what to do. Emilia'd listened politely to their advice. She hadn't mentioned that, unlike their girls, she'd actually been to school before. While Emilia's family had been staying with their cousins, in the flat on the tenth floor, Emilia had watched her cousins putting on their school clothes. At first, she'd thought it an odd thing to do, but when her aunt had told her that she'd have to wear similar clothes, she hadn't minded. It was her parents who'd refused. They'd been anxious about letting her go at all. When uniforms were mentioned they'd argued that school clothes were a waste of money, especially for a girl who was nearly grown-up and would be married before long. Her cousins had giggled and her aunt had sniffed, and reminded them that they were in England now, not Bucharest.

Later that evening, when her uncle discovered that they hadn't made any preparations for Emilia, he'd been angry. He'd been working hard to help them feel at home and he'd said that their attitude to school gave Romanian gypsies a bad name. Daniel had been offended. He'd left the flat and gone straight to one of the huge shops that never shut and bought Emilia new shoes and socks. When he'd taken them from the bag, her aunt had burst into tears and demanded why he hadn't bought black? She'd said that English children never wore red shoes in school.

Daniel had sworn under his breath. Emilia had remained silent and bitten down her nails, but she'd longed to shout: 'I *like* red!'

Despite her aunt's advice, she'd been wearing the new things when they'd stood on the step outside the school and waited for someone to let them in. Her uncle had pressed the bell again. She'd heard lots of noise from inside the building, but no one had come to the door. She'd flexed her toes. Her feet had remained warm, although the wait had been so long and cold that her uncle'd stamped his feet and rubbed his hands.

'There's no need for this,' her father spat. 'She doesn't *have* to go to school.'

Her uncle had sighed.

'They won't want her, anyway,' her father'd muttered. 'She's a good girl, in some ways, but she can't learn. She's got less brain than a child.'

Her uncle'd pressed the bell and kept his finger on the button until they heard it ringing inside. Her father had stepped back. She'd fiddled with her plaits. If the door didn't open soon, she'd lose her chance, because her father would take her away.

'Helloplease.' Silently, she repeated the lucky words in her head and willed someone to come and help. And they had.

'Hello there.' A tall, thin woman in a man's striped suit had opened the door, then struggled to hold it in the wind. 'Hello there. Come in.'

At the time, Emilia hadn't understood, but now, as she recalled that scene, she was sure that those were the words that Miss Chester had used.

'Come in! Come in!' The woman's voice had been so sharp it had sliced through the wind. 'Come on! Come in!' She'd waved her hands at them, and the wind had blown her rough red hair back from her face like flames.

Her uncle had stepped inside the school. Her father, who'd been staring up at the woman, hadn't moved.

'Come on! Come in!' The woman's mouth had opened in a crimson grin that showed her teeth and tongue.

Emilia'd smiled back. Her father'd scowled at her but she hadn't cared. She'd been waiting for this moment ever since she'd been a little girl. He'd touched her sleeve. Groups of pupils, with books and school things in their arms, had crowded behind the tall woman to watch them. Emilia'd felt Daniel's fingers closing round her wrist.

'Come on! Come in!' the woman had tried again.

Now, Emilia remembered how excitement had begun to burn through her, as she'd stood there on the step. Her father's ring had dug into her skin as he'd held her back, but somehow, she'd twisted free. She'd taken two squeaking steps in her new red shoes, and she'd been inside the school. Her father had stepped back. Her uncle had called him in. He'd sworn. The red-haired teacher'd moved to one side. She'd watched as the two men shouted at each other, and she'd tapped her teeth with a pen. When yet more students gathered around, she'd wagged a finger at them and grinned her toothy grin, and they'd moved off. Emilia had seen her father tap down his hat. She'd known that he'd expected her to turn back, but she hadn't. She'd also known that he was angry, but she'd been brave then, so she'd bitten off a crescent of fingernail and she'd stayed where she was.

'Come along,' the teacher'd touched her arm. Emilia'd taken a few more steps deeper into the school and as she'd glanced over her shoulder, she'd seen her uncle's bald head amongst streams of students thronging past. Behind them, her father had begun to walk away in his cowboy boots, moving as quickly as he could.

Emilia hadn't gone straight into a classroom but had spent some time in an office. Her uncle had talked to the teacher, but he hadn't explained to Emilia what was said. Suddenly, he'd patted her shoulder, shaken hands with the red-haired woman, and left her quite alone.

Then she'd been taken to a class. Once again, a classroom door had opened, and once again every person in the room had stopped what they were doing and looked up as she'd stepped inside. Their eyes had consumed everything about her, from her squeaking red shoes to her long fair plaits. She'd felt uncomfortable. She'd wished that she'd worn her long red skirt, because the skirt her cousins had lent her was too short: it showed her knees above her socks. A big boy in the middle row had leaned out and looked at her legs in a horrible way. She'd remained where she was, stranded at the front, with every one looking on. To avoid their eyes, she'd glanced quickly round the room, and when a crack or something in one of the corners of the room had caught her attention, she'd stared at that, while she'd waited for the laughter to begin. But it never had.

Gradually the students had stopped staring. Some had begun to chat. Others had got up and moved about. At the back of the class, an apple or maybe a ball was thrown, and caught. Only one person, a boy, sitting alone by the window, had remained indifferent to her. He was hunched over, concentrating on his book. Yet even he had glanced up once and smiled a shadow of a smile when their eyes had met. Then he'd resumed whatever he'd been working on before.

Now, she smoothed out the paper on a fresh page and began to sketch that boy: his thick, straight hair falling forward, almost covering his face, his thin wrists extending from frayed cuffs, his roughened, grimy skin, his bony shoulders sticking through his shirt.

After a few minutes the class teacher had asked a black-eyed girl to lead Emilia to the empty place beside this same boy who'd been working so hard. And that was how she'd met Sam. Yasmina had pushed her gently into the seat, and the first thing she'd noticed had been the pen in Sam's hand. It had made the finest, blackest mark she'd ever seen. The class teacher, who'd been young, had stood in front of the class and started speaking to them. Emilia had tried to understand what she'd said, but it had been as impossible as trying to grasp the wind with one's hand. She'd glanced sideways again and been astonished that Sam was drawing pictures in the white spaces on the pages of his book. The teacher had talked and talked. All around Emilia, the students whispered to each other and shifted things on the tables, and turned the pages of their books. Beside her, Sam's hand hadn't stopped. Suddenly, he'd pushed the book towards her, as if he'd wanted her to look, and she'd seen kings and queens in crowns and cloaks and fine houses on a hill. She'd also noticed that the skin on his fingers was almost bitten to the bone. When she'd looked a moment or two later, he'd turned over a page and had drawn a tiny figure of a black man, bending over a woman. Her hair streamed out. Her hands tore at his. His fingers squeezed her throat.

She'd been shocked. She'd never met someone like herself, who drew. And she'd never thought it possible to make pictures out of people like that. She'd swallowed and looked away. Sam had also glanced sideways. He'd already started a new drawing, but in that glance he'd smiled another shadow of a smile, so brief she hadn't been sure if she'd seen it at all.

In front of them the teacher had been writing something on the board. Some of the students had been calling out. Beside her, Sam had been drawing animals: a horse, a dog, a goat. Around them the other students were all talking at once. She sensed that the big boy who'd looked at her legs was looking at her again. Under the shield of the table, she'd pulled up her socks as far as they'd go, and pulled down the edge of her skirt. Sam was working on a monstrous fish, with scales and popping eyes and an open, gulping mouth so huge that it could have swallowed the little boat that sailed beside it on the page. In another part of the classroom some girls had laughed aloud. The teacher'd waved her arms, and was attempting to speak over the noise. Emilia'd sensed that the whole room was erupting. Only Sam had not been involved. As the noise strengthened he'd rummaged in a tin and brought out a sort of coloured pen she'd never seen before.

'Emilia!'

She'd jumped. Somewhere in the classroom she'd thought she'd heard her name.

'Emi – ' Then she'd heard it again. She'd tried to do nothing, and pretend she hadn't heard it. But once again every face in the room had turned towards her, like a shadow moving down a sunny street. Each pair of eyes had sought hers. For a second she'd felt like a little girl again, and almost wet her pants. Then that sound had rippled round the room.

'Emi-Emi-Emi.' But no one laughed, and the teacher hadn't banged a stick. Beside her, Sam had continued colouring in the monster fish.

Then the teacher had written something else up on the board. The class quietened down. A girl began speaking by herself and the other students appeared to be listening to her. Maybe a proper lesson had begun at last. But just as Emilia had begun to try to listen too, she'd noticed that the teacher was approaching the big boy in the middle row. She'd suddenly leant over him and changed the position of his book and everybody had laughed aloud. The boy had flushed bright red and though Emilia hadn't understood what the joke was about, she'd joined in the laughter too. And all the time she'd kept on imagining that she'd heard her own name. It had rustled amongst all the other sounds, like scraps of paper blowing in a wind.

Then a bell had rung. The students had leapt up and started grabbing bags and books, although the teacher had seemed to want them to sit down. Most continued moving to the door. Some very noisy girls were pushing to get out. Even Sam had put his pencils back in the tin and stood up. When he'd stretched his arms above his head, she'd noticed how slightly built he was and thin. She'd seen Yasmina, the black-eyed girl, struggling towards her against the tide of people going out.

'Come? Emilia? Emi come?' Yasmina had had an armful of bangles that jangled and a ring with a jewel set in her nose. '*Emi*, you come with me?' She'd repeated.

So she'd been right: she *had* detected her name, but in an English way which she'd never heard before.

Yasmina had taken hold of her arm and led her down stairs into a fenced-in place, where hundreds of other students were talking and shouting to each other and eating and running about. She'd found herself clinging to Yasmina's sleeve like a child. They'd joined a group of girls.

'Here.' One of them had held out a shiny packet. When she hadn't responded, the girl had shaken it in her face. Then another girl had dipped in her hand and taken out an orange shape like a leaf. She'd popped it in her mouth, crunched it up, and laughed. When Emilia'd done the same, the girls had clustered close, nodding to each other and clapping their hands.

Now, as she examined her picture of Sam, she remembered the odd, smoky taste of the orange 'crisps' on her tongue.

178

'Crisps, crisps,' the girls had repeated as they'd licked the salt from their lipsticked lips. They'd laughed and made her repeat the word herself. 'Crisps, crisps' she'd finally said, and then they'd all laughed again.

She'd been slightly scared of those girls at first, but in the end she'd loved them as much as she'd loved Sam. Carefully, she also drew their portraits in: Yasmina, Sonia, Kelly Jackson and Naomi, and that girl whose name she'd never known and whom everyone always called PJ. She'd got used to the smells of their scent and their smoky breath and the feel of their warm, soft hands.

She missed them now. She wanted to be with them as they painted their nails and sprayed stuff on their hair and sang. She remembered their shoes that had been as heavy as hooves on the ends of their black trousered legs. Hardly any of them had ever worn skirts, but when she'd worn her velvet one, they'd oohed and aahed and stroked it as gently as if it had been her skin. And they'd been her friends.

As she worked on in the sleeping building, she recalled them in more detail and when the group portrait was finished and she'd hidden the book away, she felt as if she'd almost been in their company once again.

Picture 11

A Circle of Friends

'Emi-ii.' Zoltan dug his thumb into her back.

'What?' It was light outside, but Emilia still wanted to sleep. She opened one eye.

'Emi.' He was bending over her. 'You remember last week, when you were ill?' His breath in her face was as hot and scratchy as wool. 'You know what you promised . . . hey! Wake up!' He pinched her cheek.

'Don't!' She drew the bedclothes up to keep him off.

'Why not?' he whined. 'Why shouldn't I?' He pinched her again.

'Stop it!' She used her elbow to keep him off. 'That *hurt*.'

'It didn't. It wasn't hard enough. It was only a joke.' He frowned, but got off the sofa. 'Anyway, I'm bored, so it's not fair if you sleep.'

'Why not? I'm tired – '

'You're not!' He kicked the side of the sofa. 'But even if you are, it's your fault.'

She rubbed the sleep from her eyes and frowned up at him.

'It's your fault,' he continued, 'because *I* know what you were doing last night.'

'How?'

'I've already looked at the book while you were asleep. You were drawing another picture, weren't you? That's why you're tired.'

'Rubbish. I'm tired because I was ill.'

'You weren't as ill as *me*. You're tired because you didn't sleep.'

'So?' She yawned in his face.

He kicked the sofa. Then he ran at it and jumped like a kick boxer, striking it with both feet. When he fell on the floor with a crash, someone below them banged and shouted 'Shut up.' Emilia stepped over Zoltan and went into the bathroom to splash water on her face. He swung on the door handle and watched. When she'd smoothed down her hair, she noticed a new red bruise on his chin.

'Anyway.' She turned on him suddenly. 'Why are you so horrible this morning?'

'Because . . .' He stared. She never asked him questions like that.

'Because?' she demanded.

'Because *nothing*! Just *because*!' He was screaming and his whole face was bright red. '*Because! Because!* Just because everything *here* is so . . . *horrible!* Can't you understand that?'

Their eyes met in the mirror.

'Do you know something?' she asked.

'What?' He swung the door to and fro so that it banged.

'You . . .' she paused.

'*What?*' This time his scream was so loud she thought his throat might crack.

'You should go to school!' She hadn't planned to say it. It had just slipped out.

'But I can't, can I?' he wailed. 'Didn't you hear what they *said*? They *said* they're going to tell people I'm ill. And that's what they'll always do, so I'll never go to school.'

'You will.'

'I won't!'

'Shut up!' she yelled at him and put her foot in the door, but he still swung it as hard as he could. She gasped.

'It was only a joke, Emi,' he looked away from the cut, 'I didn't mean to hurt you. Honestly, Emi. I – '

She ignored him. In the kitchen she filled the electric kettle with water and switched it on. Suddenly, she remembered the little kitchen in their flat in England. She'd loved it so much. It had only taken her a couple of days to learn how to use everything: the kettle, the toaster, even the washing machine. Once, when her mother had been at her aunt's, Yasmina had showed her how to bake cakes. They'd cooked them in the oven, then eaten them while they were hot.

Now, as steam rose from the kettle, she took a carton of milk from the fridge.

'You're not allowed to touch our food. Mum said.' Zoltan had followed her.

'So?' She turned on him. 'Are you going to tell?'

His mouth opened but he shook his head. She made two mugs of tea, using tea bags, and stirring in milk and sugar, just like English people did.

'Has Mum bought any biscuits?' She began to look through the cupboard.

He shrugged and took his mug into the other room. After a little while, he came back.

'Emi?' he said. 'I don't *mind* if you want a little sleep. It's just . . .' he took a gulp of his tea. 'It's just so . . . and it makes me so cross!'

'I know.' She handed him a biscuit. 'It's just so *yellow* isn't it?'

He nodded with his mouth full of biscuit and together they went to the window and looked out.

'Does it . . . ?' he pointed to her foot which the door had cut.

'Not much,' she shrugged.

'You're lucky,' he smiled up at her, 'because my chin hurts a lot.'

'Good!'

Their eyes met. He opened his mouth to protest, but changed his mind. Instead he drank his tea.

'Do you think I'll *ever* go to school?' He dipped another biscuit into the tea and sucked.

'Yes. Yes I do.'

'So, you think they'll change their minds, and let me go?'

'No.' She was reaching for words that felt too far away.

'Then, *how*?' His brown eyes glittered like those of a young animal, looking out.

'You'll have to go by yourself.' She was remembering herself at his age.

'But, you could take me, Emi, please? I've seen a school. It's over there by the park. We could go there together, if we ran really fast, and they'd never know. Because we've done it once, haven't we? We went out, didn't we, and they never knew!'

'We could try.' But as soon as she'd said the words, she regretted them.

'When?' he pulled her arm.

'Not today, Zoltan. Not yet.' As she spoke she was aware of the fear seeping back and suffocating the words in her throat.

'See?' he shouted. 'You're just as bad as *them*. That's what *they* always say: "not yet, not yet, not yet".' He flung himself on the sofa and kicked.

When she reached under it to get the book, he buried his face in a cushion so that she couldn't see him and he twisted his body as far away from her as he could.

As she took her pencils from her pocket she remembered another afternoon in England. Her school had closed early for some reason and Yasmina had suggested that they go together to the primary school to pick Zoltan up. Yasmina was the youngest child in her large family, and she'd loved playing with children who were younger than herself. She'd always made a fuss of Zoltan, holding his hand and running her fingers through his curls. He'd hated this at first, but in the end, they'd become friends.

When they'd arrived at the primary school on that afternoon, Emilia had intended to walk straight in, but Yasmina had stopped her and said they must wait. It had been cold in the playground but they'd walked up and down. As more parents arrived, Yasmina had seen someone she knew so she'd gone over to chat. Emilia'd noticed that the lights were on in one of the classrooms, so she'd crept up to a window to look. Outside, the wind had been cold, but inside, most of the children had been wearing T-shirts, and they'd all looked warm.

Now, as she planned out her next picture, she outlined the tables that she'd seen pushed to one side. Then, she copied the Christmas decorations and the pupils' paintings which had covered the walls. In the centre of the classroom, she drew the ring of small chairs. She couldn't remember the individual children's faces quite as well as she remembered details of the room, but she did recall that Zoltan's teacher and another adult had been sitting amongst the children on the same little chairs.

Emilia'd recognised Zoltan instantly. His head of black curls had been unlike any other in the room. Zoltan's teacher had been a plump young man in glasses, whose name she'd forgotten. As she took a finer pen to put the glasses on this teacher's nose, she heard Zoltan get off the sofa behind her.

'That's Mr Matthews!' he gasped as he leant over her shoulder and looked.

'Peter, Oya, Jez'n'Sue, Janice Jones and Hamid Madi, Vinnie, Paul and . . .' he was naming the children on the chairs, 'and Paul and Jack! Jack's the one who always sat by me, and look! That's *me*, isn't it? And Ben, and that girl with long hair who cried. And that tall boy, Troy Jackson. We hated him because he always wanted to fight. And Suan Po Lim, who was new like me. She was frightened of Troy because he called her Chink. And,' he was pointing to the other adult in the ring. 'Look, that's Auntie Peg.'

'Who's Auntie Peg?' Now Emilia recalled the old lady. She'd been made up with powder and eyeshadow, as though she'd been young. Her face and neck had been wrinkled like trodden mud, but her thin, cracked lips had been shocking pink. Her purple hair had sat on her skull like a cap. She'd glittered with gold which dangled from her ears and wrists and throat. Her clawed hands had been covered with rings. That afternoon, she'd been dressed in black trousers and a pink shirt. Zoltan had often talked about an Auntie Peg who helped him with his reading, but Emilia had never imagined that a teacher could look like that.

'Auntie Peg liked me a lot.' Zoltan touched her portrait on the page. 'She said I was learning reading extra fast.' He was studying the picture. 'You've done a picture of circle time!'

'Have I? What's that?'

'Circle time was in the afternoons. It was when everybody had to be quiet and listen to what other people said. *Anybody* could talk in circle time. Everybody else, even teachers, had to be very quiet and listen to what the talker said. It was really nice, Emi. I liked circle time a lot.'

Now Emilia remembered how she'd seen the tall boy, Troy Jackson, reach over and tug at the loops of Auntie Peg's necklace. She hadn't been angry. Instead, she'd taken off the necklace and handed it to the boy. He'd wriggled in embarrassment and tried to give it back. She must have persuaded him to try it on, because a moment later, Emilia had seen him fasten it round his own neck and then walk round the circle like a little king.

'How do you know about Troy doing that?' Zoltan asked.

'I saw it,' she said. She remembered how Yasmina had joined her and how together they'd watched the boy hand the necklace to the next child, who'd also tried it on. In this way the necklace had travelled round the whole ring of children. Emilia had been surprised that things like that happened in school, but Yasmina hadn't. She'd said that she had done the same thing when she'd been in that class.

'That Troy Jackson was horrible to me,' Zoltan whispered into Emilia's hair.

'I didn't know.' Emilia paused. 'I thought he'd looked quite nice.'

'That's because it was *circle time*, when you weren't allowed to be horrible. In the playground and toilets Troy Jackson was a *pig*.'

'What did he do?'

'He kicked you and pinched and called you names. He said I smelt, and whenever he was near Suan Po, he pulled his eyes up, like this, and stuck out his tongue. He called her Slitty Eyes as well as Chink. He made her cry a lot. I think Troy Jackson was bad.'

'Didn't Mr Matthews stop him?'

'No. He didn't dare because once, when Troy hit someone and Mr Matthews punished him, Troy's mum came into our classroom and tried to hit Mr Matthews back.'

'Did Troy make you cry?'

'Me? Never! I *never* cried, or not very much. When he spat in my lunch, I spat back.'

'You didn't . .'

'I *did*! And I peed in his sports bag.'

'Zoltan! Why didn't you tell me about this?'

'Because . . . because if anyone *knew*, and told Mum and Dad, they wouldn't have let me go to school! And I *liked* school, Emi, even though Troy was bad.' He pointed to the picture she'd drawn. 'That's why I liked circle time so much. You could put your hand up, like this, and say whatever you wanted, and nobody was allowed to interrupt or laugh. Even Mr Matthews had to listen, and Troy Jackson had to be quiet.'

187

'Did *you* say anything?'

'No, but I was *going to*. I was going to talk about football, but we had to leave, didn't we? So I never said my thing.'

She coloured in the classroom Christmas tree and remembered how the three of them had walked home when Zoltan's class had finished. Yasmina had been talking about 'Father Christmas' and 'stockings' but she hadn't really understood. Instead, she'd listened to Yasmina's voice and noticed that the light blue winter sky was already deepening and darkening. Shadows had been settling into corners and gutters and soon it would have been night. Streetlamps had been humming overhead and the shop windows had been full of Christmas things and tiny flashing lights.

Yasmina lived further along the street where Emilia's flat was. Her parents both worked in the restaurant below, and her large family lived in the rooms above. That evening they'd marched along the pavement three abreast, with Zoltan in the middle, holding their hands. On each third step, she and Yasmina had taken an extra big stride and swung him up in the air.

'One, two three upsadaisy,' they'd chanted as they strode along. Other folk on the pavement had smiled and stepped aside, even when they'd been struggling with pushchairs and babies and bulging supermarket bags. Emilia remembered noticing their reflection in the window of the fish and chip shop. She'd realised, then, that she'd never walked down a street in Bucharest behaving like that. She would have been ashamed of herself. But in England, she'd felt free.

Now, as Zoltan watched her signing the picture, she knew

he was remembering that afternoon too. He was chanting what they'd said as they'd swung him along: 'one, two three upsadaisy, one, two three upsadaisy.'

'When *I* go to school,' he straightened up, 'we can do that upsadaisy thing again.'

She nodded. Did he remember what had happened next?

They'd been approaching the Red Lion, which was a place where men and women went to drink. She and Yasmina had just landed Zoltan, at the end of a swing, when the pub doors had burst open and two people had stumbled out. One of them had stayed on the step. The other, a small, thin man in split shoes and a flapping shirt, had staggered down the steps and skidded across the pavement in front of them. He'd almost collided with the bus stop, but somehow, had managed to stop. He'd backed, with his elbows sticking out like wings, and he would have pitched over a low wall outside the pub if Sam hadn't rushed down the steps and held him up.

'Oh dear,' Yasmina'd groaned. 'Poor old Sam.'

The queue waiting for a bus had grumbled and shaken their heads.

'Who the man is?' Emilia'd asked.

'His dad, of course,' Yasmina replied.

They'd watched Sam's father regain his balance, then struggle to fit an opened bottle of beer into his shirt pocket. Sam had waited until the bottle was in place, then he'd grabbed his father's arm and started to walk him along.

'Come on!' Zoltan had shaken their hands, impatient to be swung again, so they'd obliged.

Their next stride had taken them up to Sam. Zoltan had laughed gruffly and Sam had looked round. He'd smiled his shadow of a smile, then waved them on. Yasmina had said something, and laughed, and when Sam's father had joined in, Emilia'd suspected that there must have been a joke, so she'd laughed as well. Sam had looked at her with his beautiful blue eyes, and almost smiled again.

When they'd reached the door to the Radus' flat, Zoltan had run up the steps, but Emilia had stayed by the entrance and watched Yasmina and Sam and his father go on down the street. Yasmina had turned into the restaurant, and then Sam had raised his free hand and waved, without looking back. Emilia, unseen in her doorway, had raised her hand and waved to him in return.

'How could you do that?' Her mother had started screaming as soon as she'd opened the upstairs door. 'After all we've said to you about being careful, what do I see when I look out of the window to check that my son is coming home safe?'

'It wasn't anything, Mum,' Emilia had tried to stay calm. 'It was just a friend from school. I think his father drank too much beer.'

'Don't you lie to me, young lady. Do you think I'm blind? Or a fool?'

'No . . .'

'So how can you lie? How can you talk about someone's father when I saw you with that girl!'

'Oh. That was *Yasmina*, another friend from school. It wasn't her father . . .'

'I don't care about her name or her father, but I saw she was *black*! Haven't we warned you to stay away from people like that? And you let her hold Zoltan's hand! How could you? After I've trusted you to keep him safe?'

'I do!'

'You're a *gypsy*, Emilia . . .' Her mother had shaken her head.

'No . . .'

' "No"? What do you mean by "no"?'

'Nothing, honestly. I only meant . . .'

'Well?' Her mother had narrowed her eyes and put her hands on her hips.

'I meant . . . I mean . . . I want . . .' Emilia'd been so upset that the words had stuck like stones in her throat.

'You "mean"! You "want!" ' Her mother had mocked. 'As if I didn't know what you really want! You've been like this, "wanting" things, ever since you were a baby! Nothing I did was ever enough. You, with your shifty eyes and your watery hair. You were difficult from the day you were born! People lifted aside your shawl to take a look at you and then they went quiet. And do you know why? Well, I'll tell you: they went quiet, because inside their hearts, they were asking themselves how I had given birth to a foreign child like you! And don't you smile at me, like that. You've always been tricky. You've never behaved like a real daughter. Always wanting things, you were, and never content to work with us; always wanting what you couldn't have! Always watching me with your eyes like ice, and messing in the mud on purpose, just to show me up.'

'I didn't mean to, I'm sorry . . .'

'You're not sorry at all! Look at you now: wanting to go to school, when there's no need! Wanting to stay a child drawing pictures, but refusing to marry and have a child of your own. Always wanting to be different from us! Always pretending you're not like us.'

Now Emilia shivered as she remembered that scene.

'What's the matter, Emi?' Zoltan was climbing on her lap. 'You've gone white. Honestly. Have you seen a ghost?'

She buried her lips in his curls, and smelt the street on his skin.

'No: it wasn't a ghost. It's just that you want to remember England, but sometimes, I want to forget.'

'Why? Has your picture made you sad? Don't you think it's good? It doesn't matter, honestly, Emi. I think it's good and it doesn't make me sad. And now the book's yours, we can keep all your pictures safe, can't we? Then I can look at the pictures, can't I, whenever I want? Because I mustn't forget what school's like. Then, when I go back, like you said, I'll know what to do.' He stroked her cheek. 'Emi? You know what you said, about going to school?'

'Yes.'

'Well, I want to go. But I don't want to make Mum and Dad mad.' He slid from her knee and kicked the table leg. 'It's not fair!' Why do we always have to choose between making them angry and doing what we want?'

They were silent. Outside on the window ledge, the pigeons moved and cooed.

'Anyway, that girl goes.' Zoltan's voice was low.

'What girl?'

'That girl in the red jacket. The one who came here, and wanted your book. She goes to school every day. I've seen her. So, do you think her family gets mad?'

'I don't know.'

'Emi?' He was looking at the picture of circle time again. 'Even if they didn't let you go to school, do you think they might let me? Then, do you think that girl would look after

192

me, like Yasmina did?' He was suddenly cheerful again. 'When I get home, after my school, I can tell you all about it and you can draw the pictures in our book. You'd like that, wouldn't you?' He was hopping about. 'I mean, I know you'd like to go, but honestly Emi, it's more important for me, isn't it, because I'm a boy? Anyway, that's what father said.'

Picture 12

Portrait of the Artist at Work

'Zoltan! Hurry up! Your father's waiting by the lift,' Elizabeta called irritably from the corridor the next morning.

'Have I *got* to come?' Zoltan was in the flat, kicking his anorak around the hall.

'Yes! I told you before. Now hurry up.'

'*Why* can't I stay? I stayed *yesterday*, and Emi and I – ' his hand flew to his mouth.

'What?' Elizabeta stepped back inside. 'What did you and Emilia do?'

'Nothing.' Zoltan picked up his anorak and put it on quickly.

'Nothing?' their mother repeated, looking at them both. 'Well, in that case, you can do "nothing" with us.'

Emilia held her breath: Zoltan had almost told their mother about the pictures in the book. Now, he stamped past her and she heard them all hurrying to the lift.

This morning the weather looked fine for the first time that year. She knew that her parents were joining another gypsy family and together they were catching a bus out of the town. The women and children would beg and the men were going to look at second-hand cars. Previously, Zoltan had enjoyed trips like that, but this morning, when the plan was being discussed, he'd said that he didn't want to go. Daniel had lost his temper and sworn at his son, which was something he never did.

Now, as Emilia looked out of the window, she saw her father waiting on the bottom step. She guessed that he was still upset because his hand shook as he struck another match. When Elizabeta and Zoltan appeared, he flung the match aside and bent down to zip up Zoltan's anorak. Zoltan twitched his shoulders and pulled back, but Daniel held on. When he'd finished he checked the street once more.

Earlier in the morning, when her parents had been discussing this trip, they'd also mentioned the broken hostel windows for the first time. Both had been distressed. The hostel manager had warned everybody to take extra care today. Apparently, there were people in this town who hated foreigners and wanted to drive them out. These people were suspected of smashing the windows and today they were holding a demonstration against asylum seekers and foreigners in the town. This was why Daniel Radu and the other gypsies had decided to stay away. They wouldn't be back until late, by which time everything should have quietened down.

Her mother had also mentioned returning to Bucharest.

'They say,' her mother's voice had hissed like hot fat, 'they say that if you buy a car *here*, and sell it in Bucharest, you'll get enough money for half a small flat. And, if – '

'No!' Her father had pushed back his hat. 'No! No! No!

Those women don't know what they're talking about. And we're *not* going back to Bucharest. Never, I'm telling you that. Or not yet. And that money won't even buy a quarter of a flat! But I've heard that Italy is the place to be, and Italy is not so far from Romania.'

Just before he'd left, her father had jerked his head towards Emilia and muttered something about whether she'd be safe, spending so long alone. When her mother'd told him not to worry, he'd left the room.

Now, as Emilia watched them walking towards the tree, she noticed that unusually, Daniel and Elizabeta were walking side by side, while Zoltan trailed behind. He was running his fingers along the tops of parked cars and kicking at their wheels. His parents had to wait under the tree until he'd caught them up.

When all three were out of sight, Emilia reached for the book. If her parents were intending to move on to Italy, or somewhere else, there was no time to lose. She wouldn't be able to draw while they were travelling, and she wanted to get as much of the diary completed as she could.

She stared at the tree and at the main road beyond it. If they moved on, she might never see this view again. At that moment a bus was moving past amongst a stream of other vehicles. The spring sun was shining and the coloured roofs of the cars glistened like wet bright glass. In England, she'd sometimes caught a bus. Once, she and Yasmina and Sam had bought tickets and sat upstairs, on one of the best front seats, and no one had told her to get off. Now, suddenly, she wanted to do that again. She wanted to walk along that busy street, with the new sun on her face, and catch the bus, and climb the swaying steps to the upper deck, and –

And she also wanted to complete the diary, because if she didn't, her life in this place would disappear without trace.

She turned past the last picture of Zoltan's class and contemplated the new blank page. She ought to be using this time to draw, but the new dread of leaving had turned her hand to stone. She knew that she wasn't like her parents, who seemed content to roam. She didn't want to move from land to land. She wanted to reach one safe place and know that it was her home.

Then, she could draw the world.

'Oi!' Outside, someone had yelled.

'No!' Another shriller voice had screamed.

She went to the window. The girl, Zeynep, was by the wall again and a booted man was leaping across the road towards her.

'Zeynep!' Emilia screamed too. She struggled to force the window up, but the yellow paint still blocked the catch. 'Zeynep!' She screamed again, but no one heard.

The man dashed the spray can from Zeynep's hand with a swing of his fist. For a second both of them froze: he towered above her, she stared up, white-faced. A woman passing on the other side of the street hesitated, then hurried on. The booted man stepped back and spat. Then he drew back his arm. Down the street, the woman was opening her car and getting in hurriedly. The man clenched and unclenched his fist.

Emilia struck the windowpane as hard as she could again and again and again. The man heard and hesitated. Zeynep ducked. He lunged at her, but missed. Immediately Zeynep ran back across the road, and up the hostel steps. The man watched from the gutter. He was tall and young and pink, with a newborn's hairless head, and a man's unshaven chin. He was staring at the hostel door and licking his lips. Then he grinned through small, bared teeth, and shouted something that Emilia couldn't understand. Suddenly, he looked up at her window and unclenched his fist. When their eyes met, she recognised him as the man from the back of the car. Once again he drew one finger across his throat, then laughed at her and walked off down the street.

She shivered. She should have hidden her face. Now it was too late. She looked up and down the street. It was utterly deserted. The woman in her car had gone. Only the pigeons still cooed on the ledge. Then, in a house opposite, she noticed a lifted curtain fall: so she wasn't quite alone. Someone else must have seen that man.

She went into the bathroom and let the cold water run over her cut hand. She hadn't realised that she'd hit the glass so hard. Her only thought had been to distract the booted man. Her knuckles throbbed but she licked off a smear of blood and then began to listen for the door. Somehow, she was expecting to hear the sound of Zeynep's steps, but there was nothing. Nothing at all: nothing but the beat of someone's music and the cry of someone's child.

When she returned to the window she saw that two new swastikas had been changed to flowers. Of course: that was why the man was furious. Zeynep had been changing his marks again and he didn't like that. Emilia flexed her fingers and took a pen from her pocket because an idea for the next picture had suddenly appeared in her head.

She'd record another day in the English school, when she'd been drawing, and someone else had messed it up.

The other boy had been one of Sam's friends, but Emilia

had never liked him. He was the big boy who'd looked at her legs on her first day at school. The students called him Frankie although their teacher, Mrs Rushmore, had always called him Francis Johnson.

Now Emilia remembered registration time: 'Sue James? Wahid Jenkins? Francis Johnson? Yasmina Habib?' She could hear the rope of names in her head. Then came the rustle of replies: 'Yesmissyesmissyesmiss'. This had usually continued until the teacher came to Sam.

'Sam Quiggley?' That's when Mrs Rushmore had looked up. 'Has anybody seen Sam?' Other students had shaken their heads or shrugged. Sam's seat was often empty. He'd come to school very little, and nobody had seemed interested, except for Frankie. 'Francis?' Mrs Rushmore had always turned to the big boy and asked him where Sam was. When Francis shook his head, Mrs Rushmore had then said 'Absent' and read out the other names on the list. 'Tony Rackman, Emilia Radu? Have we got *Emilia* here still?' After a few days, Emilia had learnt to answer: 'yes miss,' just like everyone else.

She hadn't understood what the register was, but she'd thought it was a lucky omen her name was near Sam's. Yasmina had explained things about the letters in their names, but she hadn't understood. She'd remained happy that she was near to Sam and not Francis Johnson. This wasn't because of the way Frankie looked; although he was a large boy with fat breasts and hips which some of the girls teased him about. She hadn't wanted to be near him because he'd frightened her in ways she hadn't understood.

Wherever she'd been, in class, or the library, or in the noisy hall where they'd eaten their food, she'd found

Frankie watching her whenever she'd looked up. His eyes had sought hers and when their glances met, he'd smiled and nodded in a special sort of way. Sometimes, when she'd been walking with Yasmina, he had pushed himself between. In queues, he'd stood so close she'd felt his moist breath on her cheek and she'd disliked that. Once, he'd touched her hair. He'd picked up the end of one plait and twitched it about, as though it had been a snake. He hadn't hurt her and she'd known he'd meant it as a joke, but she'd been furious and offended, although she'd never said.

When she'd been in school a few weeks, some of her new friends had teased her about Frankie.

'He *fancies* you!' they'd shrieked, before collapsing with laughter that shook them like fits. When she'd understood what they meant, she'd been disgusted and afraid. She'd never wanted anybody to think about her like that. Not even Sam. She'd also been scared of her parents hearing such gossip. Her father had continued to resent her going to school. His brother had persuaded him not to prevent her, but she'd been anxious all the time. If her father had heard that his daughter was involved with an English boy, she knew that he'd have shut the door in her face.

At the same time as friends had been teasing her about Frankie, she had discovered that she wasn't so interested in 'lessons' after all. They'd been endless and dull. She wasn't used to sitting on chairs for hours on end and she'd found it difficult to keep still. The classrooms had been too warm in the afternoons and some teachers had spoken in voices as soft as summer bees. Other students had been busy, but she hadn't been able to understand and as lesson followed lesson, she'd often fallen asleep. She'd tried hard at the beginning, but had made no progress at all. Nobody had been angry about her failure, but to her it had felt like running up a hill whose land had been constantly slipping down. She couldn't understand the words and the writing at all. In comparison with Zoltan, she'd felt a fool.

He'd already brought home notebooks with his writing in them. He'd said that they were 'words'. He'd begun to read notices in shops while she couldn't read a single word. She'd remembered how she'd watched small children reading books in Bucharest. Then, she'd thought that reading must be easy. In England, she'd changed her mind. For the first time in her life she'd wondered if it was true that people like her were stupid, as well as poor. All her life people had been describing her as an ignorant gypsy but she'd never believed them before.

Her parents hadn't minded about her failure, because they hadn't expected her to succeed. Her father had been pleased. He'd said that this proved that girls shouldn't go to school. Her cousins had giggled when they'd heard him saying this, but her uncle and aunt had frowned. Sometimes, Emilia had thought about giving up and now she realised that she might have done so if she hadn't discovered the place in the school they called the art room because the art room had changed her life so much.

Towards the end of her second week in the school, Yasmina had taken her to a different sort of lesson which had been in a different sort of room. Instead of books, the other pupils had collected large sheets of paper from a pile at the front. Their sheets already had drawings and colours on them, but hers had had nothing on it at all. The paper was the colour of milk and unusually thick. She'd never seen anything like it before, but she hadn't known what to do next, so she'd sat down in her place and stared at it. Beside her, Yasmina had been working on a drawing of houses on a street, along which lots of bicycles and people seemed to be whizzing to and fro. High up in one corner, a very yellow sun blazed yellow arms into a bright blue sky. When Yasmina had rattled the box of pencils and pens that lay on the table between them and pointed to the blank sheet Emilia'd realised that she was also expected to draw. On the table in front, Sam was working with a brush and coloured paints.

She'd wanted to be like them but she'd been over-whelmed. She'd never seen drawing things like those. She hadn't even known that such things existed in the world.

'Go on.' Yasmina had shaken the box again.

On her other side, the girl they'd called PJ had mixed a coloured powder with water, and was dabbing the creamy stuff on her paper with a bit of sponge. Emilia had felt awkward. People had been glancing at her, and smiling, but she hadn't known how to begin. The teacher had helped several people but he hadn't helped her. Sam had turned round and offered her a fine black pen, but as soon as he'd done that, this other boy, Frankie, had pushed past Sam and tried to put something else into her hand. She'd felt his skin on hers and had pulled away from him, and knocked the box of pencils to the floor. Everyone round her had left what they were doing and begun to pick them up. She'd been so embarrassed she'd tried to leave the room, but couldn't because the door she'd opened had only led into a storeroom full of paint. The teacher hadn't known what to do, but one of the girls had brought her back to her place and made her sit down again. She'd been grateful for their kindness, but she'd still have preferred to leave. As she'd sat there she'd decided that this would be her last day. Tomorrow, she wouldn't come to school.

Then she'd looked up, and realised that Sam was still holding out the pen. She'd taken it without touching his hand. He'd turned away. Beside her, Yasmina had begun humming through her teeth as she'd coloured in a little dog. In front of her, Sam was brushing sweeps of brilliant colour onto his work.

She'd made one small black mark, just to see what it was like, and the paper had accepted the ink like wood accepts a sharp blade. She'd made another mark. Then, rapidly, she'd begun to draw the facade of the President's palace in Bucharest. She'd known exactly how to fit it to the page. It hadn't been difficult. After all, she'd been looking at that building ever since she was born.

Now, as she drew the picture of herself in the school art room, she remembered how her heart had pounded as she'd extended her marks across the page. She'd never worked on a large piece of paper before, and it had felt even better than treading into unmarked snow. The teacher had stopped nearby and watched, but she'd made herself carry on. She'd been so happy with what she was doing that she hadn't heard him move. She'd been distantly aware of Kelly and Wahid chatting. Nearby, PJ had groaned, and thrown her sponge on the floor, but Emilia hadn't been distracted. She'd had a small problem with a row of windows on the fourth floor, and she'd been so busy working out what to do, that she hadn't noticed that the room had gone quiet. When she'd corrected the problem, she'd looked up.

Most of the class, and the teacher, had been gathered round the table where she was. She'd tried to turn the paper over, or hide it with her arm, because she thought she must have done something wrong. Maybe she shouldn't have drawn what ought to have remained hidden in her head. Then she'd realised that no one was angry. One or two students had been shaking their heads, as if there was something about her palace that they hadn't understood, but that was all.

She'd looked down at her work. Then, she'd understood: the class was right to be puzzled: there were no people in the square, so they couldn't have appreciated how enormous the palace actually was. She'd quickly added a minute portrait of her mother sweeping. And she'd drawn herself, squatting in the mud and holding out her hand. When she'd finished the figures, she'd been pleased. The teacher must have been satisfied too because he'd moved the class back to their own places. She'd been very relieved. He'd continued walking between the tables, looking at other people's work instead, so she'd continued filling in more and more detail until the whole page was almost covered up.

She hadn't noticed him coming back to her, but he'd suddenly reached over and taken her sheet of paper away. He'd said something she hadn't understood, but he'd been smiling, so she'd decided that he wasn't annoyed with what she'd drawn, even though it hadn't looked like anyone else's work. Nevertheless she hadn't liked the way he'd held the picture up by its corners. Her stomach had lurched. She'd thought he was going to rip it up.

Instead, he'd carried it to the front of the class, where

everybody had crowded round it and stared. Then somebody had clapped. Unexpectedly the whole class had whistled and cheered. She'd have run off if Sam hadn't turned round and smiled that shadow of a smile, that he'd smiled at her before. But once he'd smiled, and she'd known that he'd approved, she'd changed her mind and decided to stay in school. She'd also decided not to care either about Frankie, or about being bored in class. They weren't important things. What had mattered was this amazing chance to draw.

Now, as Emilia looked at the scene that she'd recreated in the book, she relived that moment when her picture'd been held up in front of her class. Even though Sam had smiled, she'd still been expecting someone to laugh at her work and sneeringly point her out. The pupils had fallen silent after they'd clapped and cheered, but they'd looked at her as though she was someone special and she'd enjoyed the sensation very much. She'd felt like a bride at her wedding feast. And she couldn't have been more delighted if the gold coins had been hung round her neck and if the banknotes had been pinned on her dress. It had been so wonderful that she'd laughed until she'd cried.

Now, she paused and recalled something Gizella had said. They'd been looking at Gizella's wedding picture again, and Gizella had taken the photograph from her and held it at arm's length. 'Was that girl *me*?' Gizella had asked, as she'd looked at herself as a bride. Suddenly Emilia realised that she was asking the same question as she stared at the picture she'd drawn of herself in the art room. 'Was that girl *me*?'

While her friends had been congratulating her, she'd felt all the heat in her body rising into her face. She'd known she was blushing, but she hadn't minded at all. Her parents had always taught her to avoid praise, but that day she hadn't followed their advice. She'd been proud of herself and so happy. She'd enjoyed the praise just as she would have enjoyed a fine sunny day. She'd suddenly understood that she'd been looking for this all her life, and on that day she'd found it in the last place she'd thought it would be. It was as if she'd been back in the square in Bucharest and this time someone had tossed her a shower of gold.

That evening, in the flat, she'd been unable to keep quiet. As she'd described what had happened in the art room, her mother had interrupted.

'Do you mean you drew a picture of *me*, as I was *then*?'

Emilia had nodded and smiled.

'You drew *me, sweeping in the square*?' Elizabeta's voice had risen to a scream.

Her father'd looked up. Emilia'd started to explain, but her mother had drowned her out.

'Are you telling me, that these . . . these *children*, looked at me *sweeping*, and whistled and clapped?'

'Yes, but – '

'And you're *happy* about that?' Her mother's voice had changed to a moan.

'Yes, but – '

'Then,' Elizabeta's lips had trembled as she spoke, 'then, you're even more of a fool than I thought! Have you no pride? Don't you care that these . . . these *animals* are laughing at us? And, if you're *happy* to make your mother a laughing stock, then you're no daughter of mine! You're evil, even more evil than I thought.' Tears had brimmed in her mother's eyes. Her father had shaken his head.

'I'm ashamed of you, Emilia.' He'd spoken bitterly. 'How could you make fun of your mother, and yourself, like that? But it's my fault too. I should never have let you go to school.'

Silence had drowned the room like a flood. Even Zoltan had understood that something was wrong. He'd stayed where he was and had kept very quiet.

'Promise me,' her father had tapped down his hat, 'promise me that tomorrow morning, you won't go back to that school.'

Now, she shivered in the yellow room as she remembered how she'd tried to defend herself, and failed. Then she'd cried, which she never, ever did. Finally, she'd promised him that in the morning she wouldn't go to the school.

But in the afternoon, she had. And she'd been late in class. Mrs Rushmore had already finished calling out the register, but as soon as Emilia'd opened the classroom door, a girl she hardly knew had jumped up, and thumped the empty space beside her, shouting: 'Emi! Sit by me!' She hadn't quite understood the words, but when she'd sat there she'd known that she'd done the right thing, because the girl had punched the air and shouted 'Ye-es!' and everybody had laughed. And she'd laughed too. She'd bent down and straightened the diamond-patterned socks. Then she'd laughed as loudly as she could. But she'd realised that from then on, she'd have to be almost invisible in the flat, if she wanted to continue in the school.

And she'd succeeded. For a week or two, she'd been less than a shadow on the wall. She'd played with Zoltan, and helped her mother as much as she could. And she'd never mentioned school. If her parents asked her about it, she'd pulled a face and said that it was boring, but not too bad, and then she'd talked about something else.

But she'd been lying. Each day she'd loved school more and more. And everything might still have been all right, if Francis Johnson hadn't blundered in again, and spoilt it all.

Picture 13

In the Art Room

Later that afternoon, while Emilia was cutting herself a slice of bread, she heard the footsteps she'd been waiting for. They stopped at her door. It hadn't sounded like her parents, but just in case, she checked that the book was out of sight. Then she crept back and listened by the lock.

'Hello?' It was definitely Zeynep. 'Hello? You are in there?'

'Yes. I am in there.' Emilia's reply was too faint for anyone to hear.

'Hello?' Zeynep raised her voice, then tried the handle on the door. 'Hello? I can come in?'

'No!' Now Emilia managed to speak louder than before.

'Please?' The handle turned again. 'Can I come in?'

'No! They lock the door.'

But she was wrong: this morning, her father must have forgotten to lock her in. She watched in disbelief as the door opened with a click, then swung slowly in.

And there she was. The black-haired girl stood in the doorway and smiled as easily as if nothing extraordinary had happened, as if she dropped by every day. She was even rolling her eyes and pulling a face, as if there was some joke about this flat that Emilia hadn't known was there.

'Oh no!' Zeynep was gasping as she looked about her. 'I am thinking my room upstairs, is bad, but it is not as bad as this!' She was pointing to the yellow walls and wrinkling up her nose. Emilia stared. Then she understood: this girl was only reacting to the colour of the paint.

'Hello, once more.' She stepped further in. 'My name is Zeynep Kara, and – ' she was holding out her hand, like foreign people often did. When she noticed that Emilia was still holding the bread knife, she hesitated, but smiled, though less certainly than before.

Emilia could think of nothing to say.

'You are . . . *cooking*?' Close to, the girl's white face was lined and she was older than Emilia'd imagined she'd be.

'Yes. I . . . cook . . .'

'Me too! I cook.' Zeynep tossed back her fan of black hair.

Their eyes met, but they both looked away again, and stared at the floor.

'I am coming to say thank you,' Zeynep whispered at last. Her hair swung over her face. She swallowed and coughed. 'I am saying thank you that you hit the glass for me this morning, and make that man to go away. Thank you *very* much.'

With the knife still in her hand, Emilia put her thumb in her mouth and bit off a ridge of skin. She was struggling to uncover some of those words that the English girls had taught her to say after 'thanks'. Another uncomfortable silence settled in the yellow air. She blinked, then kept her eyes shut a moment longer and willed Zeynep to disappear. Maybe, when she looked again, Zeynep would have gone.

210

Then she'd be alone, but at least she'd be safe within the yellow walls and wouldn't have to worry about what to say and do; and wouldn't have to fear her parents' early return.

When she opened her eyes, Zeynep was still there. Together they moved to the window with the view.

'I like it very well.' Zeynep was pointing to Emilia's picture on the wall.

Emilia couldn't speak. She'd dreamt of talking to this girl. She'd wanted to ask her everything about Lindenstrasse, and the hostel, and about where they were. There was so much she didn't know. She'd longed to discover what lay beyond the tree on the corner, and she had even dreamt of asking Zeynep about school. But now that she had her chance, and Zeynep was here, in the room, she couldn't say a word.

It had been easier alone. This girl's presence hadn't brought her any help. Instead, more fear and more anxiety were crowding into the yellow space and Emilia didn't know what to do. Ridiculously and childishly and suddenly, Zeynep's appearance had made her cry. She wanted to rush at the door and push the intruder back outside. Then she wanted to turn the key. She wanted to lock herself in. She wanted to keep the world away, and pretend it wasn't there. She wanted to double-lock the door, and crawl back under the table and . . .

Only she couldn't. Not now. Her parents had left her alone, but taken the key. So she couldn't even lock the door.

'What the matter is, with you?' Zeynep's voice was quiet.

Through tears, Emilia saw the girl looking at her kindly. She bit off another, larger piece of skin. Somewhere in her head she thought she heard Yasmina's voice: 'What's the matter, Emi? *What's up?*' That's what her English friends had said when something had happened in school: '*what's up?*' 'What's up, Emi?' They'd touched her, too. They'd put their arms around her and hugged her as if she'd been part of their family too.

' "Nothing. I'm fine thanks." ' That was the correct reply. Those were the words she'd learnt to say, so she ought to use them here. Except that her mouth was so full of tears she couldn't speak.

'I . . .'

'Yes?' Zeynep came closer and took the knife from Emilia's hand.

'I . . . I draw . . .' It was not what she'd meant to say. And as soon as the words were out, she knew she should have kept quiet. It was the only secret she had left. It was also the one subject she should have hidden from this stranger.

'You draw?' Zeynep was frowning.

For a second Emilia hoped that Zeynep wouldn't understand.

But she did.

'*What* you are drawing?' Zeynep asked.

Emilia turned away.

'*What* you are drawing? *Please*? I like to see?'

Emilia swallowed. She could still say no. Or even shout it, to be quite sure she'd made her point.

'No! No! No!' That's what she should be saying, because as soon as this girl saw the book, she'd stretch out her thin white hands and snatch it back. She'd claim it as hers. After all, this girl was someone as desperate as herself. She snatched up things in the street, didn't she? And who was

212

Emilia to blame her? Hadn't she still got the stolen drawing things in the pocket of her red skirt?

'No! No! No!' That's what her father would've said. Her mother would have done the same. They'd both have pushed this girl out of their rooms and then slammed the door in her face. They'd have cut themselves open and slid their secrets under their skin, rather than do as she'd done, and reveal them to a stranger. They were brave, not cowardly, like her. And if only she'd been like them she'd have done the same.

Instead, Emilia reached under the sofa for the book and held it out.

'Oh!' Zeynep gasped, but didn't try to snatch the book back. Instead, she sighed and shook her head.

'So: it is *here*, all the time.' Her voice was unsteady behind the shining curtain of her hair.

'Yes. It is here. But you take, please.' Emilia wiped her eyes and put her hand in her pocket and held out the pens as well. If the book was going, they might as well go too. Then she wouldn't bother to remember the past. She'd give it all up, and bury that life in a deep and silent grave. She'd do what her parents expected. She'd lead her life in their way. She'd change. She'd . . .

But Zeynep didn't take the book or the pens. Instead, she shook her head more vigorously.

'No: it is not *my* book. It is *hers*.'

'Hers?' Emilia was confused.

Together, they looked at the writing on the first page.

'See?' Zeynep was pointing out two words. '*Ka-der Ka-ra. Kader* is my *sister*, yes? She is my *big* sister, like you are the big sister to the little boy in your family, yes? Look,' she indicated a line of blue words on the first page. 'Kader Kara, born, 4-2-1978. She is my *old sister*. She has three years more than I. *This* is *Kader's* book. That *she* forgot.'

Emilia thought that she'd understood, but wasn't sure. She ran her fingers over the gold-edged pages once more, then looked up. It didn't really matter what Zeynep was saying. All that mattered was that this book could no longer be hers.

'Your sister, where is she?

'She – ' Zeynep was staring at the blue writing.

Emilia waited. Was the sister outside? Might she also walk in? Would she be angry and call Emilia a thief? Would she rip out the drawings and fling them down on the floor?

'My sister, she is . . . I don't know where.' Zeynep closed the book and smoothed down the ribbon that marked a place. 'She is not here with me. She buys a journey to go to England, before the Christmas. You know? It is, how you say, very suddenly, she goes. You understand? Kader goes by secret, in the lorry, and she is hiding in the boxes, I think.' Zeynep was speaking even more quietly, as if someone might have overheard her words. 'Everyone say me that is how you have to go, to get across the sea. To England. That is where she is being, now. I hope. Because that is where she is *always* wanting to go. And me. That is why I am studying the English so well in school – '

'She is in *England*?' Something like anger made Emilia cry out.

'Yes, I hope . . .'

'What you mean?'

'I mean, "*I hope*" because I *do not know*. My sister, Kader, she goes from here in the early morning, very suddenly, with more Turkish people who are her friends. The Turkish people, they are living *here*, in this flat, before you come. They were our good friends. That is why I knock the door before, and am asking your father about her book.'

Emilia looked away.

'You know that there is much trouble for foreigners here, in this town?' Zeynep sat down. 'And my sister, Kader, she wants so much to leave. She goes away in the morning, when I am in the school. She leaves so quick she does not take her clothes. She does not say me goodbye. She writes a little paper on the table, that I see it when I get in. It is what we always promise: that if we cannot go two together, but one only gets the chance for England, then she *must* go. Alone. But . . . for me it is sad. And then I wait. But there is *nothing*, no letter, no message for me by telephone. I am waiting all the day, outside the office, for the post, for *anything* that tells me she is safe.' Zeynep cleared her throat. 'I love my sister and I am thinking of her . . . all the time thinking, even when I'm in my school. Now, I cannot make my lessons well, like I did before, because all the time I am thinking of Kader. And I am thinking how it *is* in England for my sister? How it looks like, there?

'Then, one day, I remember this book. Always she writes her life in it, all the things that happen to her, in Turkey and here, but I never read it because it is *her* . . . how you say?' She wrinkled up her brow and touched the book.

'Her . . . diary?' Emilia whispered

'Yes! That is it! How clever you are! And diaries, they are secret, no? But I am thinking if she do not take her clothes, she do not take her diary. So, maybe I can find it and I can learn from it where she is. I look everywhere in our room,

215

but it is not there. Then I think that maybe she is leaving it *here*, in the flat of her friends because this diary it says things that she is never wanting me to know. So I knock on your door. To ask. But your father is not liking that. But I want to read her words very much, because I am *very* afraid, now, I *never* can go to England myself. And I never see my –' she coughed.

'I . . . I go . . . in England.'

'*You*?'

'Yes.'

'Oh! But you *tell* me, you *say* me how it is? Please? My sister and I, we see the films and pictures in Turkey, but we don't *know*.'

'I tell you, but . . .' Emilia was drowning amongst the words in her head.

Then, she knew what to do.

She turned over the pages until she found the first picture that she'd drawn. Then she got up and let Zeynep look through by herself. When she came back Zeynep was examining the picture of the English landscape with the autumn leaves. She watched as Zeynep traced along the arch of bare stemmed trees that had slanted up the hill.

'That is . . . beautiful. And England, it is like *that*?'

'Yes, like that, but,' Emilia turned over to the next page, 'but like *this*, also.'

Zeynep was bending over the picture of the car park in Poet's Rise. She moved her finger across the shattered van, the barking dog, and the angry crowd. She was staring at the puddle on the ground, and the great, grey blocks of flats rising up into the rain. She shook her head.

'It is *bad* in England, like in Turkey?' Then she picked the

216

book up and put her nail against the swastikas on the concrete wall. 'And *that* is in England, too?'

'Yes.'

'But my sister, Kader, how can she ever then be safe?'

Emilia shrugged.

'You are not understanding!' Zeynep was twisting her fingers. 'That is why Kader is going *from* here as quick as she can. Because here too, there are the people who draw those wicked things, like the ones on the wall. These bad people, they are not wanting the Turks and all the foreign peoples on their streets. One night they catch Kader and they are slapping her in the face just because she is a Turk. They try to do her something else as well and hurt her too much!' Her voice was shrill. 'That is why she leave quick, so quick she cannot say me goodbye!'

'In England – ' Emilia put her hand on her neck. She ran the tips of her fingers over the place where the icy blade had touched. She wanted to explain that she did understand. She longed to tell Zeynep what had happened in England, but she had no words with which to speak.

Slowly and carefully, Zeynep looked through all the pictures again. When she'd finished Emilia pointed to the earlier pages which had her sister's writing on them.

'You read?' Emilia asked.

'No. Not yet. It makes me very, very sad.' She drew a deep breath. 'My sister and me, and *all* my family, we are *not* Turkish peoples, like I tell you. I lie to you. We are Kurds. You understand?'

Emilia shook her head. Vaguely, she remembered something about Hasan, one of the boys in the English school. She'd never spoken to him, but Yasmina had said something about him being 'a Kurd', and how he and his family had fled from their country just as Emilia had.

'We are Kurds, but in Turkey they do not like us. They *kill* us and they take our land. In my village the Turkish soldiers come in the night and they take my father, my sister, my brother,' she was counting them on her finger, 'my brother's son, my uncle . . .' She went to the window and looked out. 'They are in the prison, a long, long time. My father, I think he is still there. My sister, she comes home, but she is *so* hurt. I know that she writes what they do to her in the prison in her diary. And she tells me "don't read, Zeynep". They are very bad things that they do to girls in the prison. They are . . . bad. It will make you too sad. So I *don't* read them.

'And now I am waiting for the news from England, but it isn't coming. My Kader is . . . lost. Then, I remember the diary. I am thinking: if I can look at it, maybe I am finding where she is. Maybe there is a little, little idea.'

'You find?' Emilia pointed to the lines of blue words.

'I hope, yes, when I can look.'

'Come.' Emilia crouched down and showed Zeynep where she'd found the book. There were still faint marks where the sticky tape had been, but nothing else. Zeynep sighed. Then, she turned through the pages of the book and stopped at the picture of the art room.

'It is you?' she asked, with her finger on Emilia's self-portrait. 'It is very good. I like very much.'

It was a good picture, and as she looked at it again, Emilia was still pleased. Now, she signed her name underneath. Even if it was to be the last picture that she could draw, she was still proud of it and wanted it to carry her name.

'What is *here*?' Zeynep was pointing to the next empty page.

'I draw?' Emilia asked.

'Yes!' Zeynep pointed to the wall outside. 'I *know* before that you draw very good. Now, you draw more for *me*?'

Why not? Emilia looked back at the previous picture, then thought about what to do next. Zeynep sat opposite and watched. On the ledge under the window the pigeons were cooing in the sunny afternoon. A strong spring light was falling into the room and in its shaft she noticed the way dust glistened and swirled and swam. Then she remembered another morning when she'd seen the chalk dust and the powder paint hanging in the blocks of light that had been falling through the art room windows, and patterning its floor with squares of sun.

Now, she began to retrace the outlines of that room on the fresh page. It had had windows on two sides so it had always been cold. A green board had stood at the front, and she'd loved drawing on that. On one particular morning she'd planned to draw another view of Bucharest. It had been one of her favourite subjects and also one that other people had understood. Once the students in her class had accepted that she could draw, they'd always been crowding round her: 'Draw something, Emi,' they'd said. 'Show us what it was *really* like in Bucharest.' So she tried. She'd drawn her house with the window boarded up, and Gizella's house next door, and the hospital where they'd taken Nico, and the church where the incense burners had swung. She had recreated the iron gate at the school, and the kiosks, where she'd collected papers from the ground. She'd always drawn lots of pictures of the President's palace and many people had liked those the best. 'Brilliant' had been the word which they'd used.

Occasionally, however, someone had shaken their head after they'd looked at her work. It was as if they'd doubted her, and suspected that she might have tricked them with some dangerous magic. Then she'd always felt that she'd failed, that somehow her picture had not been good enough.

The boy, Frankie, had been one of those people. He'd always shaken his head when he'd been looking at her pictures. He'd looked and looked but never once said 'wow' or 'wicked' like the other boys had. And he'd always stood too close. Sometimes, he'd touched her when he'd reached over and pointed at her work. His plump pink finger had lingered on the pictures, and he'd kept asking 'What's that? What's that?' Sometimes, he'd taken a picture away from her without even asking. Then he'd held it up for everyone to see. She'd hated that.

Sam had been so different. He'd never asked her any questions. From the moment she'd first seen him draw she'd known that he was like her. She'd known that he'd understood. That was why she'd changed her plan as she'd stood in the front of the green board on that morning in school. She decided not to draw yet another picture of the palace. She'd drawn her first picture of the fire, instead.

It had been a sunny morning and she'd felt so cheerful as she'd gone into school. She'd avoided her class and gone straight to the art room. She'd been doing that quite often and nobody had seemed to mind. Soon she was working on the new scene so energetically that she'd already snapped off several sticks of chalk and had smudged her face and hands and skirt. Sam had laughed at her when he'd come into the room a few minutes later. Then he'd leant against a table and silently watched her at work. That morning, their part of the school had been unusually quiet. Occasionally, she'd been aware of murmuring voices from another class, but usually the loudest sound had been her chalk on the board, scraping it like a claw on bark. Sometimes, she'd almost forgotten that Sam was there because he'd been so quiet. Then she'd remembered him and known without turning round that he was silently watching what she did, and she'd realised that she didn't mind at all.

'One day,' he'd broken into that silence. 'One day, I'll go.'

She had looked up, then.

'One day,' he'd repeated, pointing at her chalked-in street, 'one day, I'll go *there*. With you.'

'No!' She'd shaken her head. She'd been shocked. The thought of going back horrified her. 'No!' she cried again. 'No go there!'

'Why not?' He hadn't moved, but he'd seemed closer to her than he'd been before.

'I draw,' she'd said. 'Then you know why not!'

He'd sat down then, and watched. As she'd used the duster to rub off what she'd already drawn she'd made hurried plans in her head. At first she'd intended to recreate the fires that had destroyed her house and street, but at the last moment she'd changed her mind again. She hadn't been confident that that would truly show him how horrible some parts of their life had been, so she'd decided to draw an imagined scene. It would illustrate an incident that she'd heard talked about when she'd been living there. She hadn't seen it herself, but her father and everyone else had

221

discussed it endlessly during the final days before they'd left.

It had taken place one wet evening in another part of Bucharest, or so people said. Another howling mob had torched a block of flats where several gypsy families had been living. Most of the gypsies had escaped, but once the lower floors of the building were blazing there'd been no other way down. A young woman and a child had been trapped. They'd climbed to the roof and screamed for help. The watching crowd had covered their mouths and noses with cloths soaked in water, but no one had tried to help. The young woman had run from side to side, looking for a way down. Then she'd thrown her child. People said that bystanders had seen him twisting and waving in the air, but they'd all backed away, afraid of being struck. When the young woman had jumped, her long hair had already been alight. Or that's what people had said. So that's what Emilia had drawn. She'd never attempted a picture like that before, although such scenes had regularly been part of the deadly landscape of dreams that disturbed her nights. But on that sunny morning she'd decided to try and show Sam what their life had really been like and so explain to him why she never wanted to go back.

When she'd finished the picture, Sam had sighed. Then, he'd picked up a piece of chalk and scratched a white winged bird into the sky above the flats she'd drawn. She'd watched as he'd given it a curving, orange beak and tucked up yellow legs. He'd glanced at her and then stepped back. At first she hadn't understood. He'd pointed at the green board and handed the chalk to her.

'Now I?' she'd asked.

She'd assumed that this was an English game: to make a picture with someone else, so she'd drawn another bird. Then he'd drawn a cat. She'd drawn herself, standing apart from the crowd and looking up at the smoke and flames. Suddenly, he'd drawn her uncle's van. Then she'd shaken her head. It had become clear that he'd thought that her picture was one of England and she hadn't known how to make him see that this was a picture of Bucharest.

She'd decided to begin drawing the palace in the distance, but before she could do anything else Francis Johnson had burst into the art room. He'd been talking so loudly that she hadn't understood a word he'd said. When he'd frowned, and pointed to his watch, she'd thought he was warning her to leave the room, because another class was coming in, so she'd begun to clean the board as quickly as she could. For some reason Frankie had shouted at her even more. Then he'd grabbed her wrist. She'd jerked her arm, and got it free. Then she'd slapped his face. Sam had been shouting as well. He'd rushed at them and given Frankie a shove, and Frankie'd stumbled into a table piled up with chalks and tins of powder paint. It had overturned and Sam had charged at Frankie again. Then the two of them had fallen to the floor amongst smashed pots and scattered brushes and rising clouds of chalk and paint.

She'd been so frightened and hadn't understood why they were fighting, but she did remember looking up and marvelling at the clouds of dust and powder paint flowing in the sunlight like petrol spilt on a wet street.

'Those boys, they were fighting in the *school*?' Zeynep was shaking her head as she looked at the picture.

Emilia nodded. She crumbled up a fragment of chalk from her pocket, and threw it into the shaft of light.

'They are fighting here, in my school as well.' Zeynep pulled a disgusted face. 'But the boys in your picture, in England, *why* they are fighting?'

'Because . . .' Emilia shrugged and went to the window. She still didn't understand what had happened that morning in the art room, when the boys had been fighting and paint had coloured the air.

A teacher had dragged them apart. Sam's lips had been green and his shirt was ripped, but when he'd got to his feet, he'd laughed. Frankie, however, had stayed sprawled on the floor. A lump like a small white egg had appeared on the edge of his brow. He'd had a scratch on his cheek and as his fingers felt for more damage, he'd smeared the blood from his nose into the paint. If she hadn't been so startled, Emilia might have laughed as well.

She'd intended to finish cleaning the board before the next class came in, but an older woman teacher had pushed through the pupils at the door and clapped her hands. In the hush that followed, she'd stepped over poor Frankie and put firm arms around Emilia as if she'd been a child. Emilia had wanted to apologise for the drawing on the board, but hadn't known how, and the woman, whom she'd then recognised as the library teacher, hadn't let her go. She'd held on, and stroked back Emilia's plaits as if Emilia'd been a daughter of her own. Her behaviour had surprised Emilia so much that she hadn't said a single word. She hadn't been sorry about slapping Frankie, but as the lump on his forehead grew, and the blood trickled down from his nose, she'd wished that she hadn't slapped him so hard.

But he shouldn't have grabbed her wrist. He'd disgusted her, and as soon as she could, she'd intended to run to the cloakroom and held her arm and hand under the hot tap. She'd wanted to wash away every last feel of his flesh. But they hadn't let her do that and she hadn't been able to explain. Later, the library teacher, Mrs Morris, had taken her in to see the Head. There, both teachers had tried to get her to talk about what had happened, but she'd refused. She'd already realised that if any word of this got back to her parents, they'd have stopped her coming to school.

'They are fighting about *you*?' Zeynep suggested, pointing to the boys in the picture.

'No!' Emilia shook her head. 'Not me.'

But the girls in her class had all said the same thing. They'd said that Frankie and Sam both 'fancied' her and that's why there'd been a fight. They'd even teased her about 'pulling stupid blokes like that.' Kelly had said 'Yuk, Emi! *Poor* you! Who'd want Francis Johnson or Sam Quiggley to fancy them? You'd be much better off with Rachid: he's really cute.'

She'd refused to understand what they'd meant. She'd never lived like them, and she'd always known that it was dangerous for girls like her to think of things like that. Love was deadly and not the subject for jokes. She'd only needed to remember Gizella to know how fatal love could be. So, she'd been relieved when other people in the school had suggested that Frankie Johnson had grabbed her wrist not because he liked her, but because he hated her because she was a gypsy. Then somebody else had whispered that it was all Frankie's mother's fault: Mrs Johnson was an idiot who hated all foreigners, and her son was the same. Yasmina had explained that Mrs Johnson was campaigning to keep the gypsies away from the estate where she lived, so it was very possible that stupid Frankie was only doing what his mum wanted.

Emilia had shrugged when she'd understood that. She'd been disappointed when she'd realised that some people in England were just as horrid as some people in Bucharest, but she hadn't been so surprised. It had hurt, like a shoe that rubs, but she was used to putting up with sores.

'So, what the matter was? Why they fight?' Zeynep asked again.

'The matter was . . . I am a *gypsy*.' Emilia shrugged.

'So?' Zeynep demanded. 'What you *do*?'

'What I do?' Emilia didn't understand.

'Yes? What you do, after this fight? You tell your parents? And – '

'No!' Emilia cried, 'I tell *nothing*!' That was the one thing she'd known she mustn't do. But the next day the school had phoned her uncle and her father and asked them all to come to a meeting with the Head. And within minutes, it had seemed, her father and her uncle had been there, in school.

Picture 14

Woman with a Blue Ring

After Zeynep had left the flat, Emilia went back to the window and watched as she hurried down the street towards the main road. It had been a sunny day and it still looked warm out there, even in the late afternoon. Perhaps this was spring at last, or at least the end of winter in this place where they were. A house opposite had a tub of small white flowers with hanging heads outside the front door. Another had window boxes filled with yellow blooms and waving leaves like spears. If Emilia had dared to follow Zeynep and walk as far as the tree on the corner, she suspected that she might have been able to see its forming buds. But she didn't.

Instead, she reflected that in Bucharest, a fine spring day like this had been one of the best times for earning money. When the weather had been at its most cruel, and Emilia had been out on the streets begging with her mother, she'd learnt that no one bothered to stop and feel in their pockets for change. On the worst winter days, when they'd needed the money the most, it had never been worth working the streets because nobody gave a thing. On spring days, however, when the sun was warm, and the mud was not yet dust, people had lingered and smiled and chatted to each other, and tossed down their coins with a nod.

Since people here were probably not so different from those in Bucharest, Emilia was hoping that her parents would be having a successful trip. At the very least, Zoltan would enjoy being out of the flat and in a different area of town. Probably, he'd be playing with other children. Today he wouldn't have to sit apart and watch. If boys were kicking a football about, he would certainly have shot some goals. Then he'd come in smiling, and wouldn't be angry and sad. Her mother might be happier too. Today, she'd have chatted to other women, as well as having had the chance of earning a decent amount, for a change.

Her father would be pleased with the money, and he'd have enjoyed his day too. He'd have had a few beers with friends and, as they looked at the second-hand cars, they'd have talked about what to do next and their plans. His friends might have reassured him that this was a good town to settle in. They might have advised him to stay where he was, and then told him that he was a fool to think of returning to Bucharest. If their children were in school here, they might even have persuaded him to let Zoltan go back to school with them. So, Emilia convinced herself, when her parents and Zoltan returned to the hostel in the evening, they'd be smiling for a change.

She imagined them calling out a greeting as they opened the door and even using her name. If her father'd stretched himself on the sofa, in a good-humoured way, she might dare to crouch down and pull off his boots. In fact, if they'd only decide to settle here, and make this town their home,

Emilia decided that she would definitely try to be a better daughter and do as they expected. Then, if she was very, very careful, and didn't annoy them again, they might forget about what she'd done in England. They might even forgive her enough to let her draw . . .

Suddenly, she wanted Zeynep to be wrong about this place. Unpleasant things had happened here, but maybe it wasn't quite as bad as Zeynep had made out. Someone had smashed in the hostel windows, and sprayed that ugly stuff on the wall opposite, but wasn't this sort of thing happening everywhere, all the time? Two men had spat at Elizabeta, and others had hurt Zeynep's sister, Kader, but wasn't that just the way things were? You couldn't prevent it. There wasn't anything anyone like her could *do*, was there? Despite what Zeynep had said, these ugly things were happening in other places as well. So, if this town was no different from any other, what was the point of moving on yet again? They couldn't keep moving forever, because in the end, they'd have no place left to go. Except over the edge, or into the sea.

She looked out of the window again. The street was quiet and she was glad. She wanted her parents and Zoltan to be safe. She didn't want them to be hurt, or to witness any trouble in the street or see anybody else getting hurt. If that happened, they'd be too frightened to settle here. So, even if there was fighting, and even if there were hundreds of people out there, protesting against foreigners, Emilia didn't care, so long as the protests remained hidden and so long as her parents didn't know.

Outside, it certainly didn't look as if there was any protest going on. The main road was particularly quiet. Hopefully, this march, or whatever it was, wasn't as big as the hostel manager and Zeynep had both feared. It might even have been cancelled, because as Emilia glanced out again, she realised that strangely, nothing was moving along the main road. She couldn't see a single car, or van, or bus. So, maybe it was just a holiday here or something else like that. In the kitchen, she cut another slice of bread and smeared on jam. Maybe the hostel manager's warning had been wrong.

Maybe cars weren't moving because supplies of petrol had run out. In Bucharest, there'd often been problems like that, especially at the end of the winter. However, when the buses hadn't run, everybody'd walked. She returned to the window, and looked left and right, but there was still nothing to see. No one was walking past. Now, she noticed something else: the parked cars that usually lined the street outside had all gone.

It was as if life had stopped. Apart from the pigeons, nothing was moving. She wiped a smear of jam from the glass, then licked her finger. If she'd been able to open the window, she would have put her head out and listened for some different sound that might have given her a clue. Then, she remembered the door. She'd shut it after Zeynep had left, but it wasn't locked today.

She opened it slowly and looked out. Even the corridor was quiet. There were some sounds from next door, where she thought the doctor and his wife and child lived, but that was all. There was no music in the building, no foot-steps, no clank of the old lift door and no men's voices seeping through like smoke. She made herself walk as far as the lift, then back, more quickly. In the flat, she cut more bread. It was ages since she'd felt as hungry as this. The last time had been when she was staying in Mrs Morris's house in England. Since then, she'd hardly eaten a thing.

Restlessly, she went back to the corridor, and walked up and down as she ate. Then she remembered that she'd acted in the same way in the Morrises' house, although it was hard to believe that she'd actually lived there, now. But it was true. The day after the fight in the art room, Mrs Morris had offered to take Emilia into her own home, and she'd agreed. She'd done it as easily as she'd eaten those crisps, on her first day in school. She'd just stretched out her hand.

She recalled how Mrs Morris had shown her over the house and explained what everything was. Then she'd taken her into the kitchen, and finally got her to understand she was free to touch and eat their food. She'd understood that she could take whatever food she wanted, so long as she used a plate, and didn't make crumbs! At the time, it had seemed such a funny thing to say, because she'd never been inside a house that was so untidy, and in such need of a good clean and dust! Her mother would have been ashamed if her house had looked like that, but Mrs Morris hadn't seemed to care. And within a day or two, Emilia hadn't cared either. She'd just stopped noticing the dust and the clutter.

She'd walked into their house and lived with them, as if it had been planned all along. And once she'd settled in, and learnt their ways and learnt that nothing dreadful happened when she ate their food, she'd started to feel hungry all the time. For the first time in her life, her cheeks had been almost plump. Indeed, while she'd been staying with the Morrises she hadn't been able to stop eating, but as soon as she'd left them, she'd had no appetite at all.

Now, she finished the bread and listened at the window again. This time she thought she heard distant shouting, but wasn't sure. It could have come from the streets, but it could also have been a television on another floor. Outside, the outlines of the buildings were sharpening as the sun sank down behind. She could have enjoyed drawing a picture of this horizon of roofs, but as she smoothed out the new page, she rejected the idea. The roofs must wait. If her parents weren't returning until late, she must use the time for the next picture for the diary. Then, if Zeynep came back, she could show her the answer to that question: 'What you are *doing* about *this*?'

As soon as Zeynep had asked her about that, she'd started to feel uncomfortable, as though, somehow, she hadn't done the right thing.

She'd never mentioned the fight in the art room at home. That afternoon, she'd double-checked that her skirt hadn't been marked by the paint, then she'd climbed the stairs to their front door, just as she'd always done. Zoltan had pushed past, just as he always did, and they'd found their mother and aunt sitting in the front room drinking black tea. When her aunt had asked about school, Emilia'd shrugged and said it was all right just as she always did. Luckily, Zoltan had been longing to tell them about his day in school. He'd boasted that he'd been chosen to be a king! He'd begun chattering about actors and going on a stage. Her mother had frowned. None of them had ever seen acting on a stage, but Elizabeta was confident that she didn't approve. There had been gypsy musicians in Bucharest, and she had enjoyed their music at weddings, but her family had never been involved in anything like that, and she didn't want it for her son. Their aunt had intervened and explained that Zoltan was likely to be describing the Christmas play, about the Jesus baby, which the children in England often performed in the schools at that time of year. Her younger daughter had taken part in something like that, last year. She'd been an angel, and a friend's son had been a sheep. Their aunt told them that she'd watched the play with all the other parents and had enjoyed it very much.

'A *sheep*?' Elizabeta'd asked. 'Well, you may not care that they make your child into an animal, but I *do* care. No son of mine is going to be a beast, so that these stupid people can laugh at him!'

'I'm *not* being a beast,' Zoltan had wailed, 'I'm being a *king*! In a cloak and crown! And Auntie Peg says that I can hold her special little box, with jewels in it.'

'And you think they won't *laugh* at you, behind your back?' their mother'd retorted.

'*No*!' Zoltan had shouted back and stamped his foot. 'They *won't*. They like *me*, a lot.' His lips had been trembling as he'd left the room.

All that evening after the fight, Emilia'd nervously waited for a knock on their door. Surely, someone, like her uncle, would rush round and tell her parents about the trouble in school? In Bucharest, gossip had always travelled fast. That night she'd dreamt about the fight. In her dream, Sam's face had been smothered in green paint that had stuck like thick mud. He hadn't been able to speak or see, and she'd been unable to move and so couldn't help him claw it off.

The next morning, however, she'd left the house as usual. Yasmina had been waiting outside, and the three of them had walked to school together. It'd been cold in the night, so she'd put on an extra thick pair of red socks. Zoltan had worn his huge new anorak for the first time. He'd insisted on walking along with the collar turned up and only the top of his head sticking out. As they'd drawn nearer to the school, they'd met up with more friends and since nobody had mentioned the fight, Emilia had begun to hope that it had been forgotten. After all, people were always fighting about this or that.

In class, she'd sat by Sam and everything had seemed as it always did. She'd noticed paint in Sam's hair, and some of the girls had been teasing him about it. She hadn't understood what they were saying, but Sam had been smiling as he'd ducked and shaken his head about to try and stop them plucking out the coloured hairs. But that was all. When the register was being taken everyone was already in their place and Sam was busy with his drawings as usual. Emilia'd noticed that his shirt cuff was purple instead of white, but there was no other sign of yesterday's fight, except that Frankie wasn't there.

She'd been surprised about that. Frankie's place was empty, and he'd never missed a day before.

'Francis Johnson?' Mrs Rushmore had repeated the question and looked up from the register. She'd seemed surprised as well. When she'd asked Sam where Frankie was, everybody'd laughed. Emilia had felt guilty, especially when several people had turned round and looked at her. Had she hurt Frankie more than she'd realised, when she'd slapped his face? She'd seen the lump on his head, but surely she hadn't hit him that hard? As she'd sat in her place, she'd remembered the wet feel of Frankie's lips and nose on her palm and she'd wiped her hand on her skirt again. Had she really hit him so hard that he couldn't come to school?

Beside her, Sam had been drawing a comic figure of a plump boy stretched out on the ground, with a bump like a hill on his head and stars whirling around in the paint-coloured air above. He'd moved his arm so that she could see better. Then he'd sketched himself as a stick-thin rat, with his little paws clenched under his chin and his whiskers covered in paint. Obviously, Sam hadn't thought she'd done anything very bad. His picture showed the fight between him and his friend as a joke. So maybe it was. Maybe she shouldn't be worrying at all. Everyone else seemed to think it was a laugh, as they'd always said. So she'd decided to laugh at it as well. She'd also decided to be nicer to Frankie when he came back. Maybe he wasn't as bad as she'd thought. Maybe his behaviour to her was all part of English manners between boys and girls. And if it was, why should she worry? Or maybe it was true that Frankie and his mum didn't like gypsies and foreigners. And if that was so, why should she care? So long as her parents never heard about it, the incident could be swept away like lines in the mud.

Certainly, when the teachers had talked to her straight after the fight, she'd smiled as much as she could, and tried to show that she hadn't been hurt in the least. She'd tried to tell them that she was sorry to have caused so much mess. The head teacher, Miss Chester, who'd met her on her first day, had seemed to understand. She'd kept on grinning her lipstick grin as Emilia had struggled to find words to explain. She'd also kept on running her hands through her rough red hair, but she'd been nodding as she listened, and her eyes had never left Emilia's face. Miss Chester had spoken to Sam before seeing Emilia, and he'd emerged from her office, looking just as he'd always looked. He'd waited for Emilia outside Miss Chester's room and together with Mrs Morris, the three of them had walked as far as the playground. When Mrs Morris had gone, Sam had smiled at Emilia with his shadow of a smile, and she'd hoped that everything was going to be all right.

When she thought about it later, she'd realised that Mrs Morris was the teacher who'd been most concerned about the fight. She was the one who'd stepped straight over Frankie, when he'd been sprawled on the floor and put her arms round Emilia, and held her, so that she couldn't finish cleaning the board. She was the teacher who had been so kind, yet at the same time she was also the one who had made it all seem more complicated than it really was.

This tall, quiet woman, who'd always been in the school library, amongst all the books, had continued to keep Emilia in her arms, like a child who'd been hurt. While she'd been holding her, Mrs Morris had smoothed back Emilia's plaits again and again with her free hand. And one of the shafts of light falling from the line of windows had also fallen on Mrs Morris's hand and ring. Then, each time she'd stroked back Emilia's hair, Emilia had noticed that the stone in that ring had flashed its blue light around the white walls of the art room, like a glimpse of summer sky. At first, Emilia had wanted to get away from Mrs Morris, but the touch of the woman's hand on her skin had been cool and smooth, and when she'd closed her eyes for a moment she'd noticed a perfume that she'd never noticed before.

She remembered breathing it in and at the same time she remembered how she'd let her head rest against the other's neck, just as if she had been hurt so badly that she'd needed to be held.

Now she drew the ring with its blue stone set into fine claws of gold.

Then she paused and looked up from the portrait. There was that sound again and it had to be the sound of a crowd. Yet in the street nothing moved, although the light was fading fast. Cautiously, she opened the door again and looked out into the corridor. Then she heard a renewed roar behind her and ran back into the room. But the street was still empty and only shadows crept across her picture on the wall.

She made herself settle down and concentrate on the portrait of Mrs Morris. She told herself that nothing was going to happen. It was only the end of a quiet spring day. That was all. Nothing was going to change.

And that had been one of the things about Mrs Morris that Emilia'd liked best. She'd never changed. Wherever she'd gone and whatever she'd done, Mrs Morris had been the same. She'd always looked so nice and she'd dressed herself in colours that were soft and warm. Her long brown hair had always stayed as she'd pinned it, in a shiny coil on top of her head. And she'd always worn her ring. She'd worn it in the garden and when she'd been washing up and she'd even worn it when she'd been clearing the coal ash from the grate. She'd always been kind and calm, and she'd somehow remained like that even when Emilia's father and uncle had burst into the school the day after the fight.

The second lesson of the morning had been halfway through. Emilia's class had been copying lines of words from the board. Sam had been half-asleep and Emilia had almost nodded off as well. She'd glanced at him, then at the board. Then she'd yawned. Then yawned again. The warm rooms had always sent her to sleep. She'd tried to copy down a word or two, but there hadn't seemed much point. She could remember the shapes of buildings and streets and walls so well, but copying writing had always made her mind go blank. She couldn't see where the shapes of the letters began or went. Whenever she looked at them they seemed to shimmer and move.

Then she'd noticed a bag of those 'crisps' sticking out of Kelly Jackson's pocket and she'd felt hungry. Most of the girls used to bring chocolate to school, or fizzing drinks in cans, and they'd always shared this food with her. She'd enjoyed this, though she'd felt guilty that she'd never been able to bring anything in return.

She'd just been thinking about the crisps and looking forward to eating some in break when she'd heard something odd. Then she'd become aware of other people also looking up from their work. It had sounded as if someone was running through their part of the school. Classroom doors were being flung open so roughly that they were swinging back with a bang. The noise had got louder. Their teacher had stopped writing on the board. The students had been looking at each other and turning round. They'd been staring open-mouthed at their classroom door.

Her father had burst through it, then staggered to a halt as he'd stared wildly around. She'd heard her uncle shouting at her father to stop. She'd shut her eyes and willed them both to disappear but she'd known that there was no point.

When he'd caught sight of her, her father had moved towards her, banging against the edges of the tables as he'd pushed his way between. He'd tried to grab her wrist, but she'd wound her arms around her chair so that he hadn't been able to force her up. Kelly Jackson had shrieked and jumped up, but everyone else had gone quiet. For a second, nobody had breathed or moved. Emilia remembered bracing her legs against the table. But she'd known that if he'd wanted to, he could still have dragged her from the room.

'Why didn't you *tell* us?' he'd hissed under his breath as if the words needed to be secret, even though he must have known that no one else could understand what he'd said. 'Why didn't you tell us that some boy tried to hurt you yesterday? If I'd known, Emilia, I'd have sorted him out! I'd have beaten him until his own mother wouldn't have recognised him. Don't you trust me to look after you? Do you think I don't care? Don't you trust me to help?' He'd tipped back his hat and put his face so close to hers that she'd smelt the tobacco in his spit. 'Come along, now. You're coming home with me. Your mother and aunt will look after you now. It's where you belong and where you always should have been. But it's not too late. You've tried your best in school, but it was not to be. It hasn't worked. These people aren't like us and anyway, they don't want you here. So up you get Emilia, please.' He'd held out his hand.

She'd known that the whole class had been watching them, and she'd sensed that they were all expecting her to leave. Even Miss Chester had waited in silence, and licked her teeth.

'Come along! Your mother is ill with the upset.' Daniel had cleared his throat and tilted back his hat.

She'd shaken her head.

Now, she knew that everything would have been different if she'd only got up from her seat and said 'yes'.

But she hadn't. She'd hung her head and avoided his eyes as she'd whispered 'no.' She'd rejected his hand and she hadn't got up.

'Emilia?' He'd snatched at her wrist, and torn her fingers from the chair.

'No.' She'd spoken their language, so that only she and he would understand, so that he wouldn't feel the shame of it. But he had. He'd dropped her hand, then backed away from her, with a look of horror on his face. Then he'd cursed her like he might have cursed a dog that is frothing at the muzzle and mad. Then he'd left the classroom.

Later that morning, the police had come to the school to talk to her and her father, but it hadn't helped. Her father hadn't spoken to them at all and she hadn't been able to explain how she'd felt either to them, or to a Romanian woman who'd spoken English, as well as halting bits of the language they'd spoken at home in Bucharest.

After all, what had there been to say?

In Miss Chester's room, her father had again asked her to leave the school and go with him. She hadn't dared look at him, but once again she'd refused. When the woman had translated her answer into English, her father had suddenly stood up. In a moment he'd left the room and abandoned her without saying another thing. She'd heard him walking away as fast as he could and she'd known that her shame was so complete that even if she'd run after him, he wouldn't have given her a backward glance.

And that was the moment when Mrs Morris had offered to take her into her own home. Remembering it now, Emilia still wasn't sure how it had been arranged. At the time, she'd only been thinking about staying in the school. She'd known her father would be furious, and that he would interpret her refusal to do as he wanted as a betrayal, but she hadn't thought about the consequences and about where she would go.

And hadn't cared.

After her father had gone, she'd continued to sit quietly in the corner of Miss Chester's room but she'd felt as if she'd been floating somewhere, near the ceiling. She'd looked down on herself and been surprised that she cared so little about what she'd done. She'd recognised herself as the ungrateful daughter her mother had always said she was, but she hadn't minded. She accepted it as the way things were. She'd sat there, memorising the room from above, while the others talked and talked. And she'd waited to start feeling ashamed of herself.

Only she hadn't.

Instead of shame she'd felt excitement in a way that was wonderful and frightening at the same time. When everybody had finally stopped talking, she'd silently followed Mrs Morris out of the school, and climbed into the front seat of Mrs Morris's old car. By then, most other students had started going home and the ones who knew her had crowded round the car and waved. She'd waved back and suddenly she'd remembered the important people's cars that had driven along the main road into Bucharest and how the school children had stood in lines and waved their flags.

And she'd waved back . . . to Yasmina and Sam and Rachid and Kelly Jackson and that tall girl, PJ . . .

Now, she remembered Mrs Morris's ringed hand on the steering wheel, and the way she'd hummed to the music in the car as she'd driven through the crowded streets. Emilia'd never seen anyone do that. Then she remembered how the car had slowed down, and turned into a drive with a garden and house beyond. And she remembered how strange it had felt that she hadn't been surprised.

Once again it had seemed to her as if she'd been waiting for this all along. Mrs Morris had opened the front door and they'd stepped into a large hall with a coloured rug on the wooden floor and a jug of flowers on a small table. A cat had been asleep on a chair. It had opened its golden eyes and looked up as they'd approached, and Mrs Morris had bent down, with her keys and her bags still in her hands, and kissed its stretched-out head.

Suddenly, that had been when Emilia had felt ashamed. She'd remembered Gizella and unexpectedly felt tears in the back of her eyes. So poor Gizella *had* been telling the truth about England all along. This *was* how people lived and Gizella would have loved it so much and would have been so happy here, if she'd come. In the end, she would probably have ended up loving the cat as well. Yet Gizella hadn't been there. She had still been in Bucharest and would never know that she'd been right all along. And would never have this chance that Emilia had of a new life, in a new place.

'Don't cry.' Mrs Morris had put down her bags and patted her shoulder as they'd stood in the hall. 'We'll sort it all out with your father. And you can go back home whenever you want.'

Emilia had wiped her eyes, but she hadn't been able to explain.

Then Mrs Morris had shown her all over the house, and had finally opened the door into a little white room with a blue rug on the floor and the same pattern of blue flowers on the curtains and the pillows on the bed. It was to be 'her' room and she'd realised that she was to sleep alone in it, for the first time in her life. That evening, she'd sat at a table with Mrs Morris and her husband and she'd shared their food, and used their knives and forks and plates. It had felt very odd for a moment or two. Then swiftly and strangely it had felt all right. That night, after she was in bed, Mrs Morris had knocked on the door and put her head round.

'Are you OK?' she'd asked.

'Yes. I OK,' she'd answered in the dark. And she had been. Except that as she'd lain there, with her head on the blue flowered pillow, and thought about her family, she'd realised that she was wonderfully happy, when she knew that she should really have been feeling sad and lonely instead.

The next morning, Mrs Morris had knocked on her bedroom door again. And there she'd been, looking as she always did, with her hair piled up on her head. She'd sat on the end of the bed, and held out a mug of something warm to drink.

'Tea?' she'd asked.

Emilia had sat up and taken it. Then, as Mrs Morris had

drawn back the flowery curtains, she'd seen the blue ring on Mrs Morris's long white hand flash its colour round the room. When Mrs Morris had gone downstairs, Emilia had sipped the tea and breathed in the perfume that had been lingering in her room, and she'd let the cat settle down on the end of her bed.

Picture 15
The Sound of a Crowd

It was completely dark, so she'd put on the light to finish the portrait of Mrs Morris. Now she switched it off. When she'd looked out earlier, there were no other lights on in the houses in Lindenstrasse, or if there were, the curtains had been drawn across so carefully that no beam showed. She didn't understand this. Were these people hiding? Why didn't they want to be seen?

Then, she remembered the broken windows on the ground floor of their building. Were these people afraid of *that* happening to *them*? Had they seen the man in the back of the car drawing his finger across his throat? Did they fear him and his friends, like she did?

Because he could come back, couldn't he?

He could be out there now. He could be standing in the shadows by the wall watching their building, and planning another attack on them, or on any of the houses in the street. He could be waiting there at this very moment and none of them would know. So was it fear that had made them park their cars somewhere else and draw their curtains so tightly across?

She shivered in the hot room and bit at a corner of skin.

Anyway, she wouldn't have to stay on her own for much longer. Her family would certainly be back soon. It might have been a fine, warm day earlier but it was only spring. The nights were still very cold and her parents wouldn't want Zoltan to catch a chill and start to cough again. They wouldn't want to stay out late themselves. Especially not her father. If they'd earned good money, her father wouldn't want to be out at night with lots of cash hidden in his belt. That was asking for trouble. They all knew that.

But, if they returned to the hostel by their usual route, they'd have to walk straight past that man who might be hiding in the shadows by the wall. They might even brush against him, and never know, until it was too late. It was exactly the situation her father had always warned them against. He'd always cautioned them to be on their guard against strangers, especially if that stranger wasn't a gypsy. Never trust anyone, he'd always said. Even the most re-spectable-looking person in a street might be a thief, or an informant working for the Secret Police. You could never be sure. You could never know what was in a stranger's heart, which was why people like them must take great care. In his opinion, they should all have been as careful as he was and constantly on watch.

But that was impractical. Emilia's experience in England had taught her that it was impossible for anyone to protect themselves all the time. No matter how careful she'd been, it had still been impossible to prevent someone from hating her.

Nothing can prevent an evil person from leaping out of the shadows and grabbing their victim by the throat –

Emilia took her fingers from her mouth and touched the ends of her cut-off hair. Until she'd lived in England she'd never given much thought to being hated. But over there she'd learnt new lessons about hate and she'd learnt them in her flesh. She'd learnt that it was possible for a total stranger to hate her so bitterly that, even though they'd never spoken to her, they could still do her harm. Hate was like a disease that leapt from person to person and made them all mad. Because that was what had happened in England, on a winter night, when it had been cold and dark, and when . . .

She bit into her skin as deeply as she could. The pain stopped her remembering, and remembering frightened her too much. And fear didn't help, because at this moment she needed to concentrate on her family who would soon be walking down that street.

Even if the man didn't attack them as they walked past, he could still watch where they went. Or follow them, as unseen and silent as a rat. That's what he'd do: he'd watch her mother and father and Zoltan cross the road, and climb the hostel steps. When they'd reached the yellow door, and opened it and switched on the light, then that man hiding over there in the shadows would know exactly where they lived.

Any watcher would see them outlined against the light. They'd be framed in the yellow window, as clearly and as firmly as if they had been in a picture on a wall.

And then –

Then she remembered the unlocked door. How could her parents have forgotten that, on today of all days, when everybody had been warned that there might be trouble on the streets? How could they have neglected to make sure that she was safe? Or didn't they care?

At this moment, that man out there could be getting out of the lift and walking swiftly down the silent corridor, then turning the handle on the yellow door.

So, why hadn't they taken care? Didn't they mind what happened to her? Or had all their talk about their day out been untrue? Was it their way of hinting that they were actually moving on and leaving her behind? Was that why Zoltan hadn't wanted to go with them? Had he heard something? Had he suspected that they might be leaving the hostel forever and never coming back?

But that was a ridiculous idea. It couldn't be true. They hadn't even packed up. Nor had they taken enough food for a journey, or had they? Because her mother had certainly packed up plenty of food for the picnic that Zoltan had been talking about. So, maybe they *were* going away?

She felt her heart miss a beat.

Or, what would happen if someone suggested a move to them while they were out? It didn't have to be planned. Somebody could just say: 'Why don't you travel to this new country with us?' And they'd think: why not? And they'd go and she'd never hear where they'd gone.

She bit off another strip of skin. She knew that she must stop frightening herself. It was stupid of her. Why, even a few hours ago, she'd been happily imagining the rustle of supermarket bags at the door and the sound of Zoltan's gruff voice boasting about having kicked more goals than any other boy. She'd pictured her father stretching out on the sofa and announcing in a voice softened by beer, that despite everything, Lindenstrasse 3 wasn't such a bad place, and that he'd decided to stay here after all. Why couldn't that still come true?

She *must* stop being afraid: there wasn't anyone by the wall. No one was watching her window and waiting for the light to go on. It was all pictures in her head. It was all something that she kept on making up.

Wasn't it?

She went back to the window and rested her forehead on the glass. Across the road the white wall gleamed like skin uncovered in the dark. She looked along the other houses with their tubs of flowers still outside, but with their curtains and shutters drawn so tightly across. The street-lamps dropped unimpeded pools of silent light onto the edges of the pavement and the thick black road. And up and down the street, as far as she could see, nothing moved to spoil the stillness of the night.

Except for a sound.

It barely glanced across the glass. She pressed her cheek closer and shut her eyes in order to concentrate. And there it was again: a sound like a moan. Or a wind. Or the roar of a road. Or the sea. Or the sound of a crowd on the move.

That was it. She recognised it now and knew it, because she'd heard it once before. Somewhere out there a crowd of people was moving through the night. She snatched up the diary, then crawled across the carpet and crouched underneath the table with the book clasped like a child to her chest. When she held her breath and listened once more she realised that the crowd was moving towards her. There was no doubt any more.

But, if the crowd ran down the road and burst in, they might not notice her hidden there. At least, not at first. And when they did notice, at least by then she'd have hidden the book. Because she was going to put it back exactly where she'd found it. And she would have done so immediately, if she'd had the sticky tape, and if the diary had been finished, which it wasn't, not yet, because she needed to draw one more picture to complete it.

It needed the final picture to make it make sense.

But she couldn't draw, could she, when she was crouched under the table, like a rat in its hole? Anyway, she couldn't even see to draw, not without a light, and she was too scared to turn it on.

Wasn't she?

Then she heard it again, heard that sound of a crowd that she'd heard before. It was half a scream and half a roar as running feet pounded the ground like waves on a beaten shore. And all around the still dark night lapped at the gaps in between.

But it was louder now.

So, why was she still crouching under the table, when she needed to draw? When she needed to make one last picture before the crowd got to her? Why was she so held back, even though she knew that without that last picture the diary made no sense at all? It would be like a meal with no food, or a wedding without the bride.

What was this fear? Why was she hiding in the dark? If someone *was* out there, wishing her harm, why was she waiting like a rat, for the shovel to smash in her head?

Why didn't she draw?

Suddenly, she stood up and clicked on the light: there was nothing else for her to do now. She must make herself remember that night in England when she'd first heard that sound of a crowd's cruel roar. And she must draw it, because that was what fed her fear.

She found a pen and opened up the final page. It was too late and there was no point in being so afraid any more.

She'd been staying with Mrs Morris for some time and had settled in well, except that she'd missed Zoltan a great deal. She'd gone to school every day, and she'd continued to draw. One of the pieces of furniture in her room had been an old wooden desk. In the evenings and at weekends, she'd opened the desk out and drawn for hours and hours, as she'd never been able to draw before. And she'd been happy, so very, very happy. It had been much easier to step into this new life than she'd ever thought it would be. It was as if she'd been waiting for this all through the years.

Both her uncle and her father had been round several times to try and persuade her to return, but she had never been tempted. She'd been ashamed of herself and her feelings of indifference and each time she'd been relieved when she'd heard them walking away from the house.

On the day of the school Christmas disco that had been planned for that evening in the big assembly hall, her father had come round twice. At first he'd demanded that she return. Then he'd explained that her mother was so ashamed of what Emilia'd done that she wouldn't even leave the flat. She hadn't worked since Emilia'd left. Each night she cried herself to sleep and then woke in the early morning and cried all over again. Now she'd stopped eating as well. If Emilia didn't come back, he'd warned her that her mother might die from the disgrace. Hadn't she understood that girls like her could only leave home on their marriage day? Was she a fool as well as a disgrace?

Didn't she realise that after this incident she would suffer because no respectable gypsy family would want her as a daughter-in-law? No decent man would trust a wife who'd run away, or not without the encouragement of a huge dowry that would take him years and years to repay. Didn't she care? Didn't she understand the danger she was in? Didn't she mind being considered unclean because she'd lived with these people and shared their food and their spoons and plates?

She'd blushed and hung her head when he'd spoken of these things. He'd agreed that these laws were cruel and unbending, but he'd insisted that that was the point of them. If it was easy to be a gypsy then they'd soon be swamped by all sorts of people all wanting to live like them. Didn't she understand that it was their laws that made them so special?

She'd sat in Mrs Morris's kitchen, biting her nails as she'd listened to him. Mr Morris had remained at the sink washing the dishes more slowly than she'd ever known him wash them before.

'Just come home.' Finally, her father had almost begged. 'Just come back. Now. Then we can tell everyone that you didn't mean to leave us. We can tell them that you made a mistake and that the school people forced you to come here. We can tell everybody that it wasn't your fault, that you didn't dare say no. Anyway,' he'd shifted his hat, 'you'll have to come back in the end, for Zoltan's sake. When he's older and we're looking for a bride, what decent father will give his daughter to us, when our own daughter has run away from our home? They'll think that your mother and I are bad people. And we're not. So you might as well come back now.' He'd stood up, as if he was sure that she'd get up too.

But she hadn't moved and in the corner by the sink, Mr Morris had begun to dry up even more slowly still.

'Emilia, please?'

When Emilia hadn't replied her father had left the house abruptly and she'd listened to the sound of him walking swiftly away. And she'd been glad. Because, what could she have said? If she'd told him the truth, she'd have hurt him even more.

Later, however, she'd gone back to her room and wept. She'd always realised that she was a bad person, but until that moment she hadn't realised just how bad she was. As she'd lain on her bed she'd accepted that she was cruel and selfish. She'd despised herself for not caring more about her poor mother and Zoltan, but she hadn't changed her mind.

She'd lain there, biting the remaining bits of skin from her nails and staring at the flowery curtains, while she'd tried to work out what she should do. Around her, in the rest of the house, the Morris family had been getting ready for the disco. She'd listened to the sounds of the shower and the bath and of people running up and down stairs barefooted, and of cupboards and drawers being opened and closed. Mrs Morris's granddaughter, Katy, and a couple of her friends had been in the house as well. Emilia had listened to them chatting and laughing and she'd been reminded of a group of noisy birds. She might have drawn a quick sketch if the doorbell hadn't rung several times. Each time she'd held her breath and waited to hear the sound of her father's angry voice, but each time it had been someone else.

She hadn't even understood what a disco was, only that it was some sort of party that was being held at night. She'd agreed to go with them and had been looking forward to it, but after her father's visits she'd felt anxious and uncertain about it. Some of her school friends were meeting at Mrs Morris's house first. Then they were all travelling to the disco together, in the Morris's big old car. She'd planned to wear her favourite long red skirt and Mrs Morris had helped her wash and iron it the weekend before, but when it came to it, Emilia hadn't got ready until the last moment.

Then she'd run down the stairs in a borrowed pair of gold slippers and she'd squeezed into the back of the car beside the other girls. She'd noticed Frankie on the opposite side of the car and she'd smiled at him but he'd blushed and looked away.

They'd driven through bright night streets and listened to Christmas songs on the radio in the car. The others had waved to people they knew and the streets had seemed full of students who were all dressed up in their best clothes. Everybody appeared to have been heading in the direction of the school. The car had smelt of perfume and new material and polished shoes. Sometimes Mrs Morris had sung along to the music and sometimes the others had joined in as well.

When Mr Morris had unexpectedly jammed on the brakes they'd all slid about on the slippery seats and laughed. Crowds of people had been standing around in front of the school gates and as soon as Emilia had seen them she'd started to feel excited again. She hadn't realised that a disco was such an important event.

Then, a man in a T-shirt who'd stepped in front of their

car had suddenly leant over and tapped on their windscreen with a bunch of keys. He'd been grinning so Katy had begun winding her window down, but Mr and Mrs Morris had both shouted at her to stop. Emilia had been startled. She'd never heard any of them shout before. Behind them other drivers had begun hooting their horns. She hadn't understood why Mr Morris didn't make the car move on again. The people behind had sounded very impatient to get into the school. Just then a group of older students, who'd been trying to walk through the gate, were stopped by another man who barred their way. One of the boys had attempted to push through but the man had shoved him aside. A girl in a long black dress managed to dart past him but when another girl had tried, the man at the gate had grabbed her bare arm and hadn't let her go.

In the car everyone was shouting at once and all around them people were sounding car horns. She'd thought the Morrises were arguing about where to park, because her uncle and aunt had always quarrelled about that whenever she'd been out with them in their van. She'd been surprised that everyone had been making such a fuss. After all, they had almost got there.

She'd always hated arguments so she'd opened her car door to get out. It hadn't been far to walk, even in her golden shoes. As she'd done that they'd all stopped shouting at each other and shouted at her instead. It had been so horrible. They'd shouted, then screamed. She'd known that she must have made some dreadful mistake, but she'd had no idea what it was. It had been the worst thing in the world, to have those people, whom she loved, screaming at her like that. So she'd stepped away from the car. Then they'd shrieked even more, but she'd only half understood that they were telling her to get back in.

And she would have done so, if Frankie hadn't leant out and grabbed hold of her arm, just as he'd grabbed it before. He'd been shouting too, but she hadn't understood.

She'd pulled away.

He'd clung to the sleeve of her coat, so she slipped out of it, and it had fallen to the ground. She had taken a step and felt her golden slippers slide on the icy road, but at first she hadn't noticed the freezing night on her skin. Nor had she yet felt the fear. It had been the noise and confusion that had so upset her. Distantly, she'd been aware of another sound that had hung in the air like snow on an easterly wind.

Then that sound had grown as the crowd had started to roar. Katy had been sobbing and screaming from the car. Mrs Morris had been banging on the glass and pointing to the open door. And she would still have got back in, if the driver behind hadn't driven so close that she couldn't reach her side of the car.

'Emilia!' Everyone had been shouting her name. 'Emi-i! Emi-i! Get back in!'

She'd known that she'd done something wrong.

'Emi! Quick! Get in!'

And she would have if Francis Johnson hadn't been sitting by the other door, because she knew he'd have touched her again.

So she'd run, but not far.

Someone had stepped from the crowd. They'd opened their arms wide across her path and they'd blocked her escape. She'd still tried to get away. Her slippers had skidded on the frozen ground and she'd thought she might fall, but she'd swerved and ducked and almost got under the outstretched arms.

Almost, but not quite. Someone had caught hold of her hair and clung on. Then, hand over hand, like a fish on a hook, they'd hauled her in. She'd felt the skin stretch on her forehead and thought it would split, but she hadn't made a sound. So, step by golden step, the woman who'd captured her had dragged her across the glittering ground and reeled her in. And of course, she'd recognised her captor then.

It had been the woman from the car park, the mad woman with no skirt, who'd screamed as she'd splashed through the rain.

She'd been twisting Emilia's plaits round her hand to get a better grip. Around them, the watching crowd had breathed and bayed. Emilia'd felt her neck being bent further and further back. When she'd opened her eyes she'd seen the crowd's hot breath in the frosty air and she'd remembered her clean red skirt and been sorry that it would be ruined when the crowd surged forward and trampled her into the ground.

Then she'd seen the blade of a knife slice through the black air. When the watching crowd saw it they'd shuffled away and moaned. Another hand had gripped her throat. She'd needed to breathe but as she tried to open her mouth to find more air, she'd seen the knife's slow fall. There'd been no air, only the smell of scent and sweat and vinegar and smoke, so she'd started to choke.

The cold blade had seized her skin like an iron tooth. It had snapped at her neck and throat, once, twice and then once more. And all around her the crowd had howled and panted and roared.

Then she'd been free. They'd let her go. She'd stood there, as light as a bent stem unexpectedly released.

Suddenly, ridiculously, she'd remembered a song that singers had sung back in her Bucharest home. It had been about the old war and it had told of the black crow that had flown from the top of the chimney stacks as the devouring fires had burnt the gypsies' bodies below. She'd heard it as she'd moved her hands towards her neck and throat to feel for the wounds in her skin. But there'd been nothing there. Her arms and hands had felt so light that they might have been wings. She moved them up and down and would have flown up into the night –

But someone had laughed long and loud. She'd felt for the bloody edges of her cut throat, but found that there was still no wound there. Beside her, the mad woman had been swinging her cut-off plaits round and round in the air. Emilia'd touched the nape of her neck. Then she'd realised why the crowd was laughing at her. There was no wound because the woman had only slashed off her hair.

Now, she remembered how the biting cold had suddenly sunk in. She'd felt colder than she'd ever felt before. She'd shivered and her teeth had chattered so violently that she'd bitten her tongue.

People had starting running towards her. They'd shouted her name.

'Emi! Emi!'

But they hadn't run fast enough. Her father had got there first and she hadn't even known he was there. He'd stepped from the shadows and caught hold of her wrist. She'd looked back once, twice and tried to ask for help, but she'd been so cold that her words had frozen in her throat like a lump of ice. Or fear.

Now, she looked at what she'd drawn: a tiny figure that was hardly a figure at all. It wore her flame red skirt, and had her silent, screaming mouth and her bared skull that had lost her long, beautiful plaits of golden hair. There was no one else in the picture, and nothing else at all, except that the figure was not deserted because it was besieged all around by the sound of the terrible crowd that had gathered there, and by the swiftly growing sound of her fear.

They'd left England early the next morning, on Christmas Eve. This time, as she crossed the sea, she'd been standing on the deck of the boat and had looked down into the water. The unknowable depths of it and the steel grey waves had made her think of leaping in and allowing herself to be carried away. But she hadn't dared. Fear, like she'd never known it before, had stayed as close to her as an eager bridegroom and she'd stayed at the rail and shivered as she'd never shivered before.

A winter wind had whipped up waves with crests like breaking ice and then it had smashed them down. Beneath her, and beneath the swaying deck, she'd felt the engines drumming and pounding and driving them on towards yet another shore.

And they'd pounded just as they were pounding now –

'Come quick!' Zeynep flung open the door. 'Come, you must come *now*! Quick! They are running down our street.'

Emilia saw them now. It was a mob and it was streaming

down from the main road with its sticks and lights and its swastika banners held high.

'Run!' Zeynep was already pulling her towards the door. She grabbed the book.

'No!' Zeynep screamed as Emilia turned towards the lift. 'Not by lift! We go this way, by stair!'

They could hear the sound of the crowd outside. Zeynep was flinging herself against a metal bar on a door at the other end of the corridor. Together, they got it to move. Outside there was nothing but night, and the sounds of the crowd in the chilled, dark air.

'Hurry!' Zeynep screamed. She'd caught hold of a rail and seemed to be about to throw herself off.

But Emilia didn't want to jump. Nor go back inside. She stood there gripping the book to her chest, unable to move, as if all her courage had been gnawed away by her fear.

'Quick!' Zeynep had swung her leg over the rail and begun to climb down an old iron ladder that was fixed to the outside of the hostel wall.

Then, suddenly, Emilia made herself move. The book and her skirt hampered her and several times she thought she'd fall. She smelt the smoke when she was half way down and from somewhere inside the building she heard the crackle and fizz of flames taking hold and then she realised that the hostel was on fire. As she passed an open window she jerked away from a rush of hot air but saw the red glow of flames and a spray of sparks like a monstrous orange flower. Then she trod on her skirt, lost her balance and slipped and swung wildly in the air. But she clung on because she didn't want to fall. Not now, not when the book was still in her arms and when the ground was so near. Somehow she found the rung.

Once on the ground she realised that someone else was coming down the ladder after her. A wind was blowing black smoke in their faces but it was as thick as mud, so she couldn't see who it was. Zeynep began coughing violently and within seconds they could hardly see each other. Emilia covered her face with the book, then caught hold of Zeynep's arm and began to lead them through. When her free hand touched the rough stones of a wall, she ran her fingers over it and then felt her way along to a corner, some way from the fire. They crouched there and let the smoke stream over their heads. Zeynep was fighting to catch her breath. Then, Emilia covered her nose and mouth with her red skirt and peered quickly over the top.

By now much of the lower floor of the whole hostel was burning and beyond the flames the crowd cheered. They were waving their bent cross flags in the air and jumping up and down and jostling each other as they struggled to see more. Near the front, helmeted men who looked like police were struggling with some of the onlookers who appeared to be trying to rush up the steps of the hostel itself.

Beside her Zeynep was coughing and gasping for breath.

When Emilia next looked over the wall she saw fire engines by the tree on the far corner at the end of the street. They were moving slowly, because they couldn't get through the crowds. She put her face close to Zeynep's and pointed to the street side of the wall. She knew that they had to get there, before the smoke poisoned them both. She helped Zeynep up first and when she'd heard her drop down on the other side, she scrambled over herself. She half expected the crowd to surge towards them as soon as it saw them, but it didn't. Everybody seemed to be concentrating on what was going on in front of the hostel steps. One man even carried a small boy on his shoulders and when Emilia had taken another deep breath and looked again, she saw that this child was rocking up and down with excitement and clapping his hands.

Then something pierced the air.

'Let me go!' It was her mother's sound. 'Let me go! My child is in there!'

Now she saw her mother force her way past the police and climb the first step.

Then she saw her father and Zoltan.

'My daughter is up there!' Elizabeta screamed repeatedly although no one else could have understood her words. She was pointing to the yellow room where a single light still glimmered in the smoky air.

With the book held tightly in her arms Emilia began to push through the crowd. She saw her father trying to pull Elizabeta back.

'Don't!' he screamed. 'Let her go. She was never worth it and you can't save her now!' He retreated into the crowd, shielding his face and flailing his arms like a man drowning in air.

When her mother had climbed to the second step, she turned to the crowd and beseeched them for help because her daughter was in there.

Then she saw Emilia. She stared at her for a second and started to move towards her. The crowd moaned and backed. As her mother came closer Emilia saw that her face was blistered, her hair was burnt and her lips were bloody and cracked.

In front of them the first jets of water from the fire hoses hit the building in an explosion of steam and sparks. Behind them something had changed. The crowd had gone quieter. It was suddenly trying to get away. Strangers and people in official-looking uniforms were surrounding Emilia and her mother, touching them and talking to them and trying to help them. Someone brought her father and Zoltan to them and Zoltan flung himself against his mother and buried his face in her skirts. Stiffly, Elizabeta moved her hands down and tried to stroke his black curls but the palms of her hands were burnt. When Daniel saw that he shuddered as violently as if the pain were his.

'You witch!' he hissed at Emilia. 'You devil's slut, you filthy, evil thing, look what you've done to us *now*!'

He raised his fists and would have hit her if her mother hadn't stepped between.

'Mum?'

Elizabeta moved her cracked lips but Emilia couldn't hear what she said. Around them the crowd was vanishing. It was melting away into the dark corners and the shadowed parts of the street.

'Mum?'

People were hustling them towards an ambulance.

'Mum?'

Elizabeta stopped, then moved close.

'Mum, I'm not coming with you. Not now. Not any longer.'

Elizabeta sighed, but nodded her head. She raised her hands and touched Emilia gently where her hair had been

263

cut off, then she turned her back on her and walked slowly and heavily towards the place where her husband and Zoltan stood.

Emilia waited for another moment, then she stepped back into the black night and when she was sure that no one was watching her, she began to walk away down the street. There were other people on the pavement and she threaded her way through them but no one looked up. She passed the picture on the white wall and walked on, past the blue door to where the tree stood on the corner of the road and then she stopped.

She'd sensed that someone was following her. She'd heard their footsteps and she'd guessed that it was Zeynep hurrying to catch up. Her grip tightened on the book, but she wasn't afraid. Not now, not any more, because in a moment she knew that they would turn round the corner of the street and then she would be free to look at all that had been hidden before.